PHONY EINSTEIN
AND OTHER TALES FROM THE BRINK

P H O N Y
EINSTEIN
AND OTHER TALES FROM THE BRINK

MARC S. SILVER

For my wife Kathy who makes it all possible.

*"There are more things in heaven and earth, Horatio,
than are dreamt of in your philosophy."*

HAMLET ACT 1 SCENE 5

CONTENTS

THE WITCH OF BERGEN COUNTY

He hadn't thought about her much lately—not until he picked up that book that everybody was reading here—*Cellar Man* it's called. It's about this crazy shit that happened in New Jersey—where he's from—and that got him thinking about her again. Lying here in lockup, Bernie Stein had lots of time to think. He was doing a three-year stretch for embezzlement and mail fraud; a culmination of bad luck and even worse decisions that seemed to follow him ever since he got to California.

Patrick was his cellmate in the upper bunk. A big guy with a bald head who sweats a lot. He had some pictures taped to the wall up there that he looked at. Family photos, probably. Maybe a girlfriend. Bernie never bothered to look or ask about them. He figured it was none of his business.

Patrick read and kept to himself as much as possible, and that was fine with Bernie. They were both just trying to do their time, avoid trouble, and get the hell out before the system drove them insane. In one of his more talkative moods, he told Bernie that he was doing time because he was the fall guy for a money laundering operation and that he almost killed the guy who ratted him out. That's all he ever said about it.

So Bernie knew very little about Patrick, except he knew that Patrick snored. The noises that came out of this man were like nothing Bernie had ever heard come out of a human being before. It was so loud that inmates in other cell blocks would scream for him to shut up. It was like a freight train. A jumbo jet. A thunder storm. A landslide.

But every once in a while, something miraculous would happen. His snoring would become melodic. Rather than the cataclysmic noises that he usually made, sounds would emerge from his nose and mouth simultaneously, and he would actually make music. Not only that, he could harmonize with himself. Trumpets would come from his mouth, and he'd underscore the horns with the violins from his nose. When he really got going, it would sound a little like soulful oldies from the sixties and seventies—Aretha Franklin and Otis Redding type stuff. It would be completely fascinating if it weren't so fucking creepy.

Sometimes Bernie wondered what was going on in Patrick's head, but he preferred not to ask him about anything like that. They had an understanding about distance and not getting too personal with each other. Sometimes, however, contact became necessary. When he couldn't take the snoring anymore, Bernie would hit the side of his bunk or nudge him until the roaring stopped. Patrick would grunt and roll over, and it would be quiet for a minute, maybe an hour if Bernie was lucky, but then the rolling thunder would begin anew. Consequently, Bernie was only sleeping about two hours a night—so there was lots of time to think.

*** * ***

A lot of muddy water had gone under the bridge since Bernie was seventeen years old and deeply in love, or in lust, with an Irish-Catholic girl named Colleen Macdonald. Colleen was mysterious and beautiful. She had jet-black hair, big green eyes, was very smart, and she could sing like an angel. Bernie loved everything about her, especially her mouth and her lips. She drove him crazy with those lips. When he kissed her for the first time, she awakened an insatiable longing—that he was powerless against—as if he were under some kind of spell. Once he walked through a blizzard in the dead of night, almost froze to death, just so he could call her on a pay phone to profess his love over and over until she finally hung up on him. Colleen liked to play with Bernie's emotions.

They met at a little community theater in Fair Lawn, New Jersey. They both got cast in *Stop the World—I Want to Get Off*, a musical that was popular at the time. Bernie had aspirations of being a big movie star. He was in all the high school plays and got some strokes from easily impressed teachers in the Thespian's Club. But he really wasn't all that good, which he painfully discovered a little further down the road. Colleen, however, was very good. She was magnetic onstage and could belt out a show tune or sing a tender ballad that would bring you to tears.

Bernie and Colleen started spending a lot of time together. He had use of his family's second car, a Chevy Impala, and he'd drive her around. But mostly they would go somewhere and park because they couldn't keep their hands off each other. They'd find a quiet street and then start steaming up the windows. Heavy petting, they used to call it. They made out in the car, in the park, everywhere and anywhere, and they didn't care who saw them. They only had intercourse once, but the almost sex they had was the best he ever had. Later, Bernie would always compare his other sexual relationships to her, and none of them came close.

* * *

Eventually, Colleen invited Bernie to her house. It was a neatly kept place with an upstairs, where the bedrooms were. They also had a finished basement, where Bernie and Colleen would spend a lot of time making out. Colleen shared the house with her father who was in construction, her alcoholic mother, her quiet and reclusive younger brother who was perpetually in some kind of trouble in school, and her grandmother who was always in the living room, in her rocking chair, grinning and knitting something that she never seemed to make any progress on. There was an older sister, but she moved into her own place somewhere in upstate New York. Bernie couldn't remember any of their names, probably because he was in a sexual daze most of the time.

Colleen told him that it was the grandmother she was closest to, but Bernie didn't like her much. She had a heavy accent and was hard to understand. She was from the old country, Colleen had told him. Bernie didn't care what country she was from; he just thought she was creepy. But Colleen loved her and would get angry if Bernie said anything unkind about her.

Colleen treated her grandmother with great respect. And they had secrets together. They would whisper things to each other and then quietly chuckle over whatever they were conspiring about. Bernie always felt like they were laughing at him. Like he was some experiment they were toying with. Colleen told him once that when she would get depressed, her grandmother would rub her bottom and tell her stories about their ancestors from long ago, and that always made her feel better. Bernie thought it odd that a grandmother would rub a sixteen-year-old's bottom, but who was he to judge—he couldn't keep his hands off it, either.

The mother was a sweet woman, but when she got to drinking she'd stay locked in her room. Colleen had told him that her father would go into rages when her mother drank. They would fight, and it would get ugly and sometimes physical. The father was standoffish anyway, but on those days he would really keep his distance. While the mother stayed locked in her room, crying and moaning, he would busy himself with some kind of project in the garage.

Bernie found it odd that the father was around the house as much as he was, considering he was a working man with a construction company. But there were a lot of odd things in that house. None more so than how everyone seemed to ignore all the fooling around that he was doing with Colleen. The family must have heard them; Colleen was pretty loud. And how could they have not seen anything? He and Colleen weren't careful about it at all. They fooled around in the doorways at night, in the basement, in her bedroom, and sometimes right on the living room couch. Bernie expected that a confrontation with Colleen's father was inevitable. He was, after all, mauling his daughter and doing it right under his own roof. How could he not want to kill Bernie for that? Or maybe the old man just didn't care. Was sex just not that big a deal in that house? Or was it some weird Catholic thing where you pretend that sex doesn't really happen to people.

Anyway, there was a strange vibe in that house. Bernie didn't particularly like going there, but he couldn't stay away, either.

* * *

Early one evening Bernie was in the living room getting stared at by the creepy grandmother. He was waiting for Colleen to finish dressing so they could go out to see the movie *2001: A Space Odyssey*. Her father came in from outside, stopped in the doorway, and then he also started staring at him. Bernie figured, well, the jig is up, he's going to kill me now. But instead he says, "Come on in the kitchen and have a beer with me."

Next to fooling around with Colleen, beer was Bernie's favorite thing on Earth. Her father wouldn't be his ideal choice for a drinking buddy, but an invitation for a free Miller High Life (the fridge was always stocked with them) was an offer too good for Bernie to refuse.

Bernie sat at the table while the father checked through some mail that was on the kitchen counter. Up until that point they had probably said five words to each other. Bernie was pretty sure he was going to get some kind of warning or threat, and possibly a hammerblow to the back of the head.

He looked around the kitchen nervously. He'd been in here before with Colleen, but it somehow seemed smaller now—more claustrophobic. It had a kind of over-the-top country kitchen feel to it. More German than Irish, Bernie thought. Maybe Bavarian. There were frilly curtains on the window, and the cabinets had that kind of overly elaborate wood trim like you'd see in an Alpine ski lodge or something. There were goofy knickknacks all over the place, and they even had a cuckoo clock over the stove—very goyish, as Bernie's mother was fond of saying.

The father grumbled about the phone bill being too high and then went to the refrigerator and got two bottles of beer. He opened both bottles (screw caps had just come out a short while back), put a beer in front of Bernie, and then took a seat opposite him at the table. He took a long swig of his beer as if he were dying of thirst. Then he put the beer down, stared at Bernie again, and started tapping the beer bottle with his fingernails.

Bernie smiled because he had absolutely no idea what to say to this man, and then he noticed the father's massive arms. He had Popeye arms. How could he have not noticed that before? They looked particularly odd because they didn't really match the rest of his body. He was a thin guy, very solid, but those arms belonged to a much larger man—or a cartoon character. His hands were also unusually large. In comparison, Bernie felt like he had little doll hands and immediately hid them in his lap so as not to be judged as a lesser kind of man. Bernie figured if he was about to get throttled, it would be quick. With arms and hands like that, he should be able to break his neck in no time at all.

"My wife is an alcoholic," Colleen's father finally said in a deeply weary voice.

Bernie, startled by the confession, took a moment before he could respond.

"Bummer" was the best he could come up with.

"Makes me crazy when she drinks. She becomes another person. And I don't like that person very much."

"Yeah, that's...that's a shame. Sorry to hear that...really."

He stared at Bernie, drummed on his beer bottle again, and then guzzled the rest of it.

"Another one?" he asked.

"No, no, I'm...I'm good," Bernie said.

He was still hiding his hands in his lap and hadn't had a sip of the first one yet.

The father got up to get himself another beer. He sat back down at the table and flicked the bottle cap off with his gigantic thumb.

Bernie gulped. Yeah, if he strangles him, it will definitely be quick.

"You like my daughter?"

"Yes...we have fun together. I mean...she's very talented." Bernie cringed, worried about how *talented* might be interpreted.

"Do you love her?"

"I think I do, yes, sir."

"You better be sure."

"I'm pretty sure."

"You better be careful with her."

"I will."

"Because...she has her moods."

And then Colleen came into the kitchen.

"What's going on?" she asked.

"Just having a beer with your Jewish friend," her father told her.

She gave her father a severe look that he turned away from—as if he were afraid of her. Then he leaned back in his chair and drank his beer.

"We better get going, Bernie," Colleen said while still glaring at her father.

"Yes. We better get going. Nice talking to you, sir."

He didn't respond.

Bernie got up from the table.

"Don't you want your beer?" the father asked while staring straight ahead.

"I do, but…we don't want to be late for the movie."

He shrugged, grabbed Bernie's beer, and downed that one, too.

"Don't wait up," Colleen said with enough disrespect that Bernie thought he might kill them both right there on the spot.

But he didn't even look at her.

They left the kitchen, and Colleen went over to her grandmother in the rocking chair and kissed her on the mouth, eliciting another cringe from Bernie. She whispered something to her, and they shared a knowing grin. The grandmother started to rub Colleen's ass, which made Bernie cringe yet again.

Then they left and went to the movie.

* * *

The movie theater was packed. Bernie put his hand on Colleen's leg, caressing the inside of her thigh. She surprised him by pushing his hand away and then gave him a menacing look. She's always been receptive to his touch, so this was disturbing to him. He didn't push it, though. There'd be plenty of time to fool around later. Bernie tried to focus on the film, but it was hard to concentrate. He was distracted by Colleen's sudden coldness. It was actually making him feel a little sick. He managed to keep his hands to himself for the rest of the movie.

* * *

When they got out to the car after the movie, the Chevy had a flat tire. Bernie had never changed a tire before. He watched his father do it once, but he wasn't sure if he could actually do it himself.

It was cold outside, and Bernie suggested that Colleen wait in the car. She declined and just stood there watching him with a smirk on her face, her arms folded across her chest as if she already knew that Bernie had no idea about how to change a tire.

He got the jack and the spare out of the trunk and was immediately in trouble—he couldn't figure out how the jack worked. He was turning the thing around in his hands, trying to figure out what part goes where, when Colleen offered some advice.

"You have to use the tire iron to jack it up. The part that goes under the…let me just show you."

"No, no, I'm fine. I got it. This part is where the…uh…"

"I can't believe you never changed a tire before."

"What? Of course I have. Lots of times."

He went back to the trunk to get the tire iron and was starting to feel stupid and embarrassed and a little bit angry about the way she was talking to him.

He figured out where the tire iron fit into the jack, but then he wasn't sure where the jack fit onto the car so that he could jack it up without causing any damage to the car or to his person.

"You have to get it underneath. On the frame," she explained as if talking to a dim-witted child.

"Oh, oh, yeah…I see it now. Okay…"

"Just let me do it. I've done it lots of times before."

"I can do it!" Bernie snapped, but then immediately felt bad about being short with her. "Really, why don't you just wait in the car? I'll have this done in no time."

"Because I don't want to wait in the car."

"But it's freezing out here."

She turned her back on him, effectively cutting off any further discussion.

So Bernie struggled to change the tire. He got the car jacked up but couldn't figure out how to get the tire off. What does he use to do that? He walked back to the trunk to see if there was something in there that he might have missed. Nothing was there. When he turned to go back, Colleen was standing there with the tire iron, slapping it into the palm of her hand. The thought crossed his mind that she was going to hit him with it.

"You're going to need this," she said instead.

"Of course. I know."

"You see…this is what you use. On the other end here is the lug wrench. You put this over the nut and you pull, counter-clockwise. That's how you get the tire off."

She said this with the same sarcasm that she used with her father, and it made Bernie feel like absolute crap.

"I know how to do it. I just thought…maybe there was an-other part to it."

"There's not."

She handed him the tire iron, walked a few feet away, then turned back to watch, with the smirk returning to her face.

The lug nuts were really tight. Bernie was putting his whole weight into it but nothing was happening. His hands were really cold, too, and that made things even worse. Colleen watched him, covering her face with her scarf and occasionally com-menting on Bernie's futile attempts.

Finally, Bernie tried stomping on the tire iron with his foot, and that seemed to loosen things up a bit.

"Hallelujah," she said.

By this time his car was the only one left in the parking lot, and Colleen was pacing around to keep warm.

"Please, just go wait in the car. You're making me nervous."

"The car's on a jack, Bernie! If I get in the car, it'll probably fall and crush your legs, which would only momentarily make me feel better because then I'd have to get an ambulance and try to explain why I have a boyfriend who can't even change a fucking tire!"

It'd be one thing if she was trying to be funny, but she definitely was not. She was serious, and the tone she was using with him was like nothing he'd heard from her before. It's like how his mother talks to his father, and that made Bernie very uncomfortable.

After almost an hour, Bernie finally got the old tire off and the new one on, but a wild lug nut managed to escape and roll away somewhere into the night.

"You got to be kidding me," Colleen said while disgustedly throwing her arms in the air.

Thankfully, the parking lot had a few overhead floodlights, but even with that it took another fifteen minutes before he spotted the lug nut in a puddle under the car. So Bernie had to get on his belly and crawl where it was greasy and wet, his life depending on a car jack that he probably wasn't even using right, just to retrieve a stupid lug nut.

After surviving that, Bernie attached the runaway lug nut and then finally got the Chevy lowered onto the ground.

They got back in the car and sat there for a minute, not saying anything.

"Can we get a little heat, do you think?" Colleen asked.

He turned the key, but the car wouldn't start.

"Oh my God," she said, burying her face in her hands.

"When it's cold, it takes a few tries sometimes."

He cranked it again and then once more and then it finally started.

"You have to be careful about not giving it too much gas when you're starting up or else you can flood the engine," Bernie explained, trying to reclaim some of his eroding masculinity.

Colleen was unimpressed.

"Are you hungry? Do you want to stop and get something to eat?"

"Let's just go," she grumbled.

"I have to let the car warm up a little first."

"Swell."

He reached to put his arm around her, but she moved away from him.

"What's wrong with you?" he protested.

"Nothing's wrong! Let's just...let's just not do anything for a minute, okay?"

So they sat minding their own business, staring through the windshield at the empty parking lot.

Colleen broke the silence with a question that Bernie hoped she wouldn't ask.

"What did you think about the movie?"

Colleen loved to talk film and theater and music. She could be a damn reviewer. Bernie knew that she was his intellectual superior when it came to stuff like this. She was much more perceptive regarding story structure and all that other kind of cinematic crap that Bernie wasn't the best at recognizing and was even worse at being articulate about. He knew she was just waiting for him to say something wrong, something she didn't like, and then he'd get shit for it. He hoped something profound would come out of him, but it didn't.

"I liked when the monkey found the...thing, and then they figured out how they could kill the other monkeys with the bones. Oh, and how the bone turned into a spaceship in the air...and all that. That was pretty cool."

"But did you get the significance of what he was trying to say?"

"Who was trying to say? The monkey?"

"The filmmaker! Stanley Kubrick!"

In spite of the cold, Bernie was starting to sweat. She was really challenging him, and he wasn't sure what the movie was about or what he thought about it or what Kubrick's fucking message was. Why was she acting like such a bitch? Bernie was pretty sure that the next thing that came out of his mouth was going to determine a lot about his future with Colleen.

"That space is dangerous?" he meekly offered.

Then she slapped him. Pretty hard, too. Bernie was stunned. He wanted to cry or yell or maybe even hit her back. He didn't know what to do. He just knew that she was making him feel like shit.

"You have no idea, do you?" Colleen said, marveling at his witlessness.

"I do. I just can't really verbalize it yet."

"It's about awe. It's about wonder. It's about consciousness. It's about the destiny of man. It's the greatest fucking movie ever made! Are you an idiot or what?"

He thought that she was going to hit him again, and if she did, he was pretty sure that he would hit her back.

Instead she just stared at him judgmentally, like her father and her grandmother do. It must run in the family.

Then she abruptly turned away from him and looked out into the parking lot.

"Can we just get out of here? I want to go home now," she said.

* * *

They drove back to her house in Glen Rock and didn't say anything the whole way. In spite of this and the slap and the insults, Bernie walked her to the door.

She turned to him when they got up to the porch.

"Well, goodnight," she said.

"Goodnight." Bernie made no attempt to kiss her or to feel anything.

"I'm sorry about hitting you. I got frustrated, and I've been a little anxious lately because there's something I have to tell you. I'm seeing somebody else now."

"You're seeing somebody else?" Bernie got a little dizzy, and he was afraid that he might pass out.

"Yes, so I think we should cool it for a while."

"Who are you seeing?"

"I'd rather not say."

"Is it somebody from the theater?"

"I'd rather not say."

Then she went into the house and closed the door without giving him another glance. Bernie stood there on the porch for a moment feeling a slew of conflicting emotions, but mostly he felt sick.

He got back in the Chevy, and he just wanted to die.

***

Bernie resigned from the little theater in Fair Lawn. He didn't want to see her there or anywhere else. He had decided that Colleen really wasn't good for him. In fact, he felt she was like poison, like a drug you can enjoy and get high from but eventually—that shit will kill you.

He started going into New York City to explore the theater scene. He took acting classes and actually got himself into a bad off-off-Broadway musical. He was meeting new girls, learning a lot, and really starting to know New York.

He got an invitation to audition for a company in California. He did a song and a monologue from the musical, and lo and behold he got the job. It was a brand-new theater in Northern California, and Bernie was the happiest guy on the planet. Room and board and eighty-five dollars a week. Bernie felt sure this would be his ticket to stardom on the West Coast. It was a four-month commitment, and then who knows? He wasn't tied to anything or anyone, and the world was his oyster. He was excited about seeing new places and looking forward to whatever adventures life had in store. Whatever was coming his way, Bernie felt ready for it. He was raring to go.

Then he got a phone call. As soon as he heard her voice, the old feelings started creeping back in.

Colleen told him that she had broken up with her new boyfriend. That he had turned out to be gay and not the person she thought he was. She also told Bernie that she had heard about the musical in New York and that he had scored a big gig in California. How she knew these things, he had no idea. Colleen wanted to get together and talk, patch up their problems, and have a chance to apologize for being so mean to him. She was sweet on the phone, like she had been in the beginning, and Bernie was not able to say no to her. In fact, he managed to convince himself that he still might love her.

Turns out that Bernie's parents were going away for the weekend and Bernie had the apartment to himself, so he suggested that they get together there. He offered to pick her up in the Chevy, but Colleen said that she could use her mother's car. Bernie figured that her mother was probably locked in her room again after another bender, so she wasn't going anywhere.

Bernie got some food, some deli-type stuff for sandwiches. He also had access to the liquor cabinet. His parents hardly drank, and Bernie knew he could partake of the scotch or whatever else was in there without fear of detection. He was getting excited about seeing her again.

* * *

Colleen rang the bell at seven o'clock on the dot. Bernie opened the door, and she looked so good that he got a little weak in the knees. She was wearing her raincoat and a woman's black fedora. She looked like a sexy secret agent.

Without a word said, they came together in a furious embrace. And when they kissed, it felt so right that Bernie couldn't understand how he had lived so long without it.

They retired to the living room, and Bernie made drinks—they both had scotch. Colleen sat on the couch in her raincoat, and they role-played a secret agent game. Colleen was a Russian spy and Bernie the English attaché that she'd come to seduce. Bernie decided to commemorate the moment in pictures. He got his camera, and Colleen seductively posed on the couch for him. Then he undid her coat, and she was pulling off his sweater.

"You leave in two weeks?" she breathlessly asked.

"Yes, a week and a half."

"And then what?"

He kissed her mouth; it was deep and warm. He massaged her shoulders and ran his hands down her back, pulling her close.

"Are you going to stay there?" she asked and then bit his ear.

"I'm…" he bit her back.

"I heard you're going to LA." She ran her fingers through his hair, which he had plenty of back then, and then she roughly pulled his head back so she could peer into his face.

"How are you hearing all this?" Bernie asked.

"Are you, though?"

"I was thinking about it."

She kissed him and started undoing his belt, and Bernie was pulling off her blouse.

"Maybe I could meet you there."

"Uh…"

She bit his neck.

"Ow!"

She bit him again.

"What are you doing?" Bernie tried to push her away, to keep her off him long enough to see if he was bleeding.

"Come back here, you English dog," she said in that sexy Russian spy accent.

She made a grab for him with a crazed look in her eye, the same look a method actor had who he did a scene with in class. He had been so out of control that Bernie thought the guy was going to kill him.

Colleen got Bernie's belt off, and she was just in her bra with her pants undone. Bernie tried to get away from her, she was scaring him. He squirmed off the couch and tried to slither away across the carpet, but she was right on him, laughing and feeling his ass. Then she pulled his pants off and got on top of him. With uncanny strength, she flipped him over and started kissing him and humping against him. They'd done this kind of dry fucking before, but this felt more urgent, more real. They rolled on the carpet together, clinging to each other, clutching and groping. There was a violent desperation to it.

"Let's go in your bedroom," she said.

"Have you done it before?" he gasped.

"Of course," she said back in her Russian accent.

They ran into the bedroom together, both of them nearly naked, their clothes scattered in a trail behind them.

They jumped onto Bernie's bed and the wrestling continued, but the bed was too small for both of them.

"Let's go into my parents' room," Bernie suggested.

Completely naked, they threw themselves onto his parents' king-size bed. Bernie finally managed to get on top and pin her down. She smiled at him, and that's when it happened. He pulled her legs up and inserted himself.

While going at it, Bernie felt something that didn't seem right. It was wet—more than what you'd expect. He got to his knees to look, and his passion was crushed. There was blood all over him, all over her, and all over his parents' bed. The look of horror on his face brought a smile to Colleen's.

"What's the matter?" she innocently asked.

"There's blood," he said.

"There is?"

"There's a lot of it. I thought you said you did this before?"

"Maybe he didn't do it right."

"I have to clean this up. Holy shit!"

"Or I must be having my period."

Bernie got off the bed.

Colleen sat up in her mess and smiled at him again. It was extremely creepy.

"We're connected now—forever," she said.

"What?"

"The blood. It's not an accident. It's our destiny."

Bernie ran into the bathroom to clean himself up. When he came back to the bedroom, Colleen was still sitting there on the bed.

"Can you get up, please? I have to clean this up."

"When are they getting back?"

"Tomorrow!"

She slowly got off the bed and went into the bathroom.

Bernie charged through the apartment like a maniac, snatching his clothes and dressing while grabbing buckets and rags and all the cleaning supplies he could find, and then frantically ran back into his parents' bedroom.

"I can't believe this!"

He took a big sponge that his father used to wash the car and tried to soak up as much blood as he could.

After a while, Colleen came back into the bedroom fully dressed, back in her raincoat and black fedora. She watched as he worked.

"Do you have any rug cleaner?" she asked.

"I don't know! Jesus Christ!"

"You're a bastard."

"What?"

"Thanks for making my first time so special for me, you prick."

"I thought you said you did this before."

"I lied!"

"Why?"

Colleen stormed away. She slammed the door behind as she left the apartment, and then screamed at the top of her voice when she was out on the second floor landing. It was sort of a cross between a shriek and a howl. She stomped down the stairway, making as much noise as humanly possible just to make sure that all the neighbors knew that some weird shit just went down.

"What a bitch," Bernie muttered as he rubbed some Pine-Sol cleaner onto the stain.

* * *

Bernie thought he got most of it out. He was hoping the stain would fade as it dried and that his parents might not even notice anything. In his panic, Bernie never considered that the blood might have seeped through the bedcover to the blankets and then to the sheets underneath. Which it had.

Colleen called later that night. She was somber and apologetic, and she played Bernie like a fiddle.

"I'm so sorry to cause you all this trouble."

"If you just told me…"

"I didn't want to ruin it."

"Well…"

"And I didn't think it would be so much."

"Yeah, there was a lot."

"But I just want you to know…I really do care about you. I love you. I was stubborn and stupid and mean to you, and I will never forgive myself for that. I want to make it up to you. And I want you to know that I'm really, really, happy for you, and really proud of you because you're the only one who's making it happen. You're doing it for real—getting out of here and living your dream."

"Yeah, if my parents don't kill me first."

Bernie wasn't kidding, either. He was literally worried about getting killed. His father was a stern man, quiet and pretty much unapproachable. When he got angry, it was a scary thing and not something Bernie cared to be around. He was a strong guy, not a large man but a powerful one. He worked in a textile factory and was in charge of keeping some very tough characters in line. He dealt with labor uprisings and a lot of mob types. More than once he'd come home with bruised knuckles and blackened eyes. The trip they were coming back from had something to do with the factory. Some kind of union thing. His mother was always trying to keep up appearances. To the outside world she was funny, social, and the life of the party. In reality, she was a hysterical woman, a screamer, and a complainer. She was never satisfied and was generally an unhappy person. So this situation, if they should discover what had gone on in their bedroom, had the potential of getting ugly.

"How's it looking? Did you get it out?" Collene asked.

"I think so. Came out better than I thought it would."

"Oh, good. Thank God."

"It's still a little wet…but I think I got it."

"Bernie?"

"Yeah?"

"Did you think about me coming to meet you out there? In Los Angeles?"

Bernie had to pause a minute. He wasn't sure what he thought of that. He was hoping that when he left, he'd be leaving New Jersey and everything connected to it behind forever—including her.

"I've just…" she continued to work on him. "I've been so inspired by you. And I know I need to get out of here. It's getting really bad in the house."

"What's been happening?"

"They fight all the time now, and her drinking is getting really bad. I think she's trying to kill herself. And my brother is so strange and angry all the time. He's really starting to scare me. I need to leave. I need to be with you."

"What about college and all that?"

"I don't care about that right now."

"What about your sister? Can you stay with her for a while? I don't know if you should give up on college, you know? Are you sure you want to do that?"

"I've never been surer of anything. I love you, Bernie. Nobody can kiss me like you do."

"Nobody kisses me like you, either."

And just thinking about those kisses made him forget all about the aggravation she'd caused him and all her weirdness, too.

"We're meant to be together. We can do it, Bernie. We'll take LA by storm."

She kept at it until Bernie agreed to her plan. He even offered that maybe she should come to the theater company first so he could introduce her to everybody there, and then after that they could go down to LA together. Colleen was so happy that she started to cry. Bernie never heard her cry before. It touched him deeply, and he started to cry as well. Somewhere in his brain, Bernie knew that he was being manipulated, but he pushed that back. He just couldn't say no to her. He didn't have the power.

She wanted to get together again before he left for California, but Bernie told her that he didn't have time, that he was too busy getting everything together for the trip. She wanted to buy him dinner and then go park somewhere and pick up where they left off at the apartment. Bernie was tempted, but this time he stuck to his guns.

＊＊

When his parents came home the next afternoon, Bernie was stressed to the max. He actually prayed to God that they wouldn't notice anything. He even cleaned up the apartment in hopes of putting them in a good mood. With any luck, they wouldn't even look at the bed until it was time to go to sleep, and by then, maybe, everything would be dry, and the stain would be faded even more than it already was. He thought about asking to borrow the car so he could get out of the house and not be around if things should blow up. But then his mother decided to do some laundry.

Bernie was in his bedroom when he saw her walk by with the laundry basket. His father was watching something on TV in the den.

Then she yelled in her highest-pitched, most hysterical voice. "Jesus Christ!"

His father shouted back from the other room. "What?"

"Get in here," she yelled back. "Jesus Christ Almighty," she shrieked again.

Before complete panic set in, Bernie wondered if other Jewish families screamed *Jesus Christ* as much as his parents did.

Then his heart landed in his throat, and Bernie sat paralyzed on his bed. He thought about putting on his shoes and running out of the apartment, but he couldn't seem to move.

Then he saw his father run by.

"Jesus Christ!" he roared.

Bernie could hear them talking to each other in harsh whispers. Their bedroom was right next to Bernie's and both their doors were open, but Bernie couldn't quite make out what they were saying, probably because of the ringing that was going on in his ears. Even though he was only seventeen, Bernie was praying for a stroke. Or that his brain would just explode so he could avoid the excruciating confrontation that was about to happen.

Then they both came into his bedroom. They just stared at him with stern looks on their faces as he sat there helplessly frozen on his bed.

"What the hell happened?" his father finally asked.

"What do you mean?" Bernie stupidly responded.

"Our bed is a mess," said his mother, and then averted her eyes, finding it impossible to even look at him.

"What?" Bernie said, trying his best to seem surprised.

"Come in here and look at this," his father ordered while cracking his knuckles.

So they went into his parents' bedroom. His mother had pulled the bed cover off and the bloodstain had indeed seeped through onto the blanket. She pulled back the blanket and gasped, because it was on the sheets as well, a big reddish-brown stain for all the world to see. It seemed to have spread as it sunk in. Probably from all the shit he tried to clean it with. Bernie's mind struggled for a way out, but nothing was coming. He only stared at the bed and hoped that the shocked expression on his face was enough to convince them that he knew nothing about what had happened.

"Well?" his father asked.

His mother still couldn't look at him. She stared at the floor instead, wringing her hands like Lady Macbeth trying to rub away the blood.

Bernie took a deep breath and then came up with a story.

"I don't know what happened. I had a party, which I know I shouldn't have, but…maybe some kids came in here. Maybe they had some wine or some cranberry juice or something, and it spilled. I really have no idea. I never came in here. I'm sorry. What a drag."

They were all silent for a moment after that. He couldn't tell if they were buying it or not. His father looked at his mother who was still wringing her hands and staring at the floor. Then he grunted and left the room, bumping into Bernie's shoulder hard as he went by. His mother started taking the sheets off the bed and, miraculously, that was it. Bernie went back to his room. He lay down on his bed waiting for more hysterics or for his father to come into his room with a lead pipe and beat him to death. But nothing happened.

Bernie's family never talked about sex. He never got the birds and the bees or any advice or warnings. Bernie figured that they had to know he was lying, but they just couldn't bear to broach the subject. So rather than suffer the humiliation of having to actually talk about sex, they chose to ignore the whole thing. It was as if it never happened.

Bernie took this as a good sign of things to come.

* * *

Bernie made it out of New Jersey to begin his new life in the Golden State. He got to the theater company in the Napa Valley, and the place was beautiful. Lots of interesting, talented people were there, but the company itself wasn't exactly the professional top-of-the-line experience that Bernie was looking forward to. Not that Bernie would know what that looked like, but he was pretty sure this wasn't it.

The company members lived on a ranch out in the middle of a vineyard. The scenery was spectacular, but the food sucked, and there was no privacy. Another guy was there from New Jersey. An actor who was from a town not too far from where Bernie grew up. They kept their distance from each other, though. This guy, Harold was his name, was always talking about New Jersey and all the weird crap that went on there—UFOs and shit like that. He even thought that he had been abducted by aliens a few times. Bernie wanted no part of that, and he didn't want any reminders of the life he had left behind. Just hearing this guy's voice, that accent, even though it was probably identical to his own, made Bernie nuts. It grated on him like nails on a chalkboard. They weren't nasty to each other or anything. They just hung out with different people. Harold was more with the actors, and Bernie hung out with the tech people because that's who he wound up working with most of the time.

As it turned out, Bernie didn't do much acting with the company. Mostly he did lights or built sets. He was really hired to help the technical staff, as he painfully came to discover. He was not considered to be much of an actor by the powers that be at the theater. Harold was, though, and that grated on Bernie even more than Harold's accent. Bernie's dream of becoming a big star took its first hit in the Napa Valley, and he never quite recovered from it.

He did meet a girl, though. She was the lighting technician. Her name was Lisa and she was tall, thin, straightforward, and down-to-earth. The complete opposite of Colleen, and Bernie found that refreshing. Lisa thought Bernie was funny and talented and not getting a fair shake from the producers. She was sympathetic to Bernie's frustrations with the company because she had a few of her own.

Bernie and Lisa fell in with a group, mostly crew people, who liked to complain to each other about things around the theater. Whether it was the living arrangements, the food, the ridiculously long hours, or the late paychecks, they had plenty to complain about. They became known as the Bitter Barrys, named after their ringleader and the technical director of the theater, Barry Collin, who Bernie thought was out of his gourd.

As time went by, Bernie and Lisa became more and more of an item. Her kisses weren't like Colleen's, but the relationship was much more comfortable than what he had before—a lot less drama. Bernie moved out of the ranch and into a house with Lisa that she shared with a few other tech people. It was a little three bedroom that the company rented, and it was closer to the theater than the ranch was. The place was run-down and bare-bones, but at least they had some privacy there and a place where the Bitter Barrys could gather to bitch and moan.

By his second month with the company, four different shows were running in repertory, and they turned out to be pretty good. Bernie only got to be in one of them, and it was a small part. When he first got to the theater, time seemed to move so slowly that he almost felt like he was a prisoner. Now with a new girlfriend and the shows up and running, he was starting to have some fun, and the time was flying by.

He had been getting letters from Colleen, who was becoming more and more excited about coming out to join him. But Bernie had new plans now.

Lisa had connections in LA and was planning to head down there when the gig was up in Napa, so they naturally decided to go down there together. Lisa grew up in Orange County and knew a lot of people in the film and TV business and could take Bernie around and show him the ropes. It was a perfect way to go to LA for the first time. The only problem was he had to let Colleen know what was going on.

He put it off for as long as he could, but the inevitability of having to contact her again, the anxiety of that, was starting to torture him. He knew he should man up and call her on the phone. That would be the right thing to do. But he wrote her a letter instead. He told her everything. That he was in love with somebody new, and he apologized profusely for screwing up her plans. He went on and on with a bunch of bullshit about the mysterious ebbs and flows of life and how ultimately this would be a good thing for both of them. He put all the blame on himself and told her that it was nothing she did to cause this to happen. It was just the rhythm of the universe, and blah, blah, blah. He wished her well and said that it was just time for both of them to move on, and even though it kills him to say so, things were officially over between them.

Bernie knew if he spoke to her on the phone, he'd never be able to say these things, and she'd find a way to turn his head around to get what she wanted. Thankfully, there were no cell phones in those days, so he knew that she'd have no way of reaching him, except by mail. She could call the theater, but Bernie decided if she did, he would just ignore the call. He was done with her.

He closed his letter with something exceptionally insipid: *I hope you will still follow your dreams—all the best, Bernie.* Once the letter went out in the mail, Bernie felt a huge weight lift from his shoulders.

Somehow he had managed not to tell Lisa about Colleen. Not yet, anyway.

One of their housemates was a guy named Phil who was also in the Bitter Barrys. Phil was a big guy, with long blond hair, and he looked like a Viking. He was the audio guy for the company. Phil approached Bernie with a proposition one day. He said that he knew some guys in San Francisco who were dealing cocaine and pot and that they could make a deal with these guys, bring the stuff back to Napa, and make some serious money. Bernie told Phil that he didn't have the money to buy into something like that, but Phil said Bernie didn't need any money. His guys would front them the stuff, and they'd pay them back and keep the profits when they sold it. All they had to do was go down there and pick it up.

So on their next day off, Bernie and Phil hitchhiked into San Francisco with two suitcases to meet with Phil's connection. They arrived in San Francisco and made their way to a building in the funky Tenderloin section of town. Phil was cool as a cucumber, but Bernie was getting nervous. Too many unknowns. Too many things that could go wrong. The drug trade in those days was just starting to get nasty. There were turf wars going on in the city, and the cops were aggressively clamping down. If you should get busted for exactly what Bernie and Phil were attempting to do, you'd be looking at some serious jail time. Bernie probably went along with it in the beginning just to get out of Napa for a minute and because he really needed the money. Phil was so big and looked so intimidating that he gave Bernie a false sense of security, but now he was starting to feel like an idiot for being so naive.

They went to a third-floor apartment, and Phil knocked on the door. The marijuana smell permeated the whole building. The hallway was dimly lit, and the carpet looked like it had been used as a bathroom. A thin, long-haired hippie with a Fu Manchu moustache answered the door. He gave Phil a quick hug, pretty much ignored Bernie, checked up and down the hallway to make sure that no one had followed them, and then invited them inside.

Six decrepit-looking guys sat on the floor in a room without a stitch of furniture. Once it was determined that Phil and Bernie had not come to bust them, they resumed what they were doing before: playing guitars, banging bongo drums, snorting cocaine, and drinking wine from jugs. The joints were going around the circle of freaks in an endless stream. You could cut the smoke with a knife.

Bernie and Phil joined the circle and got swept up in the drug fest. But the drugs did nothing to alleviate Bernie's paranoia; they only made it worse.

After several hours of drug-crazed partying, some of the stoners started to stumble back to wherever they had come from, and others just passed out on the floor. Then Phil's friend who had answered the door came over with two big bags of weed and a small baggie of cocaine.

"Two pounds and a little candy for your trouble," he said. "Use it or sell it, I don't care which."

His name was Ron, and he and Phil seemed pretty tight. Ron explained the deal and broke down the costs: what they will owe him, when he wanted it by, and how much profit they'd stand to make if they could move the stuff. If they couldn't move it, they'd still have to make good on what they owed him. They had two weeks to come up with the money. Phil told him that the stuff would move fast. That they were starving for it back at the ranch. Ron's red eyes lit up when Phil told him more about the theater and all the drug fiends that were working there.

"Might have to come up there for visit," Ron said with a cackling laugh.

"Where's your partner?" Phil asked. "I was looking forward to seeing that guy."

"Skip? He's out making a collection. He should be back soon."

They talked about Skip for a minute and all the crazy stuff the guy was into. Besides being a drug dealer, he was into opera and painting, and he actually did some substitute teaching from time to time.

Bernie watched the exchange, and his drug-addled brain made a profound stoner observation. There are basically two kinds of hippies in this world: the peace and love kind, and the ruthless, drug-crazed gangster types like Ron and Charlie Manson. Ron scared Bernie, and the gun he had tucked into the back of his pants left no doubt about what group of hippies he belonged to.

Ron invited them to crash on the floor for the night and then take off in the morning. Bernie wasn't too keen on that idea, however. He'd rather sleep on the street than spend the night on Ron's floor waiting for a bust or gang war to erupt. So they packed up the weed and cocaine in their suitcases and hit the streets.

Somehow, after stumbling around the city for an hour, they managed to hitch their way back to Napa with red eyes, two pounds of weed, and a pretty good story to tell.

* * *

The stuff sold like hotcakes. They broke down the weed into lids and moved the two pounds in less than two days. Phil and Bernie made a nifty profit and split the bag of cocaine to celebrate.

Bernie and Lisa started planning their trip to LA. She already had a place for them to stay when they got there. The shows were all up and running, and with no more rehearsals or sets to build, there was a lot of free time for drinking and smoking (thanks to Bernie and Phil). Life was generally going pretty well. The bitching and moaning of the Bitter Barrys was not nearly as intense as it used to be, and Barry himself had already packed up his bad attitude and moved on to his next gig.

Bernie and Lisa were relaxing in their bedroom, looking at a travel brochure of interesting things to do while in Los Angeles, when a knock came at their door.

"Hey, Bernie. It's Phil. Can I talk to you a minute?"

Bernie got up to let him in.

"Hey, Phil. What's up?"

"Can we talk outside? It's kind of private.

Phil and Bernie went outside and sat on the porch steps. Phil had a couple of beers with him and handed one to Bernie.

"Some weird shit's gone down, dude," Phil said.

"What kinda weird shit?"

Phil looked around first to make sure nobody was listening.

"I called San Francisco to arrange a time to get them their money?"

"Yeah?"

"I couldn't get hold of them. Nobody was answering the phone. So I called this other guy I know who knows them—"

"Yeah?"

Phil leaned in close to Bernie to make sure no one else would hear what he was about to say.

"They're both dead, man. Ron and Skip were shot."

"What?"

"It was that same night we were there. They got Skip when he was out doing that pickup, and then they came to the apartment and got Ron. They found about a hundred bullet holes in him."

"Holy shit!" Bernie cried.

"Shhh."

"Sorry."

They drank some beer before Phil continued.

"So we got ourselves a situation here."

"We do?"

"We still owe them for the stuff."

"Yeah?"

"But there's nobody to give it to now."

Bernie's heart was pounding.

"Was there—?" Bernie stopped himself and leaned in close, just as Phil had before. "Was there anybody else with them? Another partner or anything like that?"

"Just them."

"So what do we do?"

"I guess…we keep it."

"We keep it? But will anybody come after us for it?"

"Nobody knows who we are."

"So we just keep it?" Bernie asked again just to be sure.

"What else are we going to do? Give it to charity?"

They sat with that for a minute and drank their beers.

"Jesus Christ," Bernie suddenly blurted. "If we didn't leave when we did—"

"Yeah, man. Dodged a bullet on that one."

Phil looked at him and a smile slowly worked its way onto his Viking face.

"Good score, bro. Guess it was meant to be."

They clinked their bottles and finished their beers.

* * *

A week later Bernie got a letter from Colleen with just two words—*I'm pregnant!*

Bernie freaked out enough to tell Lisa what was going on with Colleen. Lisa was amazingly cool about it. Bernie rambled on and on about how he didn't think it was possible for her to be pregnant.

"We only did it once and there was all that blood!"

Lisa told Bernie to relax, that he needed to call Colleen and settle things one way or another. Over the next few days, Lisa kept telling him the same thing whenever he would start to get hysterical.

"What you think will make you happy is the thing you should do."

She was calm, and there were no conditions. She told Bernie that whatever he decided to do would be fine with her—no pressure. Lisa was amazing. A drunkard's dream, as the saying goes.

Then, Bernie got a screaming hemorrhoid. He never had one before, and it seemed to come from out of nowhere. It was very painful, and made going to the bathroom an excruciating experience. The hemorrhoid tortured him for two days, and then it just disappeared.

Meanwhile, Bernie had convinced himself that Colleen was lying about being pregnant and that she was out to destroy him. At that point, she would say or do anything just to fuck up his life. It was revenge, simple as that. She always had this weird power over him, and even though she was three thousand miles away, he could still feel her pulling and tugging at him, trying to manipulate him, trying to rip him apart. He had to get away from her. Even if she was really pregnant, it didn't matter. He was trying not to get crazy about it, but he really believed that escaping Colleen was a life-or-death situation.

Bernie decided not to call Colleen. He didn't want to give her a chance to talk him into something stupid. He wanted her in the past. He wanted to turn the page on all that Jersey crap. He was done with her tricks, her games, and her cruel insults. But even still, what she had said to him that day sitting on his parents' bed, smiling at him like some demented, bloody, horror queen, it kept replaying in his head, "We're connected now—forever."

"Well, we'll see about that," Bernie said out loud to himself. "You got nothing on me now, you freak. I'm a free agent, and you're just a bad memory. So in the words of my new home-land—adios amigo!"

He got another letter before they left Napa, but he never opened it. He threw it in the trash.

Then he got another hemorrhoid. They would torture him for the rest of his life.

* * *

Bernie and Lisa arrived in Los Angeles. When he saw how big the city was, he was glad he had someone with him who knew the ropes.

They were staying with Lisa's friend Elaine in a cluttered house in the Fairfax District. The living conditions at the house were not the best. They had the back room, which was more like a storage area than a bedroom. There was a tiny lumpy bed, and the room was moldy with a lot of dust and spiders.

Elaine was a lesbian—an older Black lady who had a live-in girlfriend, a frumpy Mexican woman named Daniela who seemed to have disappeared soon after they moved in. Elaine used to be an actress. She and Lisa met years back on some theater gig they had done together. Elaine was not in great shape. She stumbled around the house with a walker and always seemed in danger of taking a fall. Worse than that, though, she was a complainer. The cost of her medicine, her mortgage, her ungrateful girlfriend, were all sources of extreme angst for her. Bernie thought she was trying to lay a guilt trip on them because they weren't paying her rent. After a few days of Elaine's attitude, tempers were getting short, and the writing was on the wall.

They needed to find their own place. Lisa was out looking for work most days, and Bernie knew that he had to do the same. He still had some money left from the San Francisco score, but he needed a job. His showbiz career had to be put on hold until they could get comfortably situated. Besides, after not getting cast in the shows up North, Bernie wasn't so sure he wanted to do the show business thing anyway.

So Bernie pounded the pavement looking for work. He was walking down Hollywood Boulevard when he got that feeling in his gut. It was the same thing he'd feel when he thought about Colleen: a momentary twinge and ache in the area where his hemorrhoids would come from—definitely enough to make him stop and take notice. He looked up and saw that he was standing in front of the Egyptian Theatre, which was one of the premier movie palaces in those days. Bernie took the twinge as a sign. He figured that his gut was trying to tell him something. Whether it was a good thing or a bad thing; there was only one way to find out. So Bernie strolled down the Egyptian Theatre's long red-carpeted walkway. He walked past statues of Egyptian queens, sphinxes, and cool-looking urns, and right up to the main theater entrance. Stationed at the door was a thin guy with long, wavy blond hair dressed in the Egyptian Theatre usher's uniform: red vest, black pants, white shirt, black bow tie, and white gloves.

"Ticket please," this guy said.

"Uh, no…I wanted to talk to the manager," Bernie told him.

"Yeah, about what?" asked the suspicious usher who's name tag said Lester.

"I'm looking for work," Bernie told him.

"Oh really?" Lester sized him up. "Well, you may be in luck because a guy just quit."

"Cool," Bernie said.

Lester escorted Bernie through the impressive Egyptian Theatre lobby to a backroom office, where he met Mr. Love, the theater manager. Little did Bernie know, but from that moment forward, everything was about to change for him. The Egyptian Theatre would become his launching pad into a life of scams, mail fraud, embezzlement, and countless other shady dealings. It was as if he got sucked into a "vortex of crime," as he later explained to the judge at his hearing. He had no aspirations for becoming a crook or a scammer, but everywhere he turned, another criminal opportunity presented itself. And once in the vortex, Bernie found it impossible to escape.

In truth, Bernie had no real skills to speak of. He never went to college and had limited life experience. Bernie could barely make change and consequently had a fear of cash registers. The Napa thing showed him that he wasn't as good at acting as he thought he was, so what else could he do? Being a criminal gave him purpose, he developed skills, and it made life exciting.

Mr. Love was a throwback from another era. An elegant man who took great care in always looking his best. He was a decent man, a trusting soul and generous to a fault. He was brutally taken advantage of by the people he employed. Bernie figured him to be in his mid-sixties. Mr. Love was planning his retirement and was training his replacement, Terry, who was a little older than the ushers, except for Helen, a strange troll-like woman who had been working there for nobody really knew how long.

Terry was an awkward guy with big, round coke-bottle glasses. He would get weekly hot combs, and he tried to match his boss stylistically but just wasn't on the same level as Mr. Love. Terry was in charge of keeping the ushers in line and scheduling their shifts. He also handled the box office receipts and made a weekly walk to the Security Pacific Bank down the street to make deposits. Terry had a gun. A big Clint Eastwood–looking .45. He would carry this cannon with him on his trips to the bank. Otherwise it was locked in the office safe. Terry was the assistant manager, but he really wanted to be one of the guys. He wanted to fit in. He was desperately lonely and in need of some friends. Terry was also taken advantage of and manipulated by the ushers.

So Bernie had his interview with Mr. Love, while Terry and Lester sat and watched. After only a few questions and a bunch of bullshit from Bernie about how important this job was to him, and how honored he would be to work for such a legendary and historic movie palace, Bernie got the job. He was immediately taken to the ushers' room and fitted for his uniform. They had tons of them in all sizes—shirts, vests, and pants. Some were clean, some of them stank. Bernie found his sizes, and although the shirt was a little rank, he lived with it. After becoming properly attired, Bernie went back to the office and signed all the necessary paperwork to become an official usher at the world-famous Egyptian Theatre.

Lester was the one who showed Bernie the ropes and took him on the Egyptian Theatre tour. He explained that all the ushers had to know how to do everything because they would be assigned to different jobs at the theater.

First they checked out the concession stand, where Andy, a good-looking Latin guy, was working. Andy looked really bored and was glad for the distraction of showing Bernie how things operated behind the counter. He showed him where they stocked the candy, how the popcorn machine worked, and how to work the concession stand cash register, and that sent a little shiver down Bernie's spine. No computers in those days to tell you how much change to give back to the customer. Bernie, of course, didn't say anything about his lack of skill in this area. He figured he could pick it up by watching the other ushers do it. Or maybe back at the house, Lisa could show him. How hard could it be?

Next, Lester took Bernie out front to the box office. Working the window was a skinny girl with the saddest, moodiest eyes that Bernie had ever seen. Her name was Deloris. Lester and Bernie went into the booth with her. Deloris was either very tired or a heroin addict. She could barely speak above a whisper, and she had the limpest, coldest handshake that Bernie had ever had to endure. Deloris tried to explain to Bernie how things worked with the tickets, but she was barely comprehensible, she just didn't have the energy. As she tried to explain things to him, her eyes grew dimmer and dimmer until she actually fell asleep. Bernie thought that she might have died, but Lester poked her, and she picked up right where she had left off.

Next, Lester and Bernie went down to the new building behind the Egyptian, where there were two smaller theaters. This was known as The Annex. It was for showing more independent features or movies that had been around for a while and weren't getting a very big turnout anymore. Sometimes they would have special screenings there. Classics and occasionally special midnight showings of cult films and campy horror films. The two theaters inside only had two hundred seats each, and The Annex had its own box office and concession stand. Most times it only took two people to run things in The Annex. The box office was not in a separate booth outside. It was just part of the concession area. Lester introduced Bernie to the two ushers assigned to The Annex that day. First there was Ali. He was from Turkey; had a cool accent; an outgoing, engaging personality; and was happy to show Bernie how everything worked. He and Lester seemed like good friends. They enjoyed a few laughs together, some inside stuff, and Bernie wasn't sure what they were talking about.

Ali surprised Bernie by asking if he liked to smoke weed. When Bernie admitted that he did, Ali got excited.

"Yeah, baby! Because I'm telling you. We have a lot of fun around here, and that's the truth!"

Then Ali described the ins and outs of working at The Annex—how the box office operated, how to handle the crowds when they got busy, and all the particulars about the concessions. He did this with such enthusiasm that Bernie felt sure that he had just scored the greatest job on the planet.

Working with Ali behind the counter was Helen, the strange troll-like woman. She didn't say anything the whole time Ali was showing him the ropes, but as soon as he got done she chimed in with a weird assumption about Bernie's lifestyle.

"You probably don't get enough sleep. Do you take vitamins?"

"Uh…probably not enough," Bernie told her.

"We'll talk about it," Helen said. "It's very important. Don't go to doctors. Take it from me. Vitamins and sleep. Look at me. How old do you think I am?"

Bernie looked her over.

"How old?" Helen demanded.

Rather than trying to guess and possibly insulting her, Bernie said, "I don't know. How old are you?"

"I'm sixty-five. Sixty-five years old just yesterday. Don't look it, do I?"

"No, not at all. I never would have guessed that," Bernie said, even though he absolutely thought she could be sixty-five, or even older.

"Well, that's what I'm talking about." Helen boasted.

When they got done with The Annex, Lester took Bernie back up to the main door where Lester was stationed. There was a box that Lester stood behind. A rectangular box that came up to Lester's waist. Lester explained that when customers come to the door with their tickets, you take the ticket from them, rip it in half, give half back to the customer, and put the other half into the box. Those tickets are counted at the end of a shift and compared to the box office receipts to verify ticket sales. Then after the last showing, and if everything matches up, the cash is locked away in the office safe until Terry takes his armed-and-loaded walk to the bank.

That first day Bernie hung around with Lester for the entire time. He answered all of Bernie's questions and explained everything about the Egyptian. And not just about how the theater operated, but about all the different personalities that he'd be dealing with—who was cool and who was not. He told him that Terry was crazy and to watch out for him because something was seriously wrong with the guy, but Mr. Love was a mellow fellow. Lester went through the entire staff in great detail, and by the time he was done, Bernie felt that he knew the employees at the Egyptian better than he knew his own girlfriend.

Lester also told him that when it got really slow, like it was now, and if he was cool about it, he could go up to the roof and smoke some dope to alleviate some of the crushing boredom that was part of the job. And just to demonstrate how it was done, Lester took Bernie up a back staircase that led to the roof, where they enjoyed the view of Hollywood and smoked a joint together. Then properly stoned, they went back down to finish their shift. No one was the wiser.

Bernie and Lester became fast friends. By the end of the day, Bernie was calling him Les and Les was calling him Bernstein (for some stony reason). Les told him that there was some other stuff that he needed to tell him about, but it would probably be best to talk about it away from the theater. He invited Bernie to his apartment, and they agreed to meet at nine that night. Les wrote down his address on an Egyptian Theatre card promoting the premier of *The Poseidon Adventure*. He wrote his address right across Gene Hackman's face—the weed was pretty good, so they both thought that was hysterical.

* * *

Bernie got home about six and had dinner with Lisa and Elaine. Everybody was excited because Bernie got a job, but when he asked Lisa to show him how to make change, she copped an attitude. She couldn't believe that he didn't know how to do that. It reminded him of Colleen when she would get nasty and mean with him. After some begging, Lisa finally taught him what he should have learned in fourth grade. It took him a minute, but eventually he got it figured out. Then he made a lot of excuses—it wasn't that he didn't know how to add and subtract, it was just that he never needed to know how to make change before, and he just wanted to make sure that he was doing it right. Bernie felt he lost Lisa at that moment. Like she had finally decided that she was living with an idiot, and she wasn't too crazy about the idea.

Bernie arrived at Lester's place right on time, which was a bit of miracle considering he took the bus to get there. Lisa went out with some friends, so she was using the car for the night. It was her car, after all. Bernie was depending on Lisa for a lot. It was her friend they were staying with, and it was her show business connections that he was hoping to get to know. But after the money changing thing, Bernie had a feeling that he might be on his own now.

Les was glad to see him at least. He had a jug of wine and some joints already rolled and ready to fire up. Les had a cool place. It was nice and roomy with comfortable furniture, book-cases, and lots of artwork. He had wood sculptures of differ-ent kinds of animals, cats mostly, and some really interesting paintings on the walls—portraits of expressive women. Some of them looked deliriously happy, and others had agonized faces that Bernie was sure he'd have nightmares about. One of them reminded him of Colleen—one of the agonized ones.

"Did you do the paintings?" Bernie asked.

"Yeah, I love doing woman's faces," Les said.

"They're really good."

"Thanks, man."

Les put a record on the turntable—Harry Nilsson's *Nilsson Schmilsson*. Les said that he thought Nilsson was the greatest singer alive. They drank wine, smoked a joint, and listened to the music for a while. Bernie agreed—Nilsson was awesome.

Then Les told him that he had to show him something, but that he had to promise not to say anything to anybody about it. Not to his girlfriend and especially not to anybody at work. Bernie was righteously stoned at this point, and his imagination ran a little wild. What was he going to show him? A severed hand? A gun? A dead guy in the closet? Is this going to turn into some weird sex thing?

"So, do you promise?" Les asked again.

"Oh, yeah. Sorry…"

Les got up and went over to the closet, but he didn't pull out a dead body. It was an attaché case. He put it on the coffee table, and then he sat back down across from Bernie.

"Open it," Les said.

"Open it?"

"Yeah, go ahead."

"What's in it?"

"Just open it. You'll see."

"It's not something that's going to freak me out, is it?"

"It might, but in a good way."

Les leaned back in his chair, ready to enjoy Bernie's reaction to what he was about to see.

Bernie polished off his wine and then opened the case. Les watched as Bernie's jaw fell open. Then he coughed and quickly closed the case and fastened the latches.

"What is this?" Bernie asked.

"Money. A lot of money."

"Yours?"

"Yup."

"How much money?"

"I think there's about two grand in there."

"Where'd you get it from?"

"That's what I wanted to talk to you about."

So Les explained that there was a thing going on at the theater. He and Ali were on the roof one day sharing a joint when they hatched this idea about how to supplement their minimum wage income with a little extra cash. Well, a lot of extra cash as it turned out to be. It would take a team to pull it off. A group of ushers they could absolutely trust. It would take some manipulation, and it was potentially dangerous, but if it worked, they'd be rolling in dough.

They would need a person in the box office, at the door to receive the purchased tickets, and at the concession stand.

In The Annex, both ushers had to be in on the plot or they wouldn't be able to pull it off in there. They had to get Terry to schedule their team on the busy nights, at premiers and all the exclusive events that looked to bring in a lot of people.

The system basically worked like this:

The team member in the box office would sell the tickets as usual, but when the ticket got to the doorman, that's when things got interesting. On every third or fourth ticket sold (depending on the size of the crowd on a particular night), the doorman would take the ticket, but instead of tearing it in half, giving half of the ticket back to the customer and dropping the other half into the box at the door, the doorman would do a little sleight of hand trick. He would only pretend to tear the ticket and instead would hand back a previously discarded torn ticket that had been collected the night before. Then one of the doormen (there're always two working the door when it's busy) would return the untorn ticket to the box office, where it would be resold. The money for the resold tickets was not recorded, of course, and was stored in a separate place.

The concession scam was a little disgusting but very effective. The way they kept track of concession sales (for popcorn and drinks—the big sellers) was by counting cups and popcorn buckets. So if those items could be collected from the trash, washed, and then resold over the course of the evening, that would turn into a nice hunk of cash as well. The big theater had over three thousand seats. If they were packed and the operation was running smoothly, well, you get the idea. The hard part was figuring how much to take without it being detected.

The other hard part was getting Terry to schedule the right people in the right place. But the team members were trained to cover all the stations, so that increased the odds of pulling off the scam. And Ali and Les knew that if they could butter him up and make him feel like their pal, they could get Terry to do just about anything.

When the plan was first hatched, Les didn't take it too seriously. He didn't think it was something they would actually do. It was just stony moron talk—just goofing and spinning tales to make the time pass. The more they talked about it, though, the more it seemed like they could actually pull it off.

Ali's the one who put things in motion. He made the overtures to the people he thought they could trust, and within two weeks the scheme was running like clockwork. They got it down to a science, and the money was pouring in. So much of it that Les was worried about putting it into the bank for fear of someone getting suspicious. In those days, most everyone paid cash for theater tickets. You never had to deal in credit.

They would meet once a week at either Lester's house or Ali's and divide the loot among the team members and plan operations for the coming week. One of the things they talked about was infiltrating the books. Everything was recorded in a book that Terry was also in charge of: the number of tickets sold, all concession sales, the ushers' shifts, and where they were stationed. If something didn't add up, Mr. Love and Terry would know who might be responsible for the discrepancy. If Ali or Les could talk Terry into letting them help with books, and if they could actually schmooze him enough to let them do the entries, well that would make their transgressions nearly undetectable. In a worst-case scenario, if something did go wrong and suspicions should arise, they could shift the blame to other ushers who weren't in on the action. They could set up a fall guy—if it should become necessary.

By the time Bernie came around, things were rolling along really well. They did manage to take over the books, and the money was rolling in. But when one of their team members quit, they needed a replacement—pronto. *The Poseidon Adventure* was going to be a huge event, and they needed to replace their lost team member to cash in on the windfall. Bernie was it. Les just had a good feeling about him. Takes one to know one.

The vortex of crime had opened and Bernie got sucked right in.

* * *

They still had a month before *The Poseidon Adventure* premiere. Bernie was picking up the tools of the swindle, and the cash was rolling in. But life in the house with Elaine and Lisa was getting more and more uncomfortable. When Bernie finally broke down and told Lisa where his newfound fortune was coming from, that was about the last straw in their already deteriorating relationship.

Bernie went back to the house after a particularly boring day shift at the Egyptian, and Lisa was gone. Elaine told him that she got a job in Oregon, took the car, made a cheese sandwich, and tripped the light fantastic out of town (Elaine often quoted lines from plays that Bernie never even heard of). She said Bernie could still stay there, but it would cost him fifty dollars a week, and if he wanted food, he had to bring in his own. Bernie told Elaine that he'd think about it and went into his room to sulk.

Sitting on the bed was a letter. He assumed it was probably a goodbye and good riddance from Lisa, but it wasn't. It was that second letter from Colleen that he had thrown in the trash back in Napa. Lisa must have picked it up and saved it for some reason. Bernie's stomach fluttered. He opened the letter. There were four words this time—*You're in big trouble.*

Bernie tore it up and threw it away, and then immediately had a sharp pain in his asshole.

The next day, Bernie moved in with Les. He pondered his failures with women and wished for a moment that he could get into a relationship that might last a little longer than those he'd had so far. Somebody who would really love him, or at least like him enough to treat him with a little respect. But the truth of it was, as with Colleen, he wasn't sad that Lisa was gone. He doubted that he would even miss her. He started to believe that he really wasn't a good person and that most likely something was wrong with him. Or maybe, he instantly reconsidered, it's not a matter or right and wrong. It's a matter of nature—

I'm a loner and a drifter. I wasn't made for long-term relationships, that's all.

Bernie began to consider that he really was an outlaw at heart and just too wily to be in a steady girlfriend-type thing.

I'm a scoundrel. A thief. A scammer. A fearless opportunity taker. I'm Butch Cassidy, and he was about the coolest guy that ever was, so give me a break, already. I'm just not the type to be tied down to some chick who wants to tell me how to behave and what to think—I'm too much of an outlaw for that.

He got himself a beer and sat on Lester's couch. He looked up at the picture that reminded him of Colleen, and then he got that uncomfortable feeling in his gut again. He shot the picture a bird, fired up a joint, and then surmised his situation.

I may be a psychopath...but, hey, there're a lot worse things you could be.

Then Bernie went into the bathroom and shit his brains out. With the new hemorrhoid that had just developed, it was an extremely painful experience.

* * *

The Poseidon Adventure premiere turned out to be a bigger deal than anyone had expected. They had to hire two extra ushers to escort all the celebrities and VIPs to their reserved seats. There were news vans on Hollywood Boulevard, and giant spotlights crisscrossed the night sky to announce the moment to the universe. The celebrities showed up in limousines, and the regular folk were lined up around the block.

But all the hullabaloo and TV attention did nothing to distract Bernie and his fellows from working their scam. Everything was positioned. They had practiced. They had the right people in the right places. They were a well-oiled machine.

Red Buttons, Irwin Allen, Jack Albertson, Roddy McDowall, and Ernest Borgnine were all there to wow the crowd. And Ali, Bernie, Lester, and Andy were there to take their money. Terry and Mr. Love were on cloud nine greeting all the big shots as they arrived. They had no idea of the great swindle that was about to take place.

There were two people in the box office—Les and Delores. Two windows, two ticket-dispensing machines, and, of course, no computers. They each had their own cash drawers. If there had to be another person in the box office who wasn't in on the scam, Delores was the preferred choice. When Les started reselling tickets, she would remain blissfully oblivious.

At the door were Ali and Bernie. The ticket box was perfectly designed for the swindle. There were two slots on top and two different receptacles inside. So the properly torn tickets would go into one slot, and the untorn tickets would go into the other. Ali would do the sleight of hand, and Bernie would take tickets legitimately. On Ali's cue, Bernie would take the whole tickets up to Les in the box office to resell.

How it worked in the box office was so simple, it was ridiculous. Instead of having a sold ticket come through the dispenser, Les did his own version of the sleight of hand trick. He would run his hand over the ticket dispenser—thereby creating the illusion that the ticket was coming out of the machine—but instead of giving the customer a new ticket, Les would give them an already sold ticket, one that he had palmed. The money paid by the customer would be stashed in a special compartment to be later collected and distributed to everyone on the team. Les had carefully set up his station. It was perfect. Sherlock Holmes wouldn't have noticed anything out of the ordinary, let alone Delores.

The box office opened two hours before the screening, and there was a steady flow right up until showtime. Terry and Mr. Love were so busy greeting celebrities and helping them find their seats that they got nowhere near where the real action was taking place.

Everything went off without a hitch, except Ali got greedy. Because of the size of the crowd, they had previously agreed that Ali would palm every fifth or sixth ticket. But Ali, in his lust for riches, was palming every third ticket instead. On three thousand seats—that was a lot of money. Mr. Love and Terry must have done some calculations and had some estimates for what kind of money the big night would be bringing in. They were going to be way short of that. Some fancy bookwork would no doubt be required.

After the premiere, Bernie was in the theater, cleaning, and collecting discarded torn tickets. Ali was in the office counting ticket sales and cleaning the books. In case Terry and Mr. Love were to finally suspect that something fishy was going on—Ali shifted culpability in Delores's direction. The sales on Les's end of the box office were switched over to Delores's.

Nothing got said that night, except Ali and Les had heated words in the lobby, and that got Terry's attention. He approached them to see what the problem was. They came up with some bullshit story about a girl they were both seeing. Terry seemed suspicious but told them not to bring their personal problems into the theater, and then let it go at that. Of course what they were really arguing about was how Ali had gotten greedy and deviated from the plan, consequently putting the whole beautiful swindle in jeopardy.

The next day, the shit hit the fan.

A meeting was called in the office, that all ushers were required to attend.

Mr. Love sat at his desk looking hurt and shaken. Terry sat off to his side, and all the ushers crowded in around them. "We have reason to believe," Mr. Love began, "that some of you may be responsible for shortages that have been occurring at the Egyptian. And last night it was particularly egregious."

There were stunned looks from the employees. Terry sat frozen with a bitter frown on his face. He stared at the red carpet on the office floor with his arms folded across his chest. Terry was fuming and seemed about ready to explode.

"The best thing," Mr. Love painfully continued, "would be for the person or persons who did this to step up and do the right thing. You need to say why you did it and how you did it. If you can do that, I will be lenient. That would be the best thing for everyone. If not, I assure you that I will get to the bottom of this, and there will be a heavy price to pay. This kind of behavior will not be tolerated at the Egyptian. I am disgusted and disappointed. In all my years…" Mr. Love had to take a moment to choke back his emotions.

Terry slowly shook his head and stared at the ushers with a weird smirk on his face as if he were just waiting for a signal to either fire everyone or take his .45 out of the safe and blast them all to hell.

"I've always thought of the staff here as family," Mr. Love continued. "And this is a devastating blow. I have nothing else to say to you."

Terry gestured with a shooing motion for everyone to leave the office.

* * *

No one stepped up.

Delores and Helen were fired the next day. Delores's numbers were obvious, and Ali had been setting up Helen for weeks in advance. They were completely stunned and terrified about what was going to happen to them next. They swore up and down that they had nothing to do with it, and of course they were telling the truth. Thankfully, Mr. Love never officially filed charges against them. I think he had a sense that although the books incriminated them, they weren't really the ones who were responsible. Of all the swindling and shady dealings that Bernie would go on to, this was the thing that irked his conscience the most. Delores had two small kids and no husband. How she managed on the Egyptian Theatre salary, he couldn't even imagine. Helen was on the verge of a nervous breakdown, and no matter how many vitamins she took, Bernie was pretty sure that this was going to kill her.

But what happened next was the thing that really turned everything around and probably why Mr. Love decided not to prosecute anyone.

After the meeting in Mr. Love's office, Terry maintained his foul mood and kept mostly to himself. On the Friday after the premiere, Terry gathered up the money in the safe. Bernie estimated that between *The Poseidon Adventure* premiere and receipts from the rest of that week, it had to be at least $26,000. Mr. Love wanted to hire a security company to transport the money to the bank, but Terry insisted that he could handle it. He stuffed the money into a Security Pacific Bank bag and armed himself with the .45. Terry had a specially made holster that he liked to show off. It fit so well under his jacket that you'd hardly know he was packing. He put the Security Pacific Bank bag into a brown paper sack, strolled down the red carpet of the Egyptian Theatre walkway, and nobody ever saw him again.

Instead of going to the bank, Terry got into his car and drove east. He got all the way to Texas before the FBI caught up with him. His car was stopped on a highway, right at the New Mexico-Texas border. Shots were fired, and Terry was killed. He was shot fifteen times, and it made the eleven o'clock news. Poor old friendless Terry stretched out dead on the highway, surrounded by a swarm of cops and suited agents and still wearing what he had worn to work that day.

All the drama was killing Mr. Love. He wanted to quickly train a replacement and then retire from the Egyptian. So despite his reservations about Ali, Mr. Love asked him to become the new assistant manager. Ali accepted, and the team of thieves were giddy with anticipation. Scamming the Egyptian was easy before, but now with their top guy in management—this was going to be ridiculous.

They had already split up the premiere money and now they were ready for more. Everybody was excited, except for Les. He had resolved his riff with Ali, but Les still didn't trust him. And now that he was assistant manager, who knows what havoc he would wreak, and who he would blame if something went wrong.

Les saw the writing on the wall and consulted with Bernie about it. Back at the apartment they broke it all down over a jug of wine. Les had a bad feeling about things, and now Bernie did, too.

In the days that followed, there were visits to Mr. Love's office by serious-looking corporate guys. They wanted to be shown the box office and the concession setup. There were also visits from other theater owners, movie studio people, and some squirrely accountants who wanted to see the books. Something was in the works.

An independent movie called *Coffy* had bought out The Annex. They were going to premiere their film there, and then exclusively run it for two weeks in both small theaters. The buzz around town was that *Coffy* was going to be a big hit. When word got out that another premiere was coming to the Egyptian, despite their worries, Les and Bernie started getting pumped up again. It was a lot easier to control things in The Annex than in the big theater. It should be an easy score.

Except for one thing. They soon came to learn that the production company for *Coffy* was going to bring in their own people to run everything, including the box office and the concessions, and they would keep their own books. They would pay the Egyptian an up-front fee for the use of The Annex, and then keep everything that came through the door.

Nobody trusted the Egyptian anymore.

This was the beginning of big changes in how movie theaters were going to do business.

The gravy train was making a stop, and Bernie was pretty sure it was time to get off.

* * *

Before the *Coffy* premiere, new box office systems that were much harder to scam were installed in both the main theater and The Annex. Things were being updated in theaters all over town. The fleecing of the Egyptian looked to be over. It was great while it lasted, and they had the additional satisfaction of knowing that what they managed to pull off was a major reason for revamping the entire movie theater industry.

A meeting was held at Ali's place to discuss developments. Ali had a huge apartment with lots of expensive-looking stuff.

Definitely a Middle Eastern decor—a lot of gold and tapestries. It made you think that Ali had a lot more going on than what he was doing at the Egyptian.

Ali was sure that they could find a way to beat the new system, that it would just take a little time to figure it out. But everybody else was done. It was too complicated, and they knew that Mr. Love was already suspicious of them. Ali tried to assure them that he could handle Mr. Love and that he really wasn't even a factor because he'd be gone soon anyway. Ali felt that it would be stupid for them not to take advantage of him in position as the new manager.

The others didn't buy it. There was too much attention on them, and it was way too risky now. Besides, how long would it take to figure out the new system? How long could they survive as minimum wage ushers?

Working at the Egyptian wasn't worth it anymore.

Ali begged them not to go, but it was decided. It wouldn't be smart to quit en masse. They would filter out slowly. One at a time over a three-week period. Ali was pissed and told them they'd be sorry, that he was going to make it work with or without them.

* * *

After the exodus from the Egyptian, Les got so bothered about what Ali might do that he decided to leave town. He wanted to be as far away from the Egyptian as he could get. He decided to move back to upstate New York, where he was originally from. He and Bernie worked it out with the landlord, and Bernie was able to take over the apartment.

Bernie thought about Colleen. He tried not to do that anymore, because every time he did something bad would happen.

Usually, he'd get sick to his stomach, and then the hemorrhoids would start popping up. But there were also the close call disasters that had started to happen. A flower pot falling out of an apartment window just as he was walking by. A large tree branch breaking and coming inches from killing him on the sidewalk. A car suddenly losing its brakes while he was in the middle of the crosswalk. On his last day at the Egyptian, he was leaving the theater and started thinking about her. When he got out to the street a crow dive bombed him and put a three inch gash on the side of his face. He carried that scar for the rest of his life. If people asked him about it, Bernie would say that it was from a knife fight.

Bernie was sure that somehow Colleen was making all this stuff happen to him, but still he longed for her. He even considered calling a few times to see how she was, and if she might be interested in coming out for a visit. He was smart enough not to do that, though.

After the Egyptian, Bernie wasn't sure what to do next. He had a nice stash of cash, but what was his next move? Should he try show business again? He got into a little dues-paying theater company, but even though he was paying them money, he still couldn't get into a show. They had classes he could take, so Bernie tried a few of those. There was a movement class and something called Shakespearian rhetoric. It was pretty boring, and he only continued going because there were a lot of hot actresses he wouldn't mind getting to know.

What he was really interested in, though, was moving on to his next score. He got to know a few people at the theater who were selling weed, and Bernie got an introduction to their connection and started doing a little dealing. He began with one-pound buys, and as his connections grew, his purchases did as well. He wasn't making a fortune, but he was doing okay. It made him nervous, though. He tried to control who he would sell to, tried to limit his customers to those who were connected to people he was already dealing with. But sometimes things would go wrong and a stranger would come to his door. After what happened in San Francisco, this made Bernie extremely uncomfortable, and it just wasn't worth all that looking over the shoulder. There must be easier ways to make a living.

Bernie sat in his apartment having a beer and a smoke and got to feeling lonely. That made him feel weak and stupid. So instead of beer, he switched over to scotch and kept telling himself over and over that he was fine on his own and that he didn't need or want anybody else in his life.

Bernie had already disconnected from his past. He had no desire to talk to anyone from weird New Jersey. It was a part of his life that he was happy to leave behind. He had only spoken to his mother once or twice since he got to California. There were a few letters in the beginning but not anymore. When he got word a few years later that his father had died, he still didn't write or call. Same thing when his mother passed away.

After a few more drinks, Bernie was feeling numb enough to forget about what was bothering him on the personal front and moved on to consider his work options, which weren't many. Then the phone rang—it was Ali from the Egyptian.

"Hey, Bernie. How's tricks?"

"Ali? Holy shit."

"Yeah, man. Good to hear your voice, my brother."

"Are you manager yet?"

"No, no. I got out of there. It was no good anymore. You guys were right."

"Yeah...it was a good run, though."

"It was a beautiful thing. How's Les doing?"

"Les? Les is gone."

"Where did he go? Is he all right?"

"He's fine. Just wanted to get away for a while."

"So where is he?"

"I'm not supposed to tell you."

"Really? Why is that?"

"Well, you know. He just wanted some distance from all that stuff, I guess."

"Oh yeah. I can understand that. Well maybe you'd be interested in this, then."

"In what?"

He never thought he'd hear from Ali again, let alone work with him. But this phone call marked the beginning of a ten-year partnership. In the vortex of crime, shit like this just kind of happens.

*⁂ * *⁂ * *⁂*

It started with a pyramid scheme and a charity donation scam. Ali had experience in how to work them both. He knew how to build them up, get the most out of them, and then get out before they crashed. They weren't on a Bernie Madoff level, but they were pretty good scores.

Ali was incredible on the phone. He knew how to flatter people, charm them, and then with an innocuous low-pressure approach, he was able to get people to gift money to what he skillfully presented as an urgently important cause. Bernie learned a lot from him. He copied Ali's style and got to be almost as good as he was.

They worked mostly Jewish and Muslim organizations, presenting themselves as representatives for an overseas charity who's primary mission was to help struggling Muslims or Jews, depending on who you were bilking at the time.

Ali and Bernie worked this scam for several years under different charity names and PO Boxes, and dozens of different checking accounts. If you want to commit wire fraud—you have to keep moving.

Bernie felt a little guilt at first for taking advantage of people in this way. Especially the Jewish people. Bernie wasn't raised religiously, but he still was a Jew. The more money that came in, though, the less guilt he felt.

They started their pyramid schemes with actors—gullible actors who were desperate for a windfall. It was presented like this:

Bernie would talk to his actor friends, and he'd tell them with great enthusiasm about this fantastic business opportunity that he just happened to fall into. He would be so excited about what he was telling them that they would beg to hear more. It was truly the best acting Bernie had ever done. He told them that he had already made $10,000 on a $1,000 investment, and he was only halfway up the pyramid, and if they got in right now, they'd stand to make a fortune. Then he'd take out his bogus diagrams and show how the pyramid worked and how new investors' money gets dispersed among the members. He explained how at first they would get smaller returns, but as they worked their way up the pyramid, they'd get more and more money, and when they finally got to the top, there was a fortune waiting for them there. The trick, he repeatedly told them, was to get in fast. And if you bring people in with you, well, that will get you to the top of the pyramid even faster. Then he'd go for the coup de grâce. The last person at the top, he'd tell them in a conspiratorial whisper (because this thing wasn't just for anybody), he just took in $200,000. And the person who replaces him at the top will probably double that. That's how big this is, and it just keeps getting bigger. By the time you guys get there…the sky's the limit.

Of course all their money went directly to Bernie and Ali. They would send investors just enough on their $1,000 investment to get them excited and, hopefully, entice others to join the pyramid.

Bernie had a line he liked to close with. He had variations of it, depending on his audience: "If it works like I think it will, you won't have to wait anymore for some producer to hire you. You can make the damn movie yourself!"

Running the pyramid scheme was scary at first. There was a lot to keep track of, and a lot of possibilities for screwups. They had to keep people interested and excited but then crash it at exactly the right time. Hopefully, nobody would call the cops.

They did several of these over the years and got better and better at it. They even got some repeat investors willing to give it another shot. When you're good, you're good.

They were taking big risks for big rewards, and they managed to run this stuff for ten years, always staying a step ahead of trouble. There were a few close calls, which they somehow managed to dodge—they were incredibly lucky. But Bernie's luck was about to change.

⁎ ⁎ ⁎

Ali and Bernie spent a lot of time working together on this stuff. They were partners in crime, but they never really became great friends. They had separate lives, and they knew very little about each other. It wasn't unfriendly; it just wasn't close. Over the years, Bernie became more and more isolated, and he preferred it that way. It was good for business, and it kept things a lot less complicated. When he chose to, Bernie could be charming and personable, but not for cultivating friendships. It was strictly business. Bernie preferred his romances to be over the phone with strangers, or when he'd get horny enough, he'd pay for someone's company. He was smart enough to realize that his lifestyle wasn't exactly a healthy one, but it didn't bother him enough to do anything about it. He thought about getting a dog once but was afraid that it wouldn't like him, so he decided against it.

The weird accidents continued over the years. There were near misses and a few direct hits. He broke his nose once walking into a tree when he thought he heard a woman call his name. And another time, when this name calling thing happened, he walked into a concrete post in a parking lot and broke his ankle.

Bernie would always curse Colleen for his misfortunes. But when he was alone in the dark, he couldn't help but think fondly of her—of those kisses and how good they felt.

One day Ali told Bernie that he was going back to Turkey to be with his family and that he probably won't be coming back. He wanted to go out on a big score. Something for the ages, he said. Something huge.

Ali had a connection with a "Muslim group" (his words) that had some money they needed cleaned. A lot of money. He told Bernie that they would need passports because they had to go to a bank in South America. His Muslim group had obtained a lot of cash, from who knows where, and they needed to run this money through a financial institution that was out of the country. They had connections to a bank in Brazil, where they knew they could stash the cash without any governmental interference and then be able to access the money as needed. In other words, they had some laundry to do.

Bernie asked why Ali needed him for this. Couldn't he just do it on his own? Ali told him that this group would have other things in the future, and if Bernie was in on this first run, and if they got to trust him, there would be much more for him down the road. And besides, it was in Rio, and Mardi Gras was happening, and it's the best party on Earth.

"How much money?" Bernie asked.

"Twenty-five grand," Ali said with a sly grin.

"That has to be cleaned?"

"No, brother. That's just our fee—not including expenses. They're cleaning a lot more than that."

* * *

So Bernie and Ali went to Rio de Janeiro with $400,000 in their checked luggage. It was a nerve-racking experience, but they survived unmolested by security. They got to the bank in the morning and made the deposit, did a little sightseeing, and then went to Mardi Gras. It was insane. The sights, the sounds, the smells. It was a once-in-a-lifetime experience. Except when two guys grabbed Bernie, forced him into an alley, and tried to rob him. Miraculously, he got rescued by some strange creatures in crazy costumes. Bernie was so drunk by the time that happened, he wasn't sure what was going on. But he wound up partying with these people all night long, and then they all landed in a bed together in some crappy hotel somewhere. They must put something hallucinogenic in the cocktails during Mardi Gras, because Bernie had no idea where he was or how he got there or if any sex had been involved. Then from across the room he heard Ali's voice.

"I knew you were crazy, brother, but this was just…I had no idea, I really didn't."

Ali started to laugh as Bernie tried to work his way free of the half-naked pile of costumed bodies. Bernie himself was only in his underwear, and he started searching the human wreckage for the rest of his clothes.

"Man," Bernie groaned. "I don't remember shit! How'd we even get here?"

"Shhh, don't wake them up. You might owe somebody money."

"Are you okay?" Bernie stopped to ask him.

"Oh yeah…I don't drink, so—"

"You don't drink?"

"No. You didn't know that? I'm a good Muslim boy. Never touch the stuff."

The irony was rich. Here's a guy who will lie, steal, and swindle, but he won't touch a drop because he's a good Muslim. Bernie had to laugh, and that made his head throb.

"Oh man…I need some coffee," Bernie groaned.

He found his shirt over the bedside lamp, and his pants under a woman who was naked from the waist down and lying in a fetal position. Bernie pulled his pants out from under her. She smiled, winked, and then returned to unconsciousness.

"In some countries, I believe you are legally married to that woman now," Ali said.

"Where'd you even come from? Were you here the whole time?"

"I've been here, but I'm a married man so I can't do orgies, and Muslims aren't allowed to fuck people dressed like flamingos."

"You're married? I didn't know that. How could I not know that?"

Bernie had been working with him for more than ten years, but he had to come all the way to Brazil to find that out? For some reason, as he stood in his underwear in a shitty hotel room, that really started to bother him.

"When's your birthday? Jesus Christ, I don't even know that!"

One of the sleeping beauties suddenly sat up with a confused look on her face.

"Where am I?" she asked.

"You're dreaming," Ali told her. "Go back to sleep."

And that's what she did.

* * *

The next day they got back on a plane and headed for home. Except for the attempted robbery, and the probability of picking up a venereal disease, the whole thing went off without a hitch. At the airport in LA, Ali told Bernie that he'd be picking up the money from the Muslim group on the following day, and then they'd get together and split up the cash.

But Bernie never heard from him. He let one day go by and then another.

When Bernie finally called Ali's house, he got a recorded message saying that his phone had been disconnected.

He stiffed me!

Bernie couldn't believe it.

How could he do this to me! After all we've been through? I'll track him down, goddammit. I'll go to Timbuktu or wherever the hell he's from!

Like everything else he didn't know about Ali, he didn't know where he was from, either. The one thing he did know was that he just got screwed out of $13,000, and there wasn't a damn thing he could do about it.

But why would he do this? Why would he even invite me to go in the first place? Just to fuck me over? Was it revenge for the Egyptian Theatre? Was he still holding that against me?

Bernie thought of trying to get a hold of the Muslim group but then thought better of it. It might be too dangerous. And with him being a Jew…Besides, he didn't have a phone number or an address, he knew absolutely nothing about them.

He purposely kept me in the dark. The fucker set me up!

He thought about going to the police, but even Bernie wasn't stupid enough to do that. What would he say? Excuse me, officer. I was a mule for a little money laundering operation, and my partner screwed me over, so could you please look into that for me? He knew Ali was going to Turkey, but that's a big country. How could he possibly find him? Look in the phone book under *Ali*?

Bernie was brewing in his anger and self-loathing when another even more distressing realization started working its way into his criminal brain.

What if he wasn't out to screw me at all? What if these guys did something to him? Maybe the Muslim group turned on him and that's why he never showed up. Maybe Ali's dead! What if they decided not to pay and just bumped him off instead? And what if I'm next? Do I have to be looking over my shoulder now for some robed, knife-wielding Muslim lunatic who's sworn an oath to Allah to off me in the most gruesome way possible? If they killed Ali, wouldn't they have to kill me, too?

Bernie didn't leave his house for two weeks. He never did hear from Ali, and he never found out what happened.

From this point on, everything Bernie touched turned to shit.

* * *

Bernie tried to run some stuff on his own, but he never reached the heights that he had with Ali. He did a pyramid that blew up so badly that he had to leave town. He tried another one in Omaha, Nebraska, that barely made him enough to get back to LA. He played around with the donation scam, but he couldn't get that one going, either. He got sloppy. He was drawing attention to himself, and the cops were closing in. Bernie lost his edge, and he couldn't seem to get it back.

So he had to try something else. Bernie had to go legit. He got hired doing telephone sales for a stationary supply manufacturer. He stayed there for a whole year, trying to give the heat he was attracting some time to cool off. They had a bunch of people on the phones who were just crap. Actors and old people who didn't really know what they were doing. But there were a few pros, and they were making a little money. They knew how to hustle this stuff. Bernie learned from them and soon got to be one of the top phone guys.

The owner took a liking to him (or so he thought) and wanted him to split his time between working the phones and doing some things in the office. What a racket this guy had going on. All kinds of things: credit card fraud, payments with no delivery, tapping into expense accounts for schools and religious institutions. He was stealing hand over fist, and I guess he recognized something about Bernie and got him in on some of the action. But, as Bernie came to discover, it was all a setup. And when the heat finally came down on Edward's Stationary Supply, it came down on Bernie. Just as they had set up the girls at the Egyptian, this guy had set up Bernie, only this time there were serious consequences.

Bernie did six months. His first real jail time. While doing time he got a hemorrhoid that was so bad it had to be surgically removed. This was done in the prison infirmary, and he got an infection that nearly killed him. That's what he got for going legit.

For the next fifteen years, Bernie followed his gut. But it seemed as if his gut was out to get him. He was in and out of jail and had one thing after another blow up in his face.

The big one was when he got another telemarketing job with a jewelry supply place and started embezzling from the company. His gut told him this was a good thing, but he was exceptionally sloppy, and he got nailed for it. At the same time, a donation scam he was running blew up. Everybody and their mother was on his ass.

Bernie gave the judge his vortex of crime speech, but that just pissed off the judge more than he already was. So Bernie got three years and wound up in a cell with Patrick, the great snoring seventh wonder of the world.

* * *

Patrick had finally stopped snoring at three in the morning. Bernie was reading *Cellar Man* in his bunk until the snoring stopped. He finally managed to fall asleep, but he had bad dreams about his parents and Colleen. They were conspiring against him. And they had scary faces that weren't human—they had possum faces. Bernie watched them from a locked cage that was suspended from the ceiling. They were trying to decide if they wanted to eat him now or fatten him up and save him for later. Colleen had the weirdest possum face because she still had those fantastic lips on the end of her extended possum snout. And the fact that he still wanted to kiss her freaked him out more than anything else.

Bernie started to cough; he couldn't breathe. He woke up to find Patrick on top of him—choking him. Bernie tried to say something, but he couldn't speak—not so much because he was being strangled, but because of what he recognized in that moment about Patrick. He had huge forearms, Popeye arms, just like Colleen's father had.

Bernie looked up into Patrick's scowling, sweating face and then started to drift. He was seeing things, reliving things: Making out with Colleen in the Chevy with the windows all steamed up. Standing on the roof of the Egyptian Theatre smoking a joint with Les and laughing as they watched a magnificent orange sunset. He saw rolling vineyards in the Napa Valley. He saw himself onstage, singing with Colleen in *Stop the World—I Want to Get Off*. Everybody looked so happy. Everything was so beautiful. What a world this is. Why was he just seeing it now? All this beauty, the symmetry, how perfect it all was, and what a fool he'd been for wasting it.

Then he was in a big open meadow with cows and bales of hay and a perfectly blue sky above him. He saw Colleen floating toward him, holding the hand of a young woman who looked just like her. They were flying like superwomen, slowly floating toward him and smiling. Bernie smiled back at them. But when they got close, they both gave him the finger. Then they laughed, as he imagined two witches would, and they floated right past him and shot straight up into the sky.

When Patrick spoke, it brought him back to his current predicament.

"I got a message for you, asshole. From Colleen."

Bernie started kicking, not because he was trying to get free or trying to defend himself. It was just his body reacting to not getting any air and having his larynx crushed.

"She wanted me to tell you that your whole pathetic life was just about getting you here right now. She's always been calling the shots. And she just wanted me to say hello—right before your last worthless breath."

Bernie was accepting of his fate. He must have known she'd eventually get him. He wondered for a moment if the pictures on the wall up there, the one's next to Patrick's bunk, if there was a picture of Colleen, and if she'd been there watching the whole time.

"Well," Bernie managed to choke out before he lost consciousness. "Tell her that I said hello, too."

* * *

Patrick, of course, was Patrick Macdonald—Colleen's brother. Although Bernie might have heard of the witches of Bergen County, he never made the connection that Colleen was a part of all that. In fact, Colleen came from a long line of witches. Way back to the old country in Ireland. Her grandmother, who had liked to rub Colleen's ass, was the supreme witch, and Colleen took her place after she died.

The talent for witchcraft seems to skip a generation. Colleen's father (her grandmother's son) didn't have it, and both he and her mother cowered to the coven's power. Colleen's sister wasn't a witch, either. It's the second child who usually gets it, and Colleen's sister got out of the house as soon as she possibly could. Patrick wasn't a witch, but he did their bidding—the really nasty stuff. The coven would cast spells and curses, and they manipulated events in local politics. They were a behind-the-scenes force, and they always got their way.

Colleen had been excited about going to California because there was a sect in Los Angeles that she wanted to connect with to expand her own coven's reach. She also wanted to use their influence to launch a career for herself in the movies.

From that fateful day when Colleen sat bleeding on his parents' bed, she was the controller of Bernie's fate. When he broke up with her, a curse was set in motion. Colleen was a powerful witch, and no matter where Bernie went or whatever he tried to do, he could never escape her reach. When she got pregnant, her plans changed, but it didn't diminish her hold over Bernie. It only strengthened it.

Fucking New Jersey. They don't let you pump your own gas, but the witches can run wild in the streets.

The lights in the house are flickering at two-second intervals. It's maddening. Maybe the wires are sweating like I am. Oh man it's hot, and the house is crawling with turtles. Little baby ones falling off the furniture. They laugh on the way down and scream when their shells crack. They're all over the fucking floor, and I've stepped on a few. *Crunch*, *squish*, it's disgusting. The cats are screaming outside. They're fucking or fighting or crying, I don't know which, but I wouldn't mind drowning a few just to teach them a lesson.

I'm soaked. I stink. My hair is awful. My face is covered in an oily sweat.

I drag my carcass into the bathroom. I look at my dick in the mirror above the toilet. I look at my eyes—I look at myself, but I don't recognize anything. Who the fuck is this person? I'm so thin. I look sick. I look old. My eyes are different. I'm somebody else. I think I'm a crook. A scammer. A schemer. Yes, that's right. I've bilked people out of their savings. But I don't know this house. I don't know how I got here. I don't know my name.

The bathroom window crashes. A large turtle lands at my feet. The lights are pulsing with my headache, and then I see her. Her head in my bathroom window. She knocks the remaining glass out of the window with a dead cat. It's Nancy Fucking Reagan. What the fuck is she doing here? She looks judgmentally at my dick, and I quickly put the thing away. She looks so dry and relaxed and in control (the bitch).

"Just say no!" she suddenly shrieks. "Just say no to drugs!"

She shakes her finger at me and gives me a condescending little mannequin smile, and I want to rip her head off and feed her some turtle fucking soup.

"Fuck you!" And having gotten that off my chest. "Fuck youuuuuuu!"

Suddenly, I'm floating away from the ex–first lady. The front door opens by itself, and I go through it. My feet are no longer touching the ground. I'm zooming down Victory Boulevard. I don't know where I'm going or how I'm getting there, but I'm off the ground, man. I'm in the air zooming like a missile right down good old Victory. It's out of control. Everything's a blur. I don't feel so good. It's too fast. The street lights are blinking, just like the lights in the house.

Wait. Good. I'm slowing down. Whitsett Street—I saw the street sign. The engines are slowing to a stop. I'm at Laurel Canyon Boulevard now. I'm coming down. I'm landing right in front of Gaylord's restaurant. Right in front of the fucking bar room door. It swings open, and it's real dark inside. A spotlight illuminates a single round table. I move toward it. Wow. It's cool in here. Some nice music from somewhere. Some jazz. Oh man, this is nice. I hear soft talking from the darkness. Comfortable, very comfortable.

The table has a red velvet tablecloth. The chair is red leather, generously stuffed and cozy. I'm fascinated by the fucking chair, and I'm feeling it up as if it were a woman. It's textures are so nice. I run my fingers over the back and along the seat. It's cool and smooth. I play with the creases in the leather. Man, I'm getting hard over a fucking chair.

The waitress comes. She is beautiful. She tells me to sit, and I do. She is tall. Long legs. Very firm. I want to feel her up, too. I want her real bad and she knows it and she likes it and she's comfortable about that, and I'm comfortable about that, too. The chair is so nice and it's so cool in here and then she puts a scotch down on the beautiful red velvet. She smiles. Her fucking teeth are perfect. Her lips are so full and rich and sweet and sexy—they remind me of someone, but I can't remember who. She puts down a pack of Marlboro Lights next to my scotch.

"Enjoy," she whispers in my burning ear.

She walks backward, gracefully, into the chattering darkness. I slowly lift the glass. The ice cubes chime lightly, delicately. I taste the aroma. I breathe in deeply. It fills my head. I've missed it so. The anticipation is so good. Let me just smell it some more. It's so good. I can't believe I ever stopped. Make this moment last. It's better than sex. It's better than the waitress. I'm so happy. Wait. The cigarettes. Let me get one going first before I drink. What a happy reunion. My old pal scotch and my best friend, Mr. Marlboro. Best damn friends a guy ever had. I'll never leave you boys again, I swear.

I put down my beloved scotch and with a deliberate slowness I gently pick up the pack, cherishing the feel of cellophane. I open it carefully, lovingly. Then they are exposed. My white, filtered beauties. God, how I've missed them. I tap the pack and take one. So delicate, so smoothly it fits between my fingers. I smell it. I put it to my lips. I explore the filter's textures with the tip of my tongue. It feels so right, so natural. I'm giddy with pleasure.

Then the waitress returns. She gets close to me, smiles, and strikes a wooden match. She offers the light. I love her. I lean into her flame. She takes a step away. I lean again and she retreats farther. She smiles, but there's something wicked about her now. Oh no. What is this shit? The chatter in the room is getting louder. Oh fuck. This is going to get scary. I know it. She steps back again and vanishes into the blackness. Nothing left of her except for a little yellow dot, but the match illuminates nothing.

What am I supposed to do? Follow her in there? Then what happens? I'll get my head bashed in by a giant Zippo lighter, that's what happens. Wait a minute. Something is crawling on my foot. It's a fucking turtle! They're all over the place. There're millions of them.

The soft chattering from the darkness suddenly stops. A moment of absolute silence…and then everything explodes. The noise is unbearable. Glasses are crashing. People are screaming in the blackness. They're fighting and fucking like cats!

I got to get out of here. I can't stand the noise. I've got to leave, but there're turtles all over the floor. I don't want to crunch them. Look at that—one of them is on the table. It's walking over the edge with my scotch on its back. *Crunch. Crack*—it's disgusting.

"Get me out of here! I'll be good. I'll say no to drugs! What kind of hell is this?"

As soon as I ask the question the place goes silent again.

And then the crazy laughing begins.

Oh, shit…

PHONY EINSTEIN

1

Howard Dudek stares at himself in the bathroom mirror. He looks closely at his graying temples and picks at the skin tabs growing on his neck.

"Age is a deformity," he says.

In truth, he looks his forty-eight years, and he sees his father staring back at him now. The similarity is undeniable and that freezes him in a kind of queasy panic. His father was a kind man who loved his wife, but she treated him like shit. His mother is a selfish, bossy woman who is never content and always angry. His dad did everything for her, but it was never good enough. For some reason he worshiped her until the day he died. Howard can't forgive his mother for how she treated his dad, and he is angry with his father for letting her walk all over him.

He pulls at one of his skin tabs. He pulls until it hurts.

"I should get these things burned off," he mutters.

But Howard lost his medical insurance two years ago, and money is a serious problem now. Last year it was a struggle just to pay rent and eat (forget about cosmetic surgery). The "acting thing" was an embarrassment. He once had a meager career, but that pretty much dissolved with the new millennium. Show business was tough on middle-aged people with skin tabs and inferiority complexes. He didn't really feel like an actor or a writer or much of anything anymore. His wife had supported him, hoping something would break—it didn't. There were no children.

"Because I was the child, if you want to be honest about it," Howard says to his face in the bathroom mirror.

She had believed in his talent at one time, and he had made her laugh. But the laughing stopped and so did the support. She lost respect for him and that made Howard feel like his father. She left him, and at forty-eight years old he was on his own and not doing very well.

"Goddamn," he says as he pokes at the dark, puffy circles under his eyes.

Howard checks his teeth and then washes his mouth out with Listerine. He combs his fingers through his thinning hair, picks up an aerosol can of Natural Color Highlights, and sprays his graying brown hair white. Next he brushes spirit gum adhesive onto his upper lip and puts on a salt-and-pepper mustache. He studies his face in the mirror.

"Ya, goot enough for the little childrens," he says in a not very good German accent.

Howard likes the face that looks back at him now. It makes him feel better about himself, and it makes his father disappear. Howard leaves the bathroom to get dressed.

His apartment is sparse—only a dresser, his computer, and a CD player furnish the bedroom. An old gray cat (his share of the settlement) lies on the bed and carefully watches him.

His costume hangs from the closet door. Howard starts dressing, his posture changing slightly as he assumes the character. The shirt has a turned-up collar, and the gray pants are baggy—like the ones his grandfather might have worn. He puts on a black tie, a black vest, and some old wire-framed glasses. Howard really looks like him now—a younger version of the Albert Einstein that we're used to seeing.

Howard gets one hundred dollars per performance for a forty-five minute one-man show that he does two or three times a week in different elementary schools around the Los Angeles area. He works for a market research company in the evenings, and on the days he isn't doing Einstein, he answers phones for AAVA, the American Association of Variety Artists, a union for people who play cartoon characters. Albert Einstein is

Howard's last connection to being an actor and the final shred of his rapidly disintegrating self-esteem. Howard runs lines in his German accent, playing to the gray cat, who listens politely.

Once a long time ago, Howard really believed that he would be a star and have his revenge on a cruel hometown. He'd make them sorry for the way they had treated him. He'd prove his worth to his overbearing mother and thumb his nose at the sarcastic relatives who had tormented him. The ones responsible for the cruel childhood pranks he had endured—the relentless bombardment of practical jokes, taunts, and mocking stares—would have to pay. If there were justice in the universe, they would pay dearly. Howard would show his father how to be a man.

Howard Dudek was like a boy named Sue. He didn't have a girl's name to make him strong, but *Dudek* sounds like *doodie*, and his cruel little friends got a lot of mileage out of that. When Howard was thirteen, they locked him in the cellar of the old abandoned house just outside of town. The story goes that a lunatic from the local mental institution escaped from his cell, broke into this house, and held the occupants, a family of five, captive in the cellar. He tied them up and gagged them and hung them upside down like smoked meat. He cut off each of their arms and legs while the others watched and screamed. To shut them up, he cut off their heads and ate their brains. Sometimes late at night, the locals say, you can still hear them screaming. Cellar Man was a point of pride, an urban legend from a mean little place in North Jersey, just outside of Paterson.

Anyway, Howard's friends tricked him in there on a dare. They locked him in and laughed as they ran away, ignoring his screams. He was there all night in the pitch-black cellar, terrified, waiting for the ax that would take an arm and then a leg and then his head to stop all the screaming. He tried to be quiet, to not cry or breathe, because he knew Cellar Man's ghost was still down there waiting for his next victim. After two hours Howard mustered up the courage to speak. Quivering and tearful, he made a pact of revenge. If Cellar Man would let him live, as payment Howard promised to kill them all, all the brats in town, and then bring Cellar Man their brains for dinner.

When his friends finally let him out, Howard was damaged but inexplicably empowered by the experience. He decided not to kill the brats right off. He would prove a point first, that he was not a loser, and he would shame them with his success. He'd become a rich and famous movie star while they would have nothing. And then one day from out of the blue, Howard would come back from his Hollywood mansion to his old hometown, where they would all be fat and bald, working the same stupid jobs, and living with ugly wives and mean children. They would want to be his friend, but he wouldn't let them. They would feel terrible for how they had treated him, but he wouldn't care. He'd rub his fame and fortune in their faces. He'd rub it in good and make it sting. That's when he'd take out his ax and chop off their heads. That would set things right.

That was the master plan of thirteen-year-old Howard Dudek. And little Howard stayed focused. He got into the school plays and began to stand out and get noticed. He kept at it. He had talent and he had motivation. In high school he was voted most talented of his graduating class. He started going with a girl in his geometry class. They got married a year after graduation and then moved out to California together. Everything seemed to be falling into place. He got an agent and immediately started booking acting jobs on TV. But over time, for some inexplicable reason, everything started falling apart.

Howard's confidence eroded with the years. The talent that had made him special became his greatest burden and rewarded him with nothing but frustration and pain. Howard's lust for revenge turned inward. He wasn't sure what was happening to him, but he was beginning to self-destruct, and auditions became torturous for him. Full of doubt and fear he stopped getting callbacks, then he stopped getting auditions, and then his agent dropped him. He tried writing after that, but he could never get anything sold.

Howard didn't know anymore what he was about or what he was supposed to do. Unless it was to fail at everything he tried in order to inspire others by his pitiful example. *Hey*, people would say. *I couldn't do worse than Dudek!*

He grew more and more distant from his wife. The things he had adored about her in the beginning now reminded him of his mother, and he began to despise his wife. They grew distant from each other. The coldness in the apartment became unbearable, and about a year ago, she told Howard that she couldn't take it anymore.

"I was good, though, wasn't I, girl?" Howard asks the cat.

But the old gray cat is already asleep. Howard watches her for a moment, wishing he could sleep so easily and then walks over and scratches her under the chin. She doesn't purr anymore. The cat hasn't been the same since his wife left.

2

oward has recently become prone to anxiety attacks while driving. Consequently, he grips the wheel ferociously as he heads down the 110 freeway.

"Shake it off. Don't think about it!" he scolds himself.

He's getting that ringing in his head, and he's starting to sweat. He can see himself doing it. One sharp turn of the wheel and right into the center divider—right into oblivion.

"Stop thinking about it!"

He tries to think about Einstein. Old Albert behind the wheel. His hair all crazy, his giant brain thinking about the curvature of space while driving to work like a regular guy, listening to the oldies and singing along in his German accent. Howard finds this hysterical and laughs so hard that he almost pukes. He punches the dashboard repeatedly, screams, and then he starts to feel a little more like himself. He checks his mustache in the rearview mirror and wipes the tears from his eyes. He tries to name all the presidents—in order—and that keeps him occupied the rest of the way.

3

He arrives safely at the Sixth Street Elementary School. The multipurpose room is where he usually performs, and he feels the comforting little rush he always gets when he first arrives. It's basically a warehouse for kids. A big empty space: part cafeteria, part auditorium, and part rumpus room. A place where the kids can run amok and expel energy for a few hours before their parents come to pick them up.

Howard does his Einstein show for an after-school program called YS Care. It's a state-sponsored day care setup, so the kids don't have to go home to an empty house after school. They usually have two or three supervisory-type people to try and keep some order. They're not really teachers—they're more like prison guards. Howard wonders where they come from. He always thought they were unnecessarily rough with the kids, and maybe a little dangerous. Anyway, Howard gets a welcomed rush when he walks into the room all dressed up like Albert Einstein, carrying his shopping bags full of props. He walks to the center of the room and takes it all in, looking around at the kids with wonderment on his face. It's part of the act. He takes advantage of their natural curiosity to draw them in. Without him saying a word, the kids gradually settle down, and the din of a hundred crazed youngsters transforms into hushed, excited whispers. Howard loves this part—the part when he first starts taking control.

My God—nobody is better at this than me.

Howard smiles his goofy Einstein smile.

"Hello, how are you? Look, there's something I have to show you. Do you like science?"

"Yeahhhhh!" the kids shout.

"Goot! Goot! Goot!"

Howard's excitement is infectious. He bounces up and down and laughs like a contented seal. The prison guard teachers settle back to take a break. Einstein is in the house.

Howard moves across the room toward the chalkboard (which has been preset for him by the prison guards) and writes some unfathomable equations at breakneck speed. The kids all gather around to see what he's up to and plop down on the multipurpose-room floor to watch the show. Once they settle, Howard steps back to examine his work. He erases something and then writes down another equation. Howard steps back again, but this time he throws his arms up in exasperation.

"Acht! Dat's not it either!"

Howard turns toward his audience with a goofy, frustrated-scientist's look on his face, and the kids start to laugh. Howard smiles back at them with a glint of mischief in his eye.

Oh yeah—this will be a good one.

And then, in an instant, Howard's whole world gets rocked. A shadow crosses over him—a large, black, almost humanlike figure. It hovers for a moment about six feet from where he's standing, and then it attacks. Howard stumbles back as if the thing punched him. The kids start to giggle—they don't know what's happening. The shadow circles Howard, forcing him to the floor. Howard covers his head and tries to defend himself.

"Stop it! Get away from me!" he screams.

The kids watch as Howard grovels on the floor, swatting at the air. They aren't giggling anymore. Now they're scared.

"Go away!" he screams again.

The shadow darts to the right at incredible speed and then goes through the wall and is gone.

The room is quiet—quieter than a multipurpose room should ever be. The kids are nervous and confused. A supervisor, a thin, young Black woman who wears a whistle around her neck and has a bad tattoo of a baby on her forearm, helps Howard get back on his feet. She looks more annoyed than concerned.

"Are you all right?" she asks.

"Ya, yes…I…uh, I…." Howard struggles, somewhere in limbo between Einstein and Howard.

"What happened?" she asks, probably wondering if she needs to call security.

"I don't know. I'm sorry. I'm okay now."

The kids are getting more and more agitated and are no longer able to sit still. The supervisor blows her whistle and that stops them from running amok.

Howard tries to regain control of the situation.

"Wait a minute. Vait a minute, everybody. Everybody sit down and don't vorry. Dat vas nothing. I've seen this happen before. Don't be scared. I'll explain everything for you."

A scared little girl stares up at him with tears rolling down her cheeks. Howard pats her head.

"You are not scared, are you?" Einstein asks with a friendly scientist smile.

"Nooo," says the kid, trying to be brave.

"Goot! Everybody come on! Ve have so much to talk about. Nobody has to be afraid vhen I'm around because I know how everything vorks, and if you know how things vork, you don't have to be afraid, right?"

The supervisor slowly returns to her seat, checking over her shoulder just to make sure Howard doesn't have another conniption.

"Ya," Einstein continues. "I vas just playing vit you here, and I maybe got a little carried avay. I apologize for dat. Vhat happened here vas just the sun playing tricks on us. Ve scientists call it light refraction. Vhat we saw was just a bird that vas backlit by the sun. The bird's shadow vas magnified by the glass in the vindow. It vas just the light playing games vit us!"

But Howard knows this was no light show. Something came to see him, and it meant business.

4

Howard sits at his computer doing a search on ghosts.

A long list comes up on his screen. There are hauntings, interdimensional beings, aliens, shadow people, and all the other usual suspects. Howard recently heard about shadow people on a late-night radio talk show, so he clicks on that one. Apparently everybody and their mothers are seeing shadow people, and that keeps him busy for a while.

After reaching the saturation point with this stuff, Howard lies down on his bed with the cat at his feet. He stares up at the ceiling unable to stop thinking about what he had seen at the school. It was different from what he read online. What he had seen was not some fleeting thing that you catch out of the corner of your eye.

"It looked right at me. It punched me!" Howard says out loud to the ceiling.

As he's mulling it over, Howard catches sight of something that darts past the bedroom doorway. He jumps up from the bed and freezes there. He tries to convince himself that it's just his imagination playing tricks on him, but he turns on the bedroom lamp anyway. He lies back down and tries to relax, but the lamp casts weird shadows all over the ceiling and walls, and that freaks him out so he shuts it off again.

He tries to sleep, but he can't. He puts a CD in the little player he keeps by the bed—some classical stuff he plays sometimes to help him relax. He takes some deep breaths and closes his eyes. He starts humming along with the Beethoven and tries to visualize a soothing bright light in his head. He had read about this kind of stuff in *The Power of Positive Visualization* about ten years ago and had really been into it for about ten minutes before he decided that it was utter bullshit. But he's willing to try anything at this point. So Howard concentrates on getting the soothing bright light to move from his forehead and radiate down through his entire body. His meditation is interrupted by a strong odor—very sour, bad, and old. Howard opens his eyes.

"What is that? Is that you, girl?" he asks the cat.

And then he gets slammed.

As he's looking at the foot of the bed where the cat is sleeping, something grips him hard around the ankle and pulls. His leg is whipped around to the side of the bed and knocks the CD player over. The violent motion stretches Howard into a painfully unfamiliar position. Howard screams. He is jackknifed, and the pain in his groin is like nothing he has ever felt before. Then the music stops, or, rather, is stuck in a weird *ummmphhhawwttt* sound that repeats over and over. Howard gasps as his other leg is pulled in the same manner. This whips his whole body around 90 degrees, and he hits his head on the wall next to the bed. It has him by both ankles now and pulls hard. Howard falls to the floor, flat onto his back. He raises his head to try and see what has hold of him and watches as his legs lift off the ground—seemingly all by themselves. Howard feels a jolt and a tug, and then he gets dragged across the bedroom floor.

"Ahhhhhh! Stop it, what the hell!"

He tries to fight it with everything he's got. When he gets just past the bedroom doorway, he is suddenly released. Howard struggles to his knees.

"Jesus…!"

Then it grabs hold of his arm, pulling with the same determination. He is dragged across the carpet on his knees toward the far wall in the living room. Now Howard can see it—the shadow. The same thing he had seen in the multipurpose room. It dissolves into the wall, but it doesn't let go. Once, twice, three times—Howard is slammed into the wall as if it were trying to pull him through to the other side. Then it suddenly lets go again, and Howard collapses face first onto the living room floor.

He struggles to raise his head, to see where it went. His eyes are saucers, and he's gasping for air.

"Leave me alone," he pitifully pleads.

Something growls from the ceiling. Howard rolls over onto his back and looks up. There he sees it again—pitch-black, blacker than anything he's ever seen—quivering like heat radiating off the sidewalk on a hot day. Its shape begins to shift, forming into something like a face. Then it tries to speak. The sound is far away and scratchy, like an old phonograph record.

"*Wake up, boy. Time to paaayyy.*"

"What?" Howard screeches.

The shadow zips around the room, laughing obnoxiously and making what sounds like fart noises. Howard struggles to his feet and backs himself into a corner. The shadow rushes toward him and punches him in the face. Then it flings itself across the room and vanishes through the wall.

Howard stands there, gasping. His legs start to shake, and he falls. He crawls back to his bed, leaving a trail of blood. His knees are shredded from being dragged across the carpet. Then his nose starts to bleed—a real gusher.

"Oh my God," Howard sputters.

He pulls himself onto the bed and flops onto his back.

"What the hell?"

And then he passes out.

5

oward wakes with dried blood all over the place. He stares again at the ceiling, not sure if he's dead or alive. The CD player suddenly comes back to life, *ummmphhhawwttt!* Howard jumps, and then he feels the pain in his groin.

"Jesus! Oh, come on! You got to be kidding me, here!"

Howard painfully reaches over to shut off the CD player. He looks for the cat, who he last saw sleeping at his feet but now is a safe distance away, watching suspiciously from the dresser.

Howard struggles to his feet. He feels like he's been hit by a truck. He stumbles into the bathroom and looks at his face in the mirror.

"Holy..."

A dried blood trail runs from his nose down his chin and all over the front of his T-shirt. The whole left side of his face is swollen. He examines himself carefully in the mirror, checking his teeth and feeling around to make sure that nothing is broken. He becomes mesmerized by his own reflection and makes tough-guy faces at himself.

"You talkin' to me? You talkin' to me?"

Then he sees his father, bloodied and beaten, staring back at him from the bathroom mirror.

The alarm clock goes off in the bedroom, and then the bathroom door slams itself shut.

Howard screams.

6

Howard cleans up, throws on some clothes, and gets out of the apartment. He doesn't know where to go, so he just drives around for a while in his green 2005 Toyota Cressida. He keeps looking behind himself, checking the back seat to make sure nothing is hiding back there. It's hot in the middle of November. Not even 10:00 a.m. and it's already a scorcher. The air conditioning is making a lot of noise but not doing much else, and he's been driving with the windows closed. Finally, realizing that the sweat is pouring from his armpits, Howard rolls down the windows to get some air.

The traffic in North Hollywood is moving in fits and lurches. People are making strange maneuvers, with no turn signals, greedily jockeying for position to get a few car lengths ahead. Sour, angry faces recklessly driving their SUV tanks through crowded city streets and cursing anyone who dares to get in their way. The city looks dirtier than usual. The soot and the dust make the trees look tired and hunched over. Howard sits behind an old woman waiting for a break in the traffic so she can make a left-hand turn.

"Come on, come on!" It's hard not to get caught up in it.

The opposing traffic moves freely, whizzing past him like shadows. With their windows rolled up, the car occupants are self-contained and safe from contact. Protected like insects inside their shinny steel shells. The old lady misses her chance. The light changes, and she never moves. The guy behind Howard leans on his horn, but there's nowhere to go. Howard taps nervously on the steering wheel, searching for something to focus his attention on. He zeros in on the congregation at the bus stop. They look like zombies entranced by what they're hearing in their headsets or on their cell phones. Disconnected from the world, they walk the earth in their own private bubbles, never making eye contact with anyone. They don't want to see. They are the zombies of North Hollywood.

Howard wonders how he never noticed it before, how sad it is out on the streets.

"Because I'm one of them, that's why," Howard answers to himself.

A jingle goes off in his head. "I'm a zombie, she's a zombie, wouldn't you like to be a zombie, too? Dr. Pepper…" Wow, that goes back. Howard actually worked with David Naughton, the Dr. Pepper guy. It was a movie of the week, his first acting job in Hollywood. Howard wonders whatever happened to him and if he ever thinks about the scenes they did together.

The guy behind him blasts his horn again. Howard hadn't notice, but the old woman has gone, and the light is just starting to turn red. Howard steps on the gas. He grins when he looks in the rearview mirror and sees the guy behind him stuck at the light and screaming his ass off.

"Asshole!" Howard yells, feeling momentarily pleased with himself.

Howard checks around to make sure no cops saw him run the light, and then he barely avoids a disaster. He slams on the brakes just in time and screeches to a stop only inches from where an old man is standing in the crosswalk.

"Oh my God! Sir, are you all right?" Howard shouts from his opened window.

The old man just stands there staring, expressionless. Howard is afraid the old guy is having a stroke. His lower lip trembles, but the rest of him is perfectly frozen, staring with the blankest, dullest eyes that Howard has ever seen.

"It's the goddamn king of the zombies himself," Howard whispers.

The guy Howard had left behind at the light races up to his rear bumper and blasts his horn again. Howard checks the rearview mirror. The guy is going berserk back there, screaming and slapping himself on the forehead. Howard is wondering if the guy might have a gun in his glove compartment when the old man suddenly comes back to life. He takes a staggering step toward the car, coughs something up, and spits it in Howard's direction. With a disgusted wave of his hand and spittle hanging from his chin, he dismisses Howard in a huff and shuffles on through the crosswalk. Howard stays put and watches to make sure the old man gets safely to the other side. The maniac behind him blasts his horn again, and Howard thinks about getting out of the car so they can kill each other and get on the evening news. Then his ears start to ring and he's sweating again, even more than before. Howard grips the wheel and guns it to get out of there fast and to get some air circulating. He hits the lights right and goes a full three blocks without stopping, and then a black shadow passes over the hood of his car. The car swerves and simultaneously he feels something touch his shoulder from behind. Howard spins around to check, and the car comes just inches from running up onto the sidewalk and taking out a Starbucks.

"I need help," Howard groans. He feels like he might pass out so he slaps himself. He punches the dashboard and then continues on his way.

7

The Imagination Factory is the company that hires Howard to do Einstein. His boss, Barry Nuessman, is always happy when someone drops by. He is a smart Jewish boy in his early fifties. Barry has big dreams. He is motivated by noble causes and genuinely cares about the state of the world, and Howard respects him for that. Barry is the son of a doctor and a graduate of Yale. He has been a teacher, a fundraiser, and a published playwright. He came to Hollywood from New York and was working as a TV writer, but he tired of all that and decided to completely change direction. In his late forties he started The Imagination Factory. He raised the seed money and built a company that now is the most respected in its class. He has twenty different shows, pays his actors, and has enriched the lives of thousands of kids in the LA area. He has a successful twenty-five-year marriage and a gifted son who was composing music at the age of eight. Barry gets things done. He is a people person, and he loves to talk. He never shuts up.

Howard sits, and Barry's motor starts running. He goes on and on about some new something or other that he's working on. Over the years Howard has learned that a smile, a nod, and the occasional "that sounds great" or "great idea" was all he needed to participate in a conversation with Barry. Barry did all the work. All Howard had to do was stay awake.

So Howard smiles, not really comprehending anything Barry is saying. He just smiles and marvels at Barry's big, thick, healthy head of hair. He is graying, but there's absolutely no thinning going on.

No sir, that mop ain't goin' nowhere. You could wash the floor and brush the dog with that thing. You holier-than-thou, Ivy League—

privileged, elitist, bleeding-heart, bushy-headed son of a bitch. And look at that outfit. Give me a break with that shit already.

Barry always wears a sports jacket and tie. It's his uniform. When he feels casual, he'll wear a button-down sweater and a tie. He is the square's square. Howard wonders if he was bullied when he was young. If he was that skinny little Jewish boy, the smart kid who the other kids would wail on?

As Barry blathers, Howard looks around the office at all his framed awards and honors, and they really start to piss him off.

He always thought that Barry held it against him and thought less of him as a man because of his failed marriage. Barry never said anything like that to him, but the fact that Howard never had a child, Howard was convinced, was something Barry just couldn't come to terms with. To Barry, raising a child is the most important thing a man has to do. It's his responsibility to pass on the lessons of his lifetime, and populate the planet with wise and healthy children.

And make the future safe for bushy-headed blazer-wearing nerds the world over.

Howard knew that Barry admired his Einstein performance, but he also believed that Barry doubted the quality of his character because he didn't fulfill this most important societal obligation.

Well, tough shit, Barry! There are enough zombies in the world, all right? You ought to thank me for it, you son of a bitch.

The phone rings. Barry excuses himself and takes the call. Howard shifts uncomfortably and suddenly feels terrible for what he was thinking about poor old Barry.

What am I doing? What's the matter with me? I'm a monster. I work with children, for Christ's sake!

Howard is freaking out. He puts a fist in his mouth. He's afraid that he might start screaming. That's when Cynthia Helrich walks into the room.

Barry looks up from his call and motions to her that he'll be another minute. Cynthia looks down at Howard sitting there.

"What the hell happened to you?" she says.

Howard looks up at her, his hand still in his mouth.

"You look like shit," she continues.

"Thansthhh," he manages to say and wonders why Barry never mentioned anything about the way he looked.

Cynthia is tall, thin, and matter-of-fact about things. She's intelligent, and talented, and Howard has always liked her. She does a show about Deborah Sampson, whoever that is. Some feminist or something, a soldier, or an astronaut, he can't remember which. She has been doing Deborah Sampson for about a year now, and before that she did an introduction to Shakespeare, but that show got cancelled—the kids kept falling asleep.

Howard thought about asking her out once, but he never did. Cynthia runs hot and cold, and he has no idea what she thinks of him. He doesn't know where she is from, or what she does outside of this job. She can be funny—dry and off the wall. She sees things clearly, better than he does, and he likes her looks, too. Howard likes women who are taller than he is. His wife was shorter.

"Did somebody beat you up or something?" she asks.

"No, I fell out of bed."

Cynthia sits down next to Howard and takes his hand. She looks deeply into his eyes, which makes him extremely uncomfortable—especially with Barry sitting right there. Howard feels like a first-timer at an AA meeting, and Cynthia is his assigned sponsor probing for the truth with big, sad eyes that are condescending and understanding all at the same time.

"Listen," she says. "If you need somebody to talk to—there's this woman in Pasadena. She's a counselor that I see at an abuse clinic, but she'll see people on the side. People like you."

"Were you abused?" Howard is saddened to hear this about her.

"Oh, yeah—big-time. Misused, abused, and confused. Hey, sounds like a country song, doesn't it? But let me tell ya, I was stuck. I needed out of it and over it and on with it." She searches for a card in her wallet. "This lady saved me. She's really good and she charges like—nothing. Five dollars an hour for people like us who don't have the cash. She does it as a community service." Cynthia gives him the card.

"Thanks. But really—I just fell out of bed."

"Okay, do what you want," she says turning away from him. "Just thought I'd offer it, that's all." She shrugs as if she's done with him.

They sit silently and watch Barry talk on the phone until Cynthia decides to give it another shot.

"Look, Howard." This time she gets very close—right up in his face. "I see that you're in trouble. It's obvious, it's written all over you, man. Don't fuck around, okay? Whatever it is—sometimes you can't fix it by yourself. It's not a crime to get help, you know?"

He thinks for a moment that she's going to kiss him and then something weird happens. This little gasp comes out of him, and then a big sob erupts and surprises the hell out of him. Cynthia grabs him in a supportive bear hug and then a second even louder sob erupts. Howard feels like an idiot.

Looking annoyed, Barry swivels his chair around to finish his conversation without further distraction.

8

Howard made an appointment and shows up the next day at The Allen House for Battered Women. He had a sleepless night anticipating another visit from the shadow, but nothing happened. In the morning he made the call.

Allen House is a big Victorian-style house in the older section of Pasadena. Howard had a hard time finding a place to park, and he almost chucked the whole idea, but then somebody pulled out of a spot, and he figured that was a sign.

Howard walks through the little garden pathway to the front door of the house. He knocks first and then sees the doorbell and pushes the button. It's one of those chimes that sound like church bells, and it keeps going on after you think it's finished. The door opens a crack, and a little wisp of a woman with stringy hair and haunted eyes peers out at him.

"What do you want?" she says.

"I have an appointment? With Ms. Washington?"

She glares at him. It's the coldest, angriest expression Howard has ever seen.

She opens the door a little wider and then rushes away. Howard stands there a moment. The urge to flee only slightly trumped by his present state of desperation. So he ventures in.

Inside is a receiving room with a couch and some wingback chairs. Howard is the only person in the room. It's kind of flowery—lots of flowers in pots and flowers on the wallpaper. There's a nice fireplace and a cool-looking staircase that goes up to the second floor. There are paintings of peaceful woodland scenes, and on the walls in ornate frames are some inspirational sayings: "You are your own best friend." "You don't have to take it." "You are stronger than you know."

Beyond the waiting room there is a hallway where the look of the place changes into a more industrial office-type environment. Several women hustle back and forth from room to room, and he can hear someone crying from somewhere down the hall. A middle-aged lady in a long skirt; red hair; a big, round face; and a tiny little mouth comes out to see him.

"She's running a little late," she says in a surprisingly deep voice. "Would you like some coffee?"

"No, no thanks."

Her little mouth makes a pursed circle, and she hustles back to where she came from.

Howard sits in one of the wingback chairs, but he feels ridiculous and uncomfortable in it so he gets up and sits on the couch instead. There's a little table with magazines next to the couch, and Howard thumbs through what they have. *Better Homes and Gardens, People, Us, O*, and a *Cosmopolitan* with an intriguing teaser for a story inside: "Ten ways to turn your man into a better lover." Howard starts to pick that one up but then becomes aware of someone watching him.

Standing on the staircase is a disheveled young woman with a terrible black eye. Even from where he sits he can see the broken blood vessels. The eye itself is completely red with just a little speck of blue in the center of it. Somebody really did a number on her. She just stands there staring at him like one of the street zombies.

"Hi. How's it going?" Howard offers.

She turns and runs back up the staircase.

Howard suddenly feels responsible for every cruel and vicious thing any man has ever done to any woman anywhere on the planet. He feels like the representative for the entire gender and nobody there is exactly thrilled to see him. The woman from down the hall starts to cry again.

"That's it." Howard gets up, deciding that he's had about enough of this particular weirdness, when the lady with the little mouth and red hair comes out to get him.

"She can see you now."

"Oh, well, you know what?"

"No, what?"

"I'm thinking…maybe this wasn't such a good idea."

She purses her lips, and it looks like she has an asshole where her mouth should be.

"Follow me, please." She turns and heads back down the hall. After a moment, Howard follows her.

He is led to the office at the end of the hall, which gives him the opportunity to peek into the other rooms along the way. They are all brightly colored, and the walls are cluttered with artwork and photographs. It reminds him of the schools he goes into as Einstein. As he passes each room, the women inside look at him with varying degrees of suspicion and concern.

He steps into the rear office, and sitting behind her desk is a large Black woman wearing a flowery muumuu that looks remarkably like the wallpaper in the sitting room. She looks up from her paperwork and smiles a great toothy grin.

"Howard!" she says as if he's a long-lost relative.

She gets up from her chair and spreads her arms wide. She couldn't be more than five feet, but she's as big as a house, with impossibly large breasts.

"Come here, come over here and give me a hug right now," she insists.

She comes out from behind her desk and marches right over to Howard. She grabs him and presses him into her largeness.

"I just think this is a great way to get started, don't you?"

Howard doesn't move. And he certainly doesn't know what to say. She makes happy little moaning noises, and the hug lasts for an eternity. In Howard's paranoid brain she is making an immediate evaluation about him. It's the hug test. Women judge men by how they hug, and this is definitely not a good hug on his part. He is tense and more than a little put off by the immediate physical contact with those impossibly gigantic gazoombas.

"Okay—that's nice," she says and then finally releases him. "Now we can talk a little, what do you say?"

Howard says nothing, so she returns to her desk leaving him frozen and silent.

"You can sit down, you know."

"Oh," he says and then takes a seat.

"So you know Cynthia Helrich?"

"Yes, we work for the same company."

"You're an actor?"

"Well, sort of, I used to be. Yeah, I'm an actor, I guess."

"She's a sweetie, don't you think?"

"Yeah.

"So what do you do?"

"What do I do?"

"With Cynthia, for the kids?"

"Oh, I do Einstein."

"I love Einstein."

"Yes, everybody loves Einstein."

"Hey, that sounds like a TV show, doesn't it? *Everybody Loves Einstein!* Maybe they'll make a show about you some day. Or maybe, *Howard does Einstein!* I like that. Sounds more like a movie."

"More like a porno film, actually. But, hey…work's work."

Howard's attempt at humor falls flat. She doesn't respond with laughter or even a smile. She studies him as if his attempt at being funny is a clue, a curious admission to his emotional state of mind.

Howard gets embarrassed and wants to punch himself in the face for being so stupid. To say a thing like that in a place like this. Not only was it not funny, it was insensitive.

Stupid, stupid, stupid!

Then somebody from down the hall starts wailing.

"Howard, would you be a dear and close that door for me? It gets a little loud around here sometimes."

He doesn't like being told what to do. But he does it anyway. Howard closes the door and then sits back down. Now he's really sorry that he came here and decides to say as little as possible to this woman. They stare at each other, sizing each other up.

"What's your last name, Howard?"

"Dudek."

"Is that…German, Polish?"

"Russian, I think."

"I'm Yolanda Washington."

"What's Yolanda…Spanish, Hungarian?"

"I have no idea, sweetie. I really don't. When I was old enough to have a name that's the one they gave me. I was in an orphanage, brought in there as a small child. Hard to believe that now, I guess."

"Believe that you were an orphan?"

She wiggles herself and laughs. "No, that I was small."

"Oh, oh…I get it."

"Yeah, had to work through some stuff, let me tell you, ooh-wee! I needed some help. Drugs, alcohol—bad folks beating me up and taking me down. Had babies to care for, but I was out stealing and whoring and drinking all day long. I had me a one-way ticket on the express goin' down and right out of this world to God only knows where. Then one day, thank the Lord, somebody got to me—shook me up a little and got me in here. I was kicking and screaming, let me tell you, but they saved my life at this place. I found out that I had a brain and a heart and a responsibility to do the right thing. Well, sir…"

My God, it's the Black female version of Barry Nuessman!

Howard nods and smiles, feeling well qualified to participate in this type of conversation.

"I started doing the work," she continues. "Still got a long way to go. I won't kid you or myself about that." She pauses to evaluate how Howard is reacting to her. "But I'm taking care of my kids. I got a good job helping people. And starting next month, guess what? I'm going for my master's."

"Your master's? That's great. Good for you," Howard contributes.

Yolanda stops talking—something Howard didn't expect.

She taps a pencil on her desk. "Are you patronizing me, Howard?"

"What? No, not at all, why would you say that?"

"Oh, nothin'. It's me…probably me. I told you, I still have some work to do."

"No, I think it's great that you were able to pull yourself up and get your life…you know, get things going in a more positive direction," Howard says most sincerely.

"Thank you. So what can I do for you, Howard Dudek? What's the problem? Why do you say you're an actor, sort of? You either are or you're not, I would think."

"Yes, I…I haven't been that…I don't do it much anymore."

"Why not?"

"Uh, I don't know. I got tired."

"You got tired?"

"Of the game, I mean. I don't like the whole show biz bullshit, if I may be so blunt." Howard surprises himself by how easily he's opening up to her.

"Please, be blunt." Yolanda's warm smile encourages him.

"Thank you. Or maybe it's a confidence thing. I think I just lost my confidence."

"But you still do the Einstein show?"

"Oh, yeah. I still do Einstein."

"Are you good at that? Do you have confidence?"

"Oh, yeah. I'm really good at that. Well, I've been doing it a long time."

"I hear that you're great at it, and the kids love you."

"Where did you hear that?" he asks suspiciously.

"Cynthia told me. She let me know you might call."

"Oh."

"So you're really good and maybe you still want to do it, but your confidence is shaky because…you're afraid of something. Is that possible?"

"I'm not sure if I want to act, to tell you the truth. I write as well. I'd rather do that, I think, except I haven't been able to sell anything yet."

"Okay, but my point is…maybe it's not because you're not sure or that you don't like it. But maybe there is a fear that is controlling you, instead of you controlling the fear. Your confidence is down and you're having doubts, Howard, because you are afraid. You know you're good, that's not the question. The question is what is sabotaging your success? There's something getting in the way. Is that a possibility, do you think?"

"Yes, that's possible. I always felt that there was something kind of gnawing away. Something beyond my control."

"Hmmm," she leans back in her chair and studies him a moment. "So what we need to do is identify the fear and how it got there. Let me ask you—how did you get into acting in the first place? What made you want to do it? What drove you to it? Was it an actor you saw or a movie or a play that inspired you?"

"It was revenge."

"Revenge? I don't understand."

"Because they said I couldn't do it. They thought I was a loser and that I'd wind up a failure."

"Who did?"

"They all did. They were mean."

"Your parents?"

"All of them. My parents, my friends, my teachers."

"Why were they mean to you?"

"I was Dudek. I was the doodie man."

Howard hears a cellar door slam shut, and he is suddenly transported to a very dark place.

"Howard?"

He's back there—a small boy in a dank cellar, trembling in the dark. He covers his eyes as a shadow creeps toward him, growing larger, encompassing him—devouring him.

"Howard?"

"What? I'm sorry, what did you say?"

"Did you deserve to be treated mean?"

"No…I don't know. They wanted me to feel stupid."

"You are not stupid. Do you know that now?"

"How do you know that I'm not stupid?"

"Because you play Einstein!"

"I'm a phony Einstein."

Yolanda taps her pencil on the desk again.

"Do you have brothers or sisters, Howard?"

"No."

"Did you get along with your mother?"

"She's a bitch."

"What about your father?"

"He was a fool for loving her. She treated him like shit…I'm sorry, that's probably not nice. That's not fair. I take that back."

"Are you angry at your father?"

"He's dead."

"But are you angry at him?"

"Yes."

"Okay…good."

"Good? I don't think so."

"It's painful and it hurts to talk about these things, but it's something we have to go through to get to the other side of it. What happened to your face?"

"Did I tell you that they locked me in a cellar once?"

"Who did?"

"My friends. They were…I don't know. There was something wrong with them in that town."

"Why did they do that?"

"It was a prank, and there was this house, and there's a murderer who lives in the cellar, his ghost…and…he…"

Howard freezes like a zombie.

"Howard, what happened to your face?"

"I have to stop now," he says.

"Okay, but, I'm concerned about—"

"I can't talk about it yet."

"Okay, Howard, that's fine. But here's what I want you to do. I have an assignment for you. Look through some magazines or newspapers, comic books, coloring books, I don't care, whatever stuff you find like that and cut out pictures or words that you think apply to your childhood. Don't think too much about it. It doesn't have to mean anything. There's no right or wrong in this, just anything that strikes your fancy or reminds you of anything about growing up. Take those pictures and paste them onto a poster board. Bring that in next week, and we'll take a look at it."

Howard stares at her.

"Okay, Howard?"

"Okay."

"Are you all right?"

"What? Oh, yeah—next week, poster board."

"Right. We've had a good start today. We're going to figure out the problem, and then we're gonna kick its ass, what do you say?"

"Do you believe in ghosts?"

"Ghosts, UFO's, little green men, Atlantis, Bigfoot. I believe it all."

"Are you patronizing me?"

"I don't play that game, Howard."

Howard gets up and walks toward the door.

"Oh, Howard?"

She heaves herself up from behind the desk. By the time Howard turns back around, she is standing in front of him with her hefty arms stretched out wide, and then she lays another squeeze on him.

"I just think it's a great way to end the session, don't you?"

"I don't know. I guess so."

"Humor me a little."

"Okay."

She lets him go, and there is so much warmth and sincerity in her smile that Howard wants to cry.

"And, Howard?"

"Yes?"

"That'll be five bucks."

9

oward looks at his face in the bathroom mirror. The swelling is down, and he looks pretty much like his old forty-eight-year-old self. He starts spraying his hair white when the can sputters and dies. He checks under the sink for a spare. He has another can, but it's not the good stuff. He has some Streaks and Tips, which isn't as good as the Color Highlights that he normally uses. He shakes the can, vigorously as instructed, and resumes spraying. Then the mirror turns black—pitch-black. Howard drops the can and staggers back.

"Cut it out, you freak!"

The mirror shakes a little, and then it clears. Howard cautiously approaches. He opens the medicine cabinet carefully and checks inside. Then he checks behind the shower curtain, just in case it's hiding in there. It's not. Howard creeps back to the mirror and continues spraying his hair white.

"This is way out of hand."

Howard puts on his mustache and maneuvers his way toward the bedroom, stepping carefully to avoid the bloodstains on the carpet. He checks over his shoulder, afraid that something might be following him. He's pretty sure about what's going on now. It's unbelievable, after all these years, but the evidence is undeniable. He's being haunted by Cellar Man, who tracked him down because of a child's broken promise of revenge. Howard realizes how ridiculous it sounds, but what else could it be?

The cat is asleep on the poster board that he had picked up at the art store. Howard gently lifts her up and puts her on the pillow that he keeps on top of the dresser so she can look out of the window and feel like a queen.

He examines the photos that he found and has glued onto the poster board. He did as Yolanda had instructed. He tried not to think too much. Any pictures that he came across, that made him pause, that made a connection for whatever reason—he cut them out and attached them to the board. Looking at it now, it made him sad. There is a young boy running on a baseball diamond in the rain. Wine bottles. Another boy rowing a boat. A man driving a race car. A dark lake. Skyscrapers. A prison. A riot in some Asian country. Angry faces. Happy faces. UFOs. And pretty girls in underwear.

He also cut out words and phrases that appealed to him: *Just Do It. How Does It Feel? Silent Partners. Huge. Mystery.* He placed the words around pictures that he thought they connected with.

"It's probably all a bunch of crap," he says to the cat.

Howard had decided to see Yolanda one more time, but he doesn't really think she'll be able to help him. He also wonders about her credentials and how qualified she is to be doing what she's doing. Besides, the thing that is going on with him—

"I need an exorcist, not a therapist."

He isn't sure that he'll be able to level with her anyway. How could he tell her what was really going on? How could he tell anybody? Who'd ever believe him?

He looks over at the cat. He's worried about her. If anything should happen to him, or if the shadow comes around while he is out, it might scare her to death.

The light above the bed starts to blink.

"Stop it!" Howard yells at the light.

And then he has a full-out tantrum, kicking at the bed and throwing things everywhere. He finds a flashlight on top of his dresser, and just as he's about to heave it at the blinking light, he suddenly stops. He looks at it in his hand and then looks up at the bedroom light. He turns on the flashlight and aims it at the blinking light as if it were some kind of laser beam weapon, like a *Star Trek* phaser. Curiously, when he does this, the light stops blinking.

Howard's frantic mood is altered by a glimmer of hope. It strikes him that a beam of light might be the perfect weapon to use against a shadow. Maybe a bright light could penetrate the shadow's blackness and cause some damage and discourage it from coming around.

Howard starts dressing as Einstein, keeping the flashlight close at hand. He's actually hoping the thing will show itself again so he could test his theory.

It doesn't, though.

10

oward grips the wheel and hopes for an uneventful trip. The traffic is moving at a fairly decent clip, which is a minor miracle for this time of day. He has to drive all the way to San Pedro for the show. That's thirty-five miles one way. A long way to go without thinking about driving into the center divider. One hundred bucks for at least three hours of his time. Barry really has to start paying more for this kind of haul. Howard had thought about retiring Einstein, just for that reason. Besides, no one else in the company was doing a show for as long as he's been doing Einstein. It's been five years already, and it's getting embarrassing. He could almost hear the office whispers: "Doesn't he have anything else to do?" "What happened to his career?" "What happened to his wife?" "She left him because he's a loser. Because he's a failure."

"Wake up already, you idiot!" Howard scolds himself as an angry parent would. "Einstein is killing you! It's a dead end. It's a trap!"

Howard has all kinds of reasons why he should retire Einstein.

He turns on the radio and gets static, which he never got before on this particular stretch of road. He picks up his flashlight, which he has handy right next to him on the seat. He shines the light at the radio, and a black line jettisons from the station indicator light. It streaks over Howard's right shoulder and then exits through the back window of the car.

"Take that, you freaking ghost."

The radio roars back to life. He swerves into the opposite lane, and the guy he almost hits blasts his horn. Howard manages to regain control of the car—with one hand on the wheel and the other on the flashlight. The thing is definitely following him, no doubt about it. But the flashlight really works. He is not completely defenseless anymore. Howard reminds himself to stop for batteries on the way home. He is going to need lots and lots of batteries.

The remainder of the trip is uneventful, and Howard surprises himself by how calm he feels. It's a cloudy day, which he always likes, even more so now—the less shadow the better. Howard starts singing along with the radio, something he hasn't done in a very long time.

11

By time he arrives at the Baxter Hill Elementary School, it's pretty dark outside. While he's getting his stuff out of the trunk, the skies open up. Rain comes down in sheets. Howard is not prepared for the weather. No umbrella, no coat—nothing. He gathers up his props and runs toward the school building.

The stuff Howard normally uses in his hair is made to wash out easily with soap and water. The stuff he used today just needs water. By the time he gets into the multipurpose room, he's a mess. The white stuff in his hair is streaking down his face and staining his black vest. The paper bags he carries the props in are soaked. Looking like a demented trick-or-treater, he stands for a moment near the doorway to catch his breath. Then the bags give way, and all the props spill out onto the floor. The kids scream with delight.

Howard masterfully gets the kids to help him gather up his stuff and then makes a group project out of getting the show set up and ready to go. A cute little girl with pigtails hands him a towel.

"Mister, your hair is leaking."

Howard looks down at her sweet little face and feels tears come to his eyes. It hits him like that. They say things sometimes that just slay him. Even after five years it still gets to him. He loves these kids, and they love him back, and he is damn glad to be at the Baxter Hill Elementary School today. And that is the truth.

"Thank you," Howard says. "I maybe vill not be as vhite headed as usual. I think I got a little younger today, ya?"

The kid giggles, takes her seat, and then Howard starts the show.

"Vhat's the matter vit me? I should introduce myself, ya? Vhere are my manners?"

Howard checks his pockets for his manners.

"No, I von't find my manners in my pocket. Dat's a joke. They are in my head, I think. My glasses—my glasses I might find in my pocket."

He looks for his glasses.

"Vhere are my glasses? I had them here a minute ago. Vhat did I do vit my glasses?"

He's already wearing them. It's part of the act. The kids scream out to let him know where his glasses are.

"Oh, thank you very much. I keep forgetting vhere I put things all the time. It's a goot thing you are here, I'll tell you dat. But anyvay…I vas famous, did you know? Look, here is a picture of me on the cover of *Time* magazine."

Howard holds up a laminated cover of *Time* with Einstein's picture on it.

"See up there it says Person of the Century? Big deal. They make such a fuss. But look—I give you a hint. Did you ever have a boy or girl in your class and no matter vhat question the teacher asks, this kid raises his hand and says, "pick me, pick me. I know the answer! Please, please, please, pick me." And you look at dat kid and you say, "jeez, who does he think he is, Einstein?" Vell, dat's me. Albert Einstein! Scientist, mathematician, and today ve are going to learn a little about my life and my vork. If you like, ve do a few experiments together, too, okay? Vould you like that?"

The kids respond enthusiastically that they would.

Then from behind the audience and against the wall where the supervisors are ignoring Einstein and texting on their phones, a big blob of a shadow begins to creep up from the floor, quickly covering the entire length and width of the back wall. The shadow begins to change shape, morphing into a face.

The lights begin to flicker in the room. Howard backs up, keeping his eyes glued to the shadow while frantically searching for the flashlight that he had put on the prop table behind him. He swipes blindly, desperately, knocking his props to the floor. He can't find it. He turns away, just for a moment, finds the flashlight, and then quickly turns back again—armed and ready. But the shadow is gone. Howard looks out at his audience. The kids are frightened by his behavior. They start getting squirmy. If you lose them, it's really hard to get them back. Howard shakes it off like a trouper and goes on with the show.

"Anyvay, vhere vas I? Oh, ya…you know when I vas your age, my parents vere vorried about me because I vas a bad student. Can you believe dat? The smartest man in the whole vorld vas a bad student?"

12

oward thought the Baxter Street show was one of his best. The kids really got into it, and they had some great questions afterward. Howard always does a question and answer session after his show. They ask things that just crack him up, and he started writing them down in a journal. He'd like to publish them one day, if he ever gets serious about writing again.

The rain has stopped and it's hot again. Howard has to make a stop at the AAVA office to pick up his check. He's only working there two days a week, but every penny is precious these days. He takes the 110 to the Hollywood Freeway, which is jammed. Howard sits sweating in traffic and thinks about his father.

Before he got sick, Howard's father was a hardy guy and much more athletic than Howard ever was. He didn't smoke or drink, he played tennis and handball, and he was well liked by everybody, except his wife. Howard remembers good times with his father, when he was little. They'd go fishing, and they used to wrestle on the living room floor and laugh their heads off. He remembers a time when he thought his dad was the greatest guy in the world. They'd go trick-or-treating together dressed like clowns, and they'd make up crazy songs as they went from house to house. His father was Howard's best friend. But that all changed as Howard got older.

The relationship between his parents became more and more disturbing to him. His mom was constantly browbeating his fun-loving dad, and it was taking its toll. He worked like a dog. He did everything for her, and all she gave him was shit—nag, nag, nag. Nothing he did was ever good enough for her. She'd scream at him as if he were a child, and the way he would just take it drove Howard crazy. Young Howard didn't understand it. He still doesn't.

The distance grew between him and his dad about the same time Howard started having difficulties at school and with his friends and the relatives on his mother's side who loved to tease him. His father became harder and harder to reach. He was exhausted and unavailable, and Howard felt disserted and angry. He remembers asking him once, "Dad, why don't you just divorce her?" Howard can't remember how his father responded to that; he wishes that he could.

Howard hates the way he feels about his father now. He doesn't want to be angry with him anymore, but he can't shake it. They should have run away before she broke his dad's spirit and his pride.

When Howard grew up and moved away, he had less and less contact with his parents. It was too painful to watch. When his dad got sick, Howard made two trips to see him, but he never could say what needed saying and what his father needed to hear.

Howard tries not to think about his father too often, but he really misses him now. He rarely speaks to his mother. She lives alone and isn't in great shape. One day he will have to deal with her, and he is dreading that. The whole thing with his parents makes him feel sick.

He doesn't want to think about his family or the shadow or anything anymore. Howard turns on the radio.

When he finally arrives at the AAVA office, it's already getting dark. He finds a spot in a fifteen-minute parking zone and figures that should be enough.

13

Normally, Howard doesn't show up places dressed like Einstein, but this was the AAVA office and nobody cares. AAVA has a cruddy office on Coldwater Canyon Boulevard. There is a small reception area in the front and two offices tucked away behind a partitioned wall. They have one computer, a copy machine, a broken coffee maker, and an old electric typewriter. They still conduct business from paper files that are stuffed recklessly into old metal file cabinets.

AAVA represents people who dress in costumes and perform at theme parks. Cartoon characters, monsters, and your usual assortment of historical figures. A shady lawyer runs the union, and all the employee paychecks come from his office in New York. AAVA is a joke, or, more accurately, a front for a few corrupt people making fairly decent money from performers' dues. They use the union as a write-off and for laundering scams that make it worthwhile for them to keep the union afloat.

Two actors who can't get any other work run the office in LA, and they have no respect for the people they represent because they don't consider them to be real actors. That has always bothered Howard. That kind of superior attitude. He identifies with the looked down upon, even though in this case the AAVA members are, in fact, pretty much assholes. The ones who come into the office or who Howard talks to on the phone are pushy and arrogant, not what you'd expect from Mickey or Pluto. So the actor reps go to meetings and pretend to negotiate on the performers' behalf, but they are no match for the high-powered attorneys from Disney and Universal, and, frankly, the AAVA reps don't really give a shit anyway. The office is disorganized and almost completely inefficient. Howard's job is to answer the phone, take messages, and deflect performers' complaints. He does some filing once in a while, but mostly he reads or does crossword puzzles.

So Howard enters the office dressed like Einstein. Nobody is at the reception desk, but someone is impatiently waiting, sitting in one of the uncomfortable metal folding chairs that are put out for visitors. He greets Howard with a sneer.

"Oh, shit. It's Howard fucking Einstein. Where's Steve, did you see him?"

"Uh, no, Rich. I came in to see him, too."

Rich is in his Yosemite Sam outfit, with Sam's head sitting on his lap, and he's looking particularly hot and bothered. Howard takes a seat, the one farthest away from where Rich is sitting. Howard can't stand the guy.

"Got a notice that I've been suspended from the union for not paying my fucking dues. What'ya think about that, Einstein?"

"I don't know, Rich. Did you pay your dues?"

"Yeah, man. I paid them right on time! So where's my money going? What about my benefits and all that shit?"

"Don't know, Rich."

"Where the fuck is Steven. I've been sitting here for twenty minutes, and nobody's fucking here? This is ridiculous!"

"I know. He probably went out for coffee or something."

"I leave messages and nobody fucking calls me back, so I gotta run down here on my dinner break. This is a fucking joke!"

"Bummer."

Howard wishes that a shadow would show up and slap Richie-boy around a little. Maybe slam him into a couple of walls, and then throw him out the window.

"Howard, do me a big favor and pull my file. Come on, man. I have to get back. You know where it is. Let's see what the fuck is going on here."

"You know, Rich. I just came in to get my check. I'm not really working now, and I shouldn't be doing that anyway."

"Unbelievable—this place is a fucking joke. First I get called in at Universal, and they give me shit about being rude to the kids. I'm Yosemite fucking Sam for Christ's sake! I'm supposed to be rude! And now this shit…I tell you, man. I've about had it. Did you see the new contract?"

"No, I didn't." The absurdity of talking contracts with a cartoon character makes Howard laugh out loud.

"What's so fucking funny?"

"Nothing. Go ahead."

"Yeah, well—it's worse than last years'! What do you guys do around here anyway?"

"We think up ways to piss you off, Rich. We have a pool going for what month you're gonna have your stroke. How are you feeling anyway? Because I got you going down on the twentieth."

"Very fucking funny."

The phone rings.

"You gonna get that?" Rich asks.

"No, I'm not working. The machine will get it."

It rings and rings and rings, and then they watch as it rings some more.

"Guess it's not on," Howard surmises.

After about ten rings it stops.

"Beautiful. Unbelievable." Rich shakes his head. "Kill me now because I really can't take this much more."

Then Steve walks into the office. He's a tall, thin guy except for his big potbelly that makes him look more pregnant than fat. Howard always wonders if there is some kind of medical condition that causes his stomach to swell like that. Steve has long, stringy hair and a bad complexion. He calls himself a film director now, but he's never directed anything in his life.

"Hey, what's going on, boys?" Steve asks with no real interest in hearing an answer.

"You guys screwed up my membership, that's what's going on! I got thrown out of the union, Steve!"

"Did you pay your dues?" Steve looks for something in the desk drawers and seems not at all concerned by Rich's predicament.

"Yeah, man! I fucking paid the fucking dues!"

"Okay, okay. Down boy. Take it easy."

Howard gets up and approaches Steve at his desk.

"Hey, Steve. I need my check."

"I didn't pick it up yet," Steve says distractedly.

"He sent it to the PO Box again? Why does he do that?" It's Howard's turn to be exasperated.

"I don't know. I'll mail it to you. But you're coming in tomorrow, right?

"Tomorrow? No. I'm not scheduled for tomorrow."

"Shit, I have a meeting about a script tomorrow. I can't find the fucking thing, though. You can't come in? I'll leave the check for you here."

"No, Steve. I can't do that."

Rich jumps up and puts his hands on his cartoon guns.

"Hey, let's go already! I got Toon-Land Jamboree in, like, forty-five minutes!"

"Okay, come on." Steve walks back behind the partition, and Rich follows him, walking just like you'd expect Yosemite Sam to walk.

"Mail it. Don't forget, Steve!" Howard calls after them.

"Yeah, I won't forget!" Steve yells back.

But Howard knows that he will forget and wishes his shadowy friend would pay Steve a visit as well.

When he gets back out to his car, there's a ticket on the windshield. Howard sighs heavily and checks the damages—

seventy-five bucks. He crumples up the ticket and tosses it through the window that he forgot to roll up. Howard has had it with AAVA.

"Right after I get this check, I quit. That's it."

He gets into the car and grumbles all the way home.

14

oward stands in the bathroom, staring at himself in the mirror. He has to wash the white stuff out of his hair. He's working tonight at Anderson Research. He does a four-hour shift from six to ten, which is about all any sane person could possibly handle. It's continuous phone calling, trying to qualify people to participate in market research surveys. If you're lucky enough to get someone to talk to you, then they are asked an endless stream of questions regarding income, buying habits, and personal relationships. Sometimes, after being put through this whole ordeal, the participant is informed that they did not qualify to participate in the research project. At this point, rejected participants tend to lose it and threaten all manner of venomous retribution. Howard hates this job almost as much as the AAVA job. They pay him a whopping fifteen dollars an hour to absorb a massive amount of abuse.

So Howard has to take a shower and be naked with soap in his hair and his eyes closed. He thought about getting a hotel room to shower in, but he has to feed the cat and change clothes and who can afford a hotel room? Besides, the shadow would just follow him anyway, so it doesn't matter where he goes. He starts to undress. He turns on the water and stands naked, waiting for it to heat up. He thinks about bringing the flashlight into the shower with him but decides that's probably not such a good idea. Then it just appears, right behind the shower curtain. A big black blob waiting for him to get in. Howard steadies himself. He grabs the flashlight that's on the vanity next to the sink. He tells himself to leave, but he can't. He has to see if it works. Howard turns on the flashlight and then pulls back the shower curtain, but it's gone.

"What do you want?" Howard demands in a particularly hysterical tone of voice.

There is a garbled response from behind him. He spins around, but again there's nothing there. Howard waves the flashlight beam around the shower stall and then all around the bathroom. After several minutes of this, he puts the flashlight back on the vanity and steps in to wash his hair. Nothing else happens.

15

At least the actors who work at AAVA still have hope, delusional as that might be. At Anderson Research, they are defeated and hopeless. Here is the final resting place of broken dreams. The older employees who work the phones are valued for being able to set their minds to numb. They can take the hits and just keep calling. Years of rejection and bitter disappointment have prepared them well. These are the writers, actors, and artists who never got a break or weren't able to take advantage of the breaks they may have been given.

Howard punches his time card. His boss, Trish, gives him her famous shy-but-sly smile. Trish is only twenty-five years old. Her life is market research, and she puts in ridiculously long hours. She oversees the phone room and checks all the questionnaires that the phone people fill in. She also analyzes all the research, sets the quotas, and pretty much organizes all the car surveys from top to bottom. Trish weighs about 250 pounds, but she is gorgeous. She has long jet-black hair and a stunning face. She is sometimes mysterious, sometimes soulful, and oftentimes funny. She has big hazel eyes, and if Howard looks at them for too long, he starts to get woozy. Her desk is in the center of the room, and she is always available to answer any question at any time about anything. In the phone room she is all-powerful and all-knowing. In juxtaposition to her authoritarian side is the little girl side and her appreciation for all things cute. Her desk is covered with gnomes, fairies, Disney characters, and a weird troll doll called a Furby that makes horrible giggling noises and says things like "I love you" and "will you be my best friend?"

"Hello, Mr. Einstein. Nice of you to join us this evening," Trish says with just a hint of seductress in her tone.

Everybody here knows that Howard still does Einstein. He is the last of them still hanging on as a performer.

"Hi, Trish. Where do you need me tonight?"

"Well, that's a little personal don't you think?" She gives him a wink and a wicked little smile. She does that once in a while, and Howard is never sure how to take it. Not knowing how to respond, Howard just goes blank.

Trish looks disappointed but then gets down to business.

"I'm putting you on the Jaguar test drive. We still need two females eighteen to twenty-four and one male thirty-five to fifty."

"For tomorrow?"

"Yup."

"How are the lists?"

"Thin. Try Orange County. I think there's still some first calls on those."

"Where is the test?" Howard asks, not expecting good news.

"Santa Monica Airport."

"Jesus…I'll see what I can do."

Howard hates when the phone lists get down to Orange County and the event takes place somewhere else—like way the hell out in Santa Monica. That's a huge drive to ask somebody to make and booking the survey becomes almost impossible.

Howard gets his list from the Orange County file and then finds an open cubicle. He sits next to Sharon Stuts, who is a real piece of work. Hopefully he won't have to talk to her. In her day, she was a makeup artist. She has fifteen cats and always some hardship story to tell. You can see that at one time she was a beautiful woman. Now she uses too much makeup to recreate that *one time*. Too much fun in the sun has made Sharon look considerably older than her fifty-two years. She makes a lot of personal calls from her cubicle and freely doles out unwanted life advice, even though her own life is constantly on the brink of disaster. If you get her started, Sharon will talk your ear off, and then when she's done boring you to death, she'll ask you for a favor. Sharon always has something for someone else to do.

"Hi, Sharon," Howard says just to be neighborly.

Thankfully, she is involved with a personal call and can only offer a quick gesture of greeting before she hunkers back down into her cubicle.

Howard settles in and looks over his list. "It's going to be a long night," he mutters to himself. Then he dials the first number.

The phone rings about five times, and Howard expects the call to be picked up by voice mail, but then an old woman answers.

"Helloooo?"

"Hello, this is Howard Stanley" (that's the name he uses here) "calling from Anderson Research, and we are conducting a special market research test drive survey that we're hoping Mr. Jacobs might be interested in participating in. Is Mr. Jacobs at home this evening?"

"Hellooo?"

"Is Mr. Jacobs available to come to the phone?"

"Mr. Jacobssss isss dead…" Ssssssshhhhhhhhhttttttttttsssssss.

The old lady goes out, and the line starts hissing with static. He crosses the name off his list. Dead men don't test drive. Howard hangs up and tries another number. This time the line goes immediately to static. Howard gets up, gathers his paperwork, and tries another cubicle. He picks up the new phone. Static again—but then very faint but clear enough to make out—

"Go home…"

Howard, properly spooked, hangs up and goes over to talk with Trish.

"I'm having trouble with the phones," Howard tells her. "Is there something wrong with the lines tonight?"

"I don't think so."

"Will you do me a favor? Can you make a call on my phone?"

"Really? Just try another one, Howard."

"I did!"

His forcefulness takes Trish by surprise.

"I'm sorry, but please…I'm just curious about something."

"My, aren't we manly tonight? Honestly, Howard, my heart is pounding, and I'm feeling a bit swoon-ish."

Trish mocks fanning herself to keep from overheating. She gives Howard another sly smile, and then Howard follows her to his cubicle. She picks up the phone and listens and then dials a number.

"Shelly? Any cancels, really? Oh, crap. Okay, I'll be in." Trish hangs up.

"Any static or anything?" Howard anxiously asks.

"It's fine. Might have been a police radio signal. That can screw up the lines sometimes. It's fine now."

"Oh. That's weird. Okay, thank you."

"You're welcome. Just lost a female, though. Better get busy. I have to go in to see Shelly. Hold down the fort for me will you?"

"Sure."

Shelly is the owner of the company. She has a nice office and a cute butt that she knows how to show off and use to win lots of clients. There are rumors that Shelly and Trish have a thing going, but nobody knows anything for sure.

Trish makes an announcement to the phone room before she leaves.

"Twenty-five dollar bonus for an eighteen- to twenty-five-year-old female for the Jaguar test drive—tomorrow! Twenty-five is good for thirty minutes. If you get it in ten, I'll make it thirty-five. Thank you, people!"

Howard watches Trish leave the phone room. He loves to watch her in motion and how gracefully she carries herself. She doesn't move heavily; she moves like a dancer. Trish doesn't worry about her weight. It's not an issue for her at all, and Howard admires her for that. She is what she is, and if you don't like it, tough titty, as Trish says from time to time.

Howard sits back down at the cubicle and picks up the phone—instant static.

And then, much clearer and louder this time—"Go home!"

Howard hangs up and leaves the building, not saying a word to anyone.

16

"Come on—its wet food. You have to eat, girl."

Howard puts half the food into the cat's dish. He calls again, but she doesn't come. The cat just isn't interested in food anymore. Not since his wife left. The poor thing can barely make it to the litter box. Howard thinks she might be going deaf as well.

"It's okay, you're a good girl. I'll keep it out for you, and when you're ready, it'll be here. Okay, girl?"

She used to meow when he talked to her; not anymore. Howard puts the rest of the cat food back in the fridge.

Why "go home?" He came home and nothing happened. He looks all over for shadows or a sign of some significance. He checks his own phone for static, and there is nothing. It was trying to communicate something to him, but he isn't getting the message. Why "go home?"

Howard gets back on the computer to see if he can find any answers. He happens onto a site called Strange New Jersey. They have lots of stories about weird things that have supposedly happened in the Garden State. UFOs over reservoirs, swamp monsters, Jersey Devils—and then he finds it—in all its urban legend glory—"The Story of Cellar Man." Howard leans into the computer and reads furiously. According to this article, Cellar Man is no myth. He was a real flesh-and-blood crazy-ass ax murderer. Nothing that Howard doesn't already know but rewarding to find it posted nonetheless.

17

nticipating yet another warm reception, Howard rings the bell at the Allen House. After what seems like a long time, he rings the bell again, trying not to push the button too hard or for too long for fear of disturbing the fragile creatures whimpering inside. He's carrying his poster board with all the stuff that he cut out. He feels silly about the whole thing but is also curious about what Yolanda will have to say about it. As he stands there waiting for some damaged female to answer the door, he wonders if he should cut the crap and just tell Yolanda what's really going on. How would she handle it? She would automatically assume that he was nuts, of course.

But everybody here is nuts. She specializes in nuts. Nuts is us.

The door opens a crack. It's the redheaded lady with the little round mouth. She seems surprised to see him.

"Oh, do you have an appointment today?"

"Yes, I do."

"With Yolanda?"

"Yeah, I thought I did anyway. Didn't I?"

"Well, she's not here yet."

"She's not here? Where is she?"

"She had a problem with one of her kids. She should be here soon."

"How soon?"

"Soon."

"Should I wait?"

Her mouth gets smaller and rounder as she opens the door a little wider.

"We had a little episode here last night," she says in a deep raspy whisper.

"An episode?"

"Yes. One of our women, her husband showed up, and we had to get the police. He was drunk, and it got confrontational."

"Is everybody all right?"

"He was arrested."

"Did he hurt her?"

"Not physically this time."

"Oh…well, that's good."

"So everybody is a little out of sorts. If you wait, maybe you should wait in her office instead of the waiting room. You know, because they might see you, and everybody is…"

"Out of sorts?"

"Yes."

"Well, I don't want to upset anyone. I just—I had an appointment."

"I know, and I'm sure you are a nice man."

"Yes, I'm very nice. I have a cat."

She considers this for a moment and looks like a fish while she's doing it, her tiny round mouth puckering in and out.

"Okay, then. Follow me."

She opens the door the rest of the way, and he follows her in.

Howard looks down at the floor as he walks into the house. He doesn't want to see any black eyes or accusatory looks. He can feel the tension in the place and wants no part of it. He walks down the hall and past the offices, keeping his head down the whole way. No haunted faces, no damaged hearts, no angry, vengeful stares. He's had enough of that. Howard walks into Yolanda's office while the redheaded lady stands in the doorway.

"She shouldn't be too long. Are you all right to wait in here?"

"Sure, it's fine."

"Would you like some coffee?"

"No thanks."

"Do you mind if I close the door?"

"No, go ahead."

She closes the door.

Howard has an urge to howl like a werewolf, but he doesn't. He walks around the office, looking at the stuff on the walls. There's a poster, like the one he had made but much more artistic than his, he decides. Or maybe it's just more feminine—prettier maybe. He can sense the pain that the artist was feeling, and yet it's so pretty at the same time. Women are more sensitive. They are natural born artists, he thinks. There are a lot of childlike drawings on the walls as well. Again they remind him of the schools he goes to. He isn't sure if they were made by children or by adults who were thinking like children. On Yolanda's desk are photos of, Howard assumes, her kids. A girl of maybe eighteen, another girl a little younger, and a boy of about ten or so. None of them are smiling. They have identical zombielike expressions.

I wonder what kind of shit these kids went through.

Howard decides that his own problems pale in comparison to what his therapist is probably dealing with. A single parent in today's world? That's a heavy load. That's a lot of pressure and responsibility, and Howard feels great respect for her.

What burden do I bare? I shouldn't even be wasting her time.

Howard looks at some of her papers. She has a lot of her mail on the desk spread out all over the place. He finds her phone bill and looks it over. She has a ton of long distance charges—it's a $500 bill.

How does she swing that?

He checks her address. She lives downtown near USC. Howard folds up the phone bill and puts it in his back pocket.

The door opens and Yolanda comes in.

"Howard, I'm sorry."

"What happened?"

"My boy. Got into some trouble at school."

"Oh, what grade?"

"Fifth. He got into a fight. He's been suspended again."

She goes to her desk and drops down into her chair.

"I don't know what to do anymore. He needs a man around, I think. Fifth grade and he's out of control already."

Yolanda taps a pencil on her desk and tears begin to roll down her face.

"Where is he now?" Howard asks with true empathy.

"He's with a friend. She'll watch him till I get back."

There is a silence that makes Howard uncomfortable. He wants to say something, to support her and give her some comfort. Howard feels something he hasn't felt in a long time. He feels needed.

"There was this kid," Howard begins. "One time I went into a school, and he was hiding under his desk. He wouldn't come out. I got down there with him, just him and me, and I said to him that I needed his help with the show. He wouldn't talk at first. He must have had a bad day, and, of course, I didn't know how his home life was, you know? It was probably not so good. But I told him that I needed him to be my assistant. That I had a feeling he was the only kid in the whole world who would be able to help me. He wouldn't talk, but I was getting to him. Well, Einstein was getting to him. I was doing the German accent and being silly, and he was starting to smile. He was trying to hide it, but I could tell that I was getting to him. I did a little magic trick for him. Just him and me under the table. I made a coin come out of his ear. That's all it took—a little attention from Albert Einstein. I started the show, and I got him to be my assistant. When it was over, I had him take a bow with me, and he was a completely different kid. Something clicked for him. It happens that way. If you stay with it, it just happens and they change. I never saw him again after that. I went back to that school the next year, but he wasn't there anymore and nobody seemed to know anything about him. I hope he's doing okay. I hope somebody…I hope he has somebody like you."

Yolanda is moved by Howard's story.

"Thank you, Howard."

"I know. It's a tough job, being a parent."

"You don't have kids, Howard?"

"No."

"You'd be a good father."

"I don't know. I see the kids in the schools, and I enjoy being with them, but, you know. I'm there for an hour—in and out. Having to be there all the time, every day? I admire you for it."

"It's a challenge, no doubt about it."

Howard nods in agreement.

"Cynthia mentioned that you are divorced. How did that go?"

"Wow. I have to talk to Cynthia. I don't know if I like her being so open about my stuff like that." His leg twitches, as if he's having a spasm. "That's a little weird I think."

Yolanda studies him.

"We're not officially divorced. She just left. I don't even know where she is. I threw out all her stuff, so if she comes back we're probably going to have a problem."

"Was it ever physical?"

"You mean…sexually?"

"No, I mean violent?"

"Oh! No. She wanted to hit me a few times, but it never got to that."

Yolanda pauses again. She takes out a notepad from her desk drawer and writes something in it and makes her little *hmm* moaning noises as she does. She puts the pad back into the drawer and then spreads her arms wide.

"I almost forgot!" she says with a big smile.

She pushes herself up from the desk and comes toward him, reaching out to him. They hug and it's much better than last time. Howard doesn't seem to mind it at all.

"Thank you, Howard. I needed that one." Yolanda returns to the desk. "Anyway, let's take a look at what you did for me."

"The poster? Yes...I don't know if it's any good or not, I just—"

"Well, you don't have to worry about that. Remember what we talked about last week? There's no right or wrong with this."

She takes the poster from him and studies it. She leans back in her chair with the poster standing up in her lap so that Howard can't see her face. She starts making little moaning noises again.

A shadow pops up behind her, hovering over her shoulder as if it's also carefully examining the poster. Howard puts a fist in his mouth to keep from screaming.

Then the shadow becomes a mist and vanishes. Howard takes a deep breath.

Yolanda puts the poster down on her desk and starts tracing with her finger, making connections from one photo to the next.

"The boy here is you?" she asks.

"Yes, that's what I was thinking when I did it."

"You're in a dunce cap going to..."

"To the school."

"Oh, yes, I see...but it looks like a prison."

"Well, the school was like a prison."

"Uh, huh. Interesting imagery. A lot of towers and tall buildings."

"Yes," Howard agrees.

"A little boy running toward a baseball diamond. A little boy in a boat with a large oar." Yolanda makes some clicking noises with her tongue. "Very literal and definitely some of the things we hit upon last time. Wine bottles. Women in underwear—"

"I didn't think about it, I just did it." Howard is starting to get uncomfortable again.

"Yes, exactly right. Running, running, running a lot. Toward or away from? Running to love, or away from love. Frightened of love. Worried about your size, I think."

"My size? What size?"

"Your penis size."

"Oh." He is mortified.

"Yes, it's all over the place here. You have been made to feel inadequate. It's really pervasive." Yolanda looks up from Howard's poster. She considers him with a look of concern and compassion. "I want to talk about your family today, Howard. I think you're going to have to accept that a lot of the problems you're having today are a result of the abuses you suffered as a child."

"Yes, I understand that," Howard responds, not exactly enlightened by her evaluation.

"Good. So, we need to identify what it was, address it boldly, and see if we can't forgive and move on. We need to break a pattern. I want to talk about your mother, Howard."

"My mother?"

"I'm getting a lot of repressed anger here. Specifically about your mother and about your penis."

"Oh. I'm sorry."

"No, that's okay. That's good, that's absolutely fine."

"This is awkward," he says, and then his ears start to ring.

"I know, it's never easy," she assures him. "But I think we're ready to tackle this now. Are you ready, Howard?"

"I don't know. I hope so."

"You're doing fine. So I want to go back to the house that you grew up in. Where was it again, that you're from?"

"West Paterson, New Jersey."

"Yes. Let's go home to West Paterson."

The ringing stops. Howard's jaw falls open, and he has a stunned look on his face.

"Howard, let's go home and look around, okay?"

Howard leaps to his feet. "That's it! Go home—to Paterson!"

He gets up and excitedly paces the room.

"Do you ever feel like…like there's something you can't remember? If it's a dream you had, or if it was real, and that there's something you might have to do to make things right, but you can't remember what it is, or what you need to do? I think I just figured it out!"

"Do you feel there's something that you did wrong, Howard?"

Howard shakes his head. She's not getting it.

"I have to go. I have to leave," he says.

"We still have time."

"I know. We'll talk about it next time, I promise. Thank you, Yolanda. You're a genius."

Howard starts for the door but then abruptly turns back to her.

"How about a hug?" he says and then extends his arms to invite her in.

Yolanda obliges. She gets up and they hug. The strength of his embrace startles her.

"Oh my."

"I'm sorry. I'm a little excited. Did I hurt you?"

"No, just surprised me a little, that's all."

Howard smiles at her, a warm and sincere smile.

18

Howard drives hard, riding bumpers and getting nowhere fast. His mind is racing. The shadow wants him in New Jersey. Then what? Should he see his old friends? Should he kill them and give their brains to Cellar Man? And Yolanda—what was that crap all about? Howard didn't want to be angry with her, but he couldn't help himself.

"What a bunch of shit!" he yells. "I'm done with Allen House. Yolanda is way off base, here. Way off! The solution to the problem is in New Jersey and has nothing to do with my fucking penis size. No more posters, no more damaged little women, and no more fucking hugs!"

Howard believes the only thing Yolanda has to offer, from a therapeutic standpoint, revolves around her limited experience with abuse cases. Consequently, all diagnoses lead to the same conclusion. It will always be abuse, and her way of dealing with it is formulaic at best.

"Worried about your size? Jesus Christ that is just unbelievable! Women are so fucking weird. Controlling, selfish, manipulative bitches. Sure, they talk about feelings and kindness and world peace, but all they really want is a big dick and lots of money!"

Howard is getting so angry that it scares him. He switches gears instantly and becomes much more reasonable.

"Maybe I do have a problem with women…"

But then he explodes again, pounding his fist ferociously onto the dashboard. A sharp pain explodes through his hand and all the way up to his elbow.

"Shit!"

He anxiously checks on his hand. It's stiff but hopefully not broken because there's still so much to be done. Howard takes a deep breath and tries to quiet his mind. He's feeling a tad schizophrenic again, and there's no time for that right now. He has to focus. Cellar Man means business, and it's time to face the music.

Howard's head starts to throb. If he has a stroke right now, he decides, that probably wouldn't be such a terrible thing.

19

oward combs his hair in the bedroom mirror and is having a hard time getting it right. All the hair spray has taken its toll. His hair is getting thinner and less manageable every day, and he's starting to look like Einstein whether he wants to or not.

"Are you going to miss me, girl?"

The cat is sleeping on the bag that he has already packed and left open on the bed. It's an overnight bag and definitely small enough to carry on the plane.

"Don't worry. I'll just be a day or two. I have somebody coming in to check up on you, so you won't get too lonely."

Howard gives up on his hair and opens the top dresser drawer, where he has some curious things: several different wallets, a stack of driver's licenses bound with a thick rubber band, plastic bags filled with jewelry, neat rows of film containers, and stacks of money neatly organized by denomination—also bound with rubber bands. There are piles of tens, twenties, fifties, and hundreds. He goes through the licenses and selects one. He takes some money from each pile and then uses an expensive-looking money clip to bind it together. He selects a wallet and a few film containers and then closes the drawer.

Howard detects that bad smell again. He draws his flashlight and whips around like a gunslinger.

"I'm going, I'm going, what more do you want?"

He goes into the kitchen and pours a big bowl of dry food for the cat and fills up her water bowl.

"What else? Oh God, don't forget the extra flashlights!"

He grabs two flashlights from a kitchen drawer and heads back to the bedroom, checking for shadows as he goes.

He puts the flashlights into the zippered compartment that the cat isn't sleeping on and packs the stuff he took out of the drawer. Then he gently lifts the cat and places her on her special pillow by the window. Howard scratches her under the chin. She doesn't purr. She doesn't even seem to notice.

"I'll be back soon. Guard the house, okay?"

Howard zips up the bag. He checks his hair in the mirror one more time, grimaces, picks up the hairbrush, but then decides to avoid another exercise in futility and puts a hat on instead. Howard grabs his keys and his sunglasses. He picks up the travel bag, and he's on his way.

20

American is flying three flights into Newark. The lady at the desk said that he was first on the standby list and should have a pretty good shot at it. She told him his name would be called as soon as something opened up. So Howard sits in the terminal at LAX with his bag on the floor between his feet. Security took the flashlight he was carrying, but the two in his bag got through. Why they didn't take those, he wasn't sure. Two kids are running around playing and making a lot of racket. He makes faces at them as they rush past. He does his Einstein thing to draw them in, making them curious about him, and sure enough, they gradually get closer and closer.

"Hey, what are you guys doing?" Howard asks.

"Nothing—playing," one of the kids says.

"What are you playing? Can I play too?"

"No," says the kid. The other one, a little girl, doesn't feel like talking and just stands there staring at him.

"No? Why not?" Howard asks with his most charming smile.

"'Cause you're old," the kid tells him.

And then they laugh and run away.

Howard looks after them, smiling, but the smile morphs into something more like a sneer. Then the lady at the desk calls his name, but it's not Howard Dudek.

Ralph Thompson is the name the lady calls. Howard checks his wallet just to be sure. Yes, that's him.

21

Howard sits on the plane wedged in between an old woman and a girl he guesses to be about seventeen. The girl is wearing earbuds and has pretty much disappeared from the world. A zombie at thirty thousand feet. Howard gives up his arm rests, keeping his arms squeezed against his sides, trying not to touch either one of them. He steals glimpses at the girl. He could probably look directly at her, even blow in her ear, and she wouldn't notice. She's gorgeous, though—perfect skin: no runs, no hits, no errors. Howard wonders about her story—who she is, and where she's going. He'd never know; so young, so distant. The old lady is already where she is going—outer space. She smiles at him, and Howard smiles back. A nice grandmotherly type, heading, no doubt, to see the grandchildren. Just a sweet old lady with candies in her bag and that old lady perfume that makes him want to gag. Howard is sure that she's kind, generous, and just a little bit out of her mind. He figures that she'll be dead in about two years. Both women have ordered food. He stares straight ahead at the seat in front of him. The old lady drops her plastic fork on the floor between them, and Howard wants to kill her.

22

Newark airport is a zoo. Every flight on the planet seems to have come in at the exact same time. Howard stands in line for over an hour at the Budget Rent a Car, but it works out in his favor because they run out of compacts, and Howard gets a nice Buick LeSabre at the same price.

Once he gets away from the airport, things move along pretty well. It's cold but not terrible. Howard hadn't thought about the weather, but even if he had, he doesn't have a winter coat anyway. He turns on the heat and is impressed with how quickly the car achieves and maintains the desired temperature. The Buick even has a digital readout to let you know the temperature inside and outside of the car. Howard is not used to that kind of luxury. He takes one wrong turn and misses Highway 4 from Route 17, but he gets back on track without too much trouble. From there it all comes back, and he knows exactly where he is. The timing couldn't have worked out better. He is missing the serious rush hour traffic by about an hour, so he is really dodging a bullet on that one. But the closer he gets to his destination, the more apprehensive he becomes.

23

He drives slowly, taking it in. The street is beat up and neglected. The sidewalks are buckled, and the grass is overgrown. Weeds have pushed up through the concrete, and it looks like something out of a science fiction movie—giant six footers that would burst their seed pods and turn you into a zombie. The whole area looks deserted, not a soul in sight.

Howard takes a left turn, and then he sees it set off by itself, way back from the street. A shiver goes through him. He stops the car and gawks at it like a kid at a freak show. Howard can feel its power. Pure evil—a house of horrors to be sure. He maneuvers the car onto the long, winding driveway and slowly drives toward the house. It looks exactly the same to him, only smaller. The house is impervious to time. It will always be there because no one would dare touch it.

Howard parks the car. He takes a flashlight out of his bag and sits perfectly still, staring at the house for a full hour.

Just as it starts to get dark, Howard stirs. He opens the car door, gets out, and walks purposefully toward what needs to be done. Pushing back some annoying second thoughts, he stands at the threshold and shines his flashlight on the cellar doors. They are locked. There's a hinge and a padlock—a shiny new Schlage that looks out of place on the old, decrepit doors. Howard feels a cold breeze blow past him. It rattles the dead trees as if summoning those whose presence is now required.

Howard seems to receive a message about what to do next. He stomps his heel into the lock. His foot goes right through the rotted wood, sending the lock, the hinge, and splinters of wood tumbling down to the cellar floor. The odor of decay is overwhelming. It's the same smell that was in his apartment when the ghost was approaching. He stumbles, barely avoiding a disastrous fall through the cellar doors and into whatever horror awaits him below.

Howard puts the flashlight in his mouth and while keeping the light aimed at the doors he reaches down with both hands to grab hold of the old metal handles and flings open the doors. Howard starts down the concrete stairs using the flashlight to illuminate the way, but the dark is all-encompassing and seems to devour the light He carefully negotiates the stairs, moving slowly and feeling with his feet what his flashlight fails to identify.

Arriving on the cellar floor, he hears a scraping noise and turns sharply toward the sound. He trips on the concrete floor, which is buckled and broken as if someone had pushed it up while trying to escape from underneath. He is gasping as he regains his footing. Every move, even the smallest motion, exhausts him. He searches the cellar with his flashlight, straining to see. He can make out some shapes—some old trunks and boxes. It's a long cellar, and he can't see the entire length of it. Support posts are lined up like soldiers marching off into darkness. There is very little headroom, not the way he remembers from when he was locked down here as a kid. It's claustrophobic and oppressive, to say the least, and the bad childhood memories are coming on strong.

A wave of nausea hits him, and his legs get shaky. He collapses to the floor in a sitting position, and then a cramp in his gut doubles him over. A high-pitched ringing explodes in his head, obliterating his equilibrium, and Howard falls flat on his back. He drops the flashlight, which rolls away from him. From his prone position, he searches frantically, clutching, grabbing, and cutting himself on the broken concrete floor. When he tries to get up, he can't. He can't move. The whole cellar is spinning. Howard rolls over and throws up.

"Take it easy. You're okay now, son," says a voice that sounds familiar.

"Who is that?" Howard gropes again and finds the flashlight. He aims it up at the ceiling. A shadow face looks down at him.

"Could you shut that off, please? This is hard enough as it is. Please, shut it off."

Howard shuts off the flashlight.

"Okay, now we can talk," says the face.

Howard sits up. The room has stopped spinning, and he starts to feel better.

"Who are you?" Howard asks.

"I'm your father, Howard."

There is a kind of whooshing sound, and suddenly Howard's dad is sitting right next to him on the cellar floor.

"Dad?" Howard asks again, just to be sure.

"Yup, weird, huh?" His dad smiles at him just like he did when Howard was a little boy and they were best friends. "I don't have it all figured out yet, but I can talk to you here because of what Cellar Man did. There's a negative energy from what happened here that I can ride like a wave. Opposites attracting—just like magnets. It's really fascinating stuff. I can stay here longer than other places, and that's why I had to try and get you back here."

"Oh," is all Howard can think to say.

"Howard, there are things that were never said between us—important things. There's something you have to know before it's too late."

"Know about what, Dad?"

"About me and your mother. About love, Howard."

"She ruined you, Dad."

"She didn't."

"How could you let her treat you like that?

"Your mother was a beautiful lady, Howard. She was everything I could ever want in a woman. We were completely devoted to each other. You remember the happy times, don't you, Howard."

"Yes, I remember."

"The mistake I made was later, when you got older, because I didn't tell you the truth." Dad sadly shakes his head and sighs. Howard thinks that he's about to cry.

"What truth, Dad?"

"Your mother got sick. It was an emotional kind of sick that made her into somebody else. She didn't want you to know so I never told you, but it made her act the way she did sometimes. It was a sickness, Howard. We didn't understand what it was when you were little. Later she was diagnosed, and we got drugs that helped, but she was ashamed and never wanted you to know the truth. That's what happened. I was devoted to her no matter what. I was in love with her no matter what, and I made her a promise that I now regret. We should have told you the truth. It was a mistake, and you suffered for it. I hope you can forgive me. And I hope you can understand that whatever I did, I did it for love. And that's not such a terrible thing, is it?"

"No, probably not," Howard says.

"What I'm trying to say, Howard. What I've come all this way to tell you is that love is the most important thing. Even more so over on this side. Without it you're just kind of pissing in the wind, son. I did everything in my life for love. We couldn't be talking like this now without it. Let it guide your way, Howard. It will give you strength and comfort."

A ripple goes through the room that makes Howard shudder.

"Uh, oh. Did you feel that?" asks his father's ghost.

"What's going on? What was that?"

"We're running out of time."

"Were you the one who's been doing all that stuff?

"What stuff?"

"The shadows, the lights, the phone calls?"

"Some of it was me. I was trying to keep him away and get your attention. Howard, go home. See your mother. I think you'll be surprised."

"Do you talk to her?"

"Oh, yes. And don't give up on Einstein. You do a wonderful thing with those kids. You don't know it, but you're having a tremendous impact. You inspire them, Howard."

"I won't give it up, Dad."

"I love you, son. You're just getting started. The best is yet to come for you. I have to go now. I'm fading, and Cellar Man… you have to go before he comes back. Hurry."

"Will I see you again?"

"Go home, son. Good luck. Do what's right. Do it for love."

"I'll try, Dad."

Dad turns back to shadow and then jumps back up to the ceiling.

"And close the door on the way out, will ya?"

And then he is gone.

Something else laughs from the darkest part of the cellar. Howard slowly turns to face it.

24

Howard stumbles out of the cellar and falls to the ground. He gets up and staggers back to the car. He flings the car door open, heaves himself inside, and then sits, zombielike.

Then he explodes.

"What a bunch of crap! Do it for love? Don't you get it, Dad? She's got you, and he's got me. So thanks for nothing! I appreciate the effort, but it just does me no fucking good whatsoever!"

Howard grabs his bag. He roughly turns the rearview mirror so that he can see his face. He takes a deep breath and then applies some glue to his lip and puts on the Einstein mustache.

25

oward hasn't seen his mother for quite some time, but she still lives in the same house, on the same quiet street where he grew up.

He knocks on the door, dressed like Einstein, and he's wearing latex surgical gloves. He knows it might take her a while to get to the door. She's got bad joints. He knocks again, louder, in case she didn't hear. She already had a hearing aid the last time he saw her, but she never used it, which Howard thinks is just so typical of her.

"That's great, Ma. Make everybody else shout because you can't put in the goddamn hearing aid."

She answers the door, and he almost doesn't recognize her. She has really aged and is using a walker now.

"Yes?" Apparently she doesn't recognize him, either.

"Hi, Mom. It's me, Howard."

"Howard? What happened? You grew a mustache?"

"Yeah. How are you?"

"Not so good. What can I tell you?"

"You got a walker now?"

"What?"

"You got a walker now?" he says a little louder.

"Yeah, yeah…the hip, the knee. What can I tell you?"

"Can I come in?"

"You want to come in?"

"Yeah, can I?"

"What?"

"Can I come in?" he repeats, his voice rising in frustration.

"What are you shouting for? I get nothing from you in all these years, and then you come over here to shout at me?

Some son I got. You want to come in? Come in already, what do I care?"

She turns herself around and shuffles her way back into the living room. Howard follows her in and closes the door. It's the same modest place that he grew up in. Nothing has changed. Three bedrooms, a kitchen, a living room with ugly brown paneling, and a TV that is always on. She arrives at her TV chair and with great difficulty situates herself into a position where she can plop herself down directly from the walker and into the chair. Howard watches this without offering any assistance.

"Oy," she says.

Jeopardy is on the TV, and it's turned up loud.

"Do you want something to eat?" she begrudgingly offers.

"No."

"Well, what do you want, then?"

"I just vanted to see how you vere, dat's all."

"What?"

"I vanted to see how you vere."

"I'm lousy, are you satisfied."

She looks at the TV with a depressed expression that Howard remembers well.

"Are you taking your medicine?" he asks.

"Huh?"

"Your medicine—are you taking your medicine?"

"Yeah, yeah," she waves disgustedly at the air. "I take so much that I don't know what I'm taking anymore."

"I spoke to Dad."

"You what?"

"I spoke to Dad. He told me to come see you."

"He's dead. What are you talking?"

"I saw his ghost."

"You what?"

"He told me that he loved you and it vasn't your fault dat you vere such a bitch to him. He told me you vere sick in the head."

"Your father was weak. He wasn't a smart man. Why are you talking like that? You got an accent now?"

"He told me—"

"He told you? He told you what? What do you want? You come back here…what do you want after all this time, talking about your father?" She waves a hand at him as if to shoo him away. "Leave me alone, already."

Howard moves in a little closer to her.

"You talked to your father—what kind of shit is that. What, are you crazy or something?"

"No, I saw him, Mom. I really did. And he said dat he talks to you, too. Do you talk to him, Mom?"

"I don't talk to nobody."

"He said dat you vere beautiful."

He inches closer and is making her nervous.

"Where are you going? Get away from me. Your father was a fool. He was a lousy businessman, and he had no backbone. He let people walk all over him. Your father was a loser, Howard! A dumb Polack! The biggest mistake I ever made. Look at me now, look at what I got—nothin!"

Howard leaps at her, and they both go over backward in the chair. He drags her into the middle of the room and gets on top of her. He grabs her around the neck. She starts to scream in pain and fear—a horrible sound. He has already broken her arm, and her hip, and has dislocated her shoulder. Howard covers her mouth with his hand to stop all the screaming.

"This is from Dad, you bitch. This is vhat he should have done to you a long time ago."

Howard jerks her head violently until he hears her neck snap. She goes instantly limp. Howard stays on top of her for a while, staring at her face. Then he gets up and goes into the kitchen. He finds a big carving knife. He thinks about cutting out her brain, but he plunges the knife through her neck instead, impaling her to the floor.

Howard stands over her and admires his work.

"Ya, okay, your brain probably tastes like shit anyvay." He scoops up a little of her blood with the film container. "Now, let me see, let me see—vhat do ve do?"

He finds her pocket book, removes the money from her wallet, and then turns over some furniture. He goes into her bedroom, opens the dresser drawers, and tosses her clothes all over the place. Next he goes to the hutch where she keeps various knickknacks. He takes a marble egg and a little crystal dog that he always liked and puts them into his pocket. He goes back to the body and takes the wedding ring from her finger.

"Very nice to see you again. I hope you're feeling better now. I vill send you a postcard from California—swimming pools; movie stars. You'd love it there. It's sunny and varm and the food is vonderful. Bye-bye, Mrs. Dudek."

Howard leaves the house. He gets back into the Buick, takes off the latex gloves, and stuffs them into the plastic film container with his mother's blood. He takes Mom's valuables and zips those up into a plastic bag. He puts everything into his suitcase and then drives to the airport.

26

oward stays as Einstein. He has another middle seat for the trip back. The people on either side of him have fallen asleep. On his left side is a middle-aged guy in a suit. On his other side is a rocker-type dressed all in black, maybe twenty years old with a ring in his nose. You'd probably never stop and talk to this guy on the street, but as Howard watches him now peacefully sleeping, he just seems like a sweet innocent kid.

A little boy in the seat in front of him keeps popping up and looking back at the man with the funny mustache. They play a game together. The kid pops up, Howard makes a funny face, and then the kid drops back down into his seat laughing, only to appear again five seconds later. This game apparently has no end.

Then Howard notices a bloodstain on his pants that he hadn't seen before. It's on his right leg, on his upper thigh. A sudden wave of panic makes his stomach flip. It isn't bright red. It has dried and just looks like a small dark blotch. It could be anything, but Howard thinks he can smell it now. He can smell his mother's blood. He takes a magazine from the seat pocket and puts it over the stain just as the kid's mom is trying to get his attention.

"Excuse me, sir?"

If you were casting a young mom, that would be her. Blonde, thirties, probably put on a little weight since the kid but still attractive. Big blue eyes, big smile, and great teeth.

"Ya?" Howard smiles back.

"I hope he's not bothering you too much. I'll tell him to stop if he is."

"No, no, it's fine, really. It makes the time pass, and dat's okay by me. To tell you the truth, I velcome the distraction. So don't vorry. He doesn't bother me one bit."

Howard figures that she lives in one of those little bedroom communities off the 101. Agoura Hills or Thousand Oaks, one of those four-bedroom jobs out there. She is doing okay—living the dream. Probably has one more at home and an architect husband and they've been talking about having a third.

"Are you sure?" she says, still looking sorry for the trouble her little devil is causing.

"Ya, absolutely sure," Einstein says.

"He really likes you. I've never seen him take to somebody like this."

"Ya, I have a vay vit the childrens. They are attracted to me, somehow. It happens all the time."

"Well, you must be a nice man then."

"Ya, I'm very nice. I have a cat."

"Really? We do, too! And two dogs."

"Ya, there is so much to learn from the animals."

"Yes, I think you're right. Well, nice talking to you."

"And you as vell, my dear."

She smiles and sits back down in her seat. The little kid pops up, Howard makes a face, and the kid drops back down again.

Howard reaches for his bag, which he had put on the floor under the seat. He is careful not to disturb his neighbors. He manages to pull the bag up onto his lap and open one of the zippered compartments. He retrieves an envelope and looks it over carefully. It's the telephone bill from Yolanda's desk, the address clearly visible in the envelope window: Yolanda Washington, 143 Adams Boulevard, Los Angeles, CA 90026.

The kid pops up again. Only two more hours to go.

27

When the jet lands at LAX, it is still early evening. Picking up those three hours coming back extends the time for all he has yet to do. Howard is glad to be home. He takes the shuttle bus to his car, which he had left at the Get Away Airport Parking Lot. Once in his car, Howard takes off his mustache and cleans his lip with an adhesive remover that he always keeps in the glove compartment. He applies some fresh glue and puts the mustache back on. He sprays some more white into his hair and then checks himself out in the rearview mirror.

"Ya, goot enough for the little childrens."

He pays the attendant cash and tells him that he doesn't need a receipt.

28

It takes him almost two hours to get to Yolanda's house. Her place is on a main drag, and there's a lot of traffic. It's a little place right in between two dorm houses. USC students rush back and forth to wherever they are going, oblivious to the derelicts and the drug addicts who share the neighborhood with them. Pretty girls in tight jeans shake their asses right past the drunks who are peeing blood in the street. He drives around the block once, casing the neighborhood, and then he finds a place to park.

Howard walks briskly, smiling at the pretty girls along the way. There's a lot of activity down here, more than Howard would have liked, but he is feeling powerful now. So no problem—piece of cake.

Howard, bag in hand, walks up the steps to Yolanda's house and knocks on her door. After a moment she answers and looks surprised to see him.

"Howard?"

"Hi, can I talk to you?"

"How did you—"

"I had a show in the neighborhood, I hope you don't mind."

"But how did you find my house?"

"I have to tell you something. You were right and I owe you an explanation."

"Howard, you shouldn't come to my house. We can talk at the office."

"No, I couldn't wait because it's an emergency."

"Howard, I want you to leave. Call me tomorrow and I'll set something up for you. You have to leave, Howard."

"All right, but it's just—"

Howard staggers, his legs buckle and he falls onto the stairs.

"Oh my God, Howard!"

"I'm sorry, I'm sorry. I've been passing out a lot."

A big sob erupts, just like the one that happened with Cynthia at The Imagination Factory. It seems he's trying to control it but can't. He's gasping for air and sobbing uncontrollably. It's very convincing. One of his greatest performances ever.

Yolanda takes the bait. She reaches out to help him.

"No, I'll go," he manages. "I'll call you tomorrow. You're right. I'm sorry."

"It's all right. Come inside. I'll get you some water. My God, Howard, what happened?"

Howard notices that they have drawn a small audience. He gives them the Einstein goofy scientist smile to assure them that everything is all right and then lets Yolanda help him inside.

They stumble over to the sofa, and Howard collapses in a heap.

"Thank you," he says in a damaged whisper.

"I'll get you some water," Yolanda offers and then rushes off to the kitchen.

Her place is comfortable but not fancy. She has a lot of artwork, though. African masks and stuff like that. A lot of plants. There's an upstairs where he guesses the bedrooms are. Howard unzips his bag.

Yolanda returns with the glass of water.

"Thank you," Howard says and then greedily drinks as if he's dying of thirst.

Yolanda sits in a chair opposite him.

"What's going on with you, Howard?" she asks.

"Is your son here? I don't want to disturb anybody. I'm sorry about this, I really am."

"He's upstairs. It's all right, Howard. You won't disturb anybody. Tell me what's happening."

"What about the other kids? Are they around?"

"No, they're not here. They're away at school."

As soon as she says it, she knows it's a mistake.

Howard smiles at her and then puts the drinking glass into his bag. Yolanda swallows hard.

"I'm being haunted. It's a pretty serious situation I got myself into. You believe in all that stuff, so I know you won't patronize me, and I appreciate that. You're the only one I can talk to. You were right about the abuse. There was a lot of abuse. By the way, nice place. Love the artwork."

"Did you do something, Howard?"

"Did I do something? Ya, I did something. I just got back from New Jersey actually. I went back to the cellar, and I got some instructions. Ya, I spoke to my father's ghost, but he vasn't making much sense. He didn't understand vhat vas going on vit me, I'm afraid."

"What's going on, Howard?"

"I vill tell you. I have an agreement vit another fellow. He is Cellar Man, and there is a quota that I must fulfill, a certain number of souls that I am required to collect for him."

Howard takes out a film container and shows it to her.

"What is that, Howard?"

"I keep them in here. Ya, just a little drop of blood or a hair. That seems to do it. I have lots of them."

He opens the container and takes out a pair of latex gloves.

"It's easier than chopping out all the brains, anyvay."

"Why are you talking like that?" Yolanda's voice is shaky.

"Like vhat?"

"Howard, I think you should leave."

"I vill in a moment, don't vorry. I just vanted to explain this for you. Please, it vill just take another moment, and then ve'll be done."

Yolanda gets up.

"Sit down!"

She does, and now she is terrified.

"Please, let me explain, and then I vill go," he says, becoming so reassuringly calm that she could almost believe him. "You are really the only person I can talk to now."

Howard gets up and starts putting on the gloves. He circles her chair to be sure she doesn't get up again—ever.

"I don't think the penis has anything to do vit it really. I don't know vhere you vere going vit all that."

"Howard…please," she pleads.

Howard leans down and gets very close to her terrified face. "Shhhhh."

"Oh my God!" Tears are coming down, and she's trembling.

"Look at you—all jiggly wiggly."

"Howard—"

"Shhh!"

"Okay, okay…I'm sorry."

"You don't vant to vake the boy, do you?"

"You won't hurt him will you, Howard?"

"Don't be silly. I love the childrens. I would never hurt them. Please relax. I just vant to tell you vhat is happening, and then I vill go. Ya, this is goot?"

"Okay, Howard."

He circles her again.

"So it seems to vork in cycles. I do vhat is required of me, then it stops and I forget, and then after some time he comes back to remind me and it starts all over again. Okay? Are you following me?"

"Yes."

"Goot. So I am back in the cycle, and I just got back from New Jersey. I killed Howard's mother for him, and now I have a few more. I vanted to tell you that you vere right. It vas abuse. A traumatic event that he had, and he vas never able to recover. It's a shame really. But a deal's a deal, so vhat can you do?"

Howard picks up a stone sculpture of an African tribesman.

"So now you know, and dat's it. Dat vasn't so terrible, vas it?"

"Don't hurt me, Howard, please! I have a small child. I'm going for my master's."

"Hurt you? I love you, Yolanda. You are my best friend. Vhy would I hurt you? Don't be silly. Oh, and remember the little boy Howard told you about at the school, the one under the desk?"

"Yes, I remember."

"You know vhy he vasn't around anymore? That nobody knew vhat happened to him?"

She tries to get up, but he pushes her back down into the chair.

"I killed him," Howard whispers into her ear, as only a true maniac can.

He pats her on the head like he does with the cute kids at the schools. Then he starts circling again.

"I've killed lots of the little brats. I don't vant to, you see, but I have to. So the situation is this. I have told you everything, and I'm grateful to you for dat. I feel much better. You really are a goot doctor. But the problem ve face is this—"

He jumps out in front of her with a big smile on his face.

"Now you know too much!" Howard seems completely delighted by the predicament.

"Howard, stop, please. I can get you help. I can get you to the right people. Please, let me help you, Howard. You need help!"

"Ya, I tell you something, my friend. You are the one dat needs the help."

"Howard, please!"

"Do you vant to scream? It might make you feel a little better."

She doesn't scream.

"Maybe ve should hug. It's a great vay to end the session, don't you think?"

He hits her on the head with the sculpture. One, two, three times, and then she is dead.

Howard starts up the stairs with the sculpture to visit with the boy.

29

oward showers in Yolanda's bathroom. His dirty Einstein clothes are piled on the floor, and his makeup items are neatly arranged on the sink counter. He steps out of the shower wearing Yolanda's blue shower cap. He puts on another pair of latex gloves and then takes his soiled clothes to the laundry room. He studies her washer and dryer and then carefully measures out the detergent. He puts the Einstein clothes into the washer and runs the machine. He goes back into the living room and sits naked on the couch (except for the shower cap and his latex gloves) and stares at Yolanda's bloody corpse while waiting for the laundry. The phone rings, but Howard ignores it. He doesn't even hear it. When the wash cycle is finished, he returns to the laundry room, puts the clothes into the dryer, and then goes back upstairs to the bathroom.

He removes the shower cap and touches up his hair with the Natural Color Highlights and then glues his mustache back on. There is no reflection in the mirror. The mirror is pitch-black.

When the clothes are dry, Howard takes them into the living room and gets dressed in front of Yolanda. He finds her pocket book and takes the cash. He overturns some furniture and throws some of her things around. He takes a paperweight from Yolanda's coffee table and holds it up to the light. It's a glass ball with what looks like a little solar system trapped inside. Howard thinks it's the coolest paperweight he's ever seen. He puts the little solar system into his bag. He checks around to make sure he didn't get careless and leave any clues. Satisfied, he waves goodbye to Yolanda and leaves the house.

Nobody on the street even looks at him. He gets back to his car and drives home. The traffic isn't bad at all.

30

The first thing Howard does when he gets home is open a window. It's oppressively stuffy. The cat is still on her pillow by the window, and he scratches her under her chin. She doesn't purr.

"Miss me, girl?"

Howard unpacks. He opens the dresser drawer and adds to his secret collection. Three more film containers, which he places neatly and carefully next to the many others that are already there. The cash is placed onto the proper piles and secured with rubber bands. He takes the marble egg, the glass dog, the tiny solar system, his mother's wedding ring, and puts them into the plastic bags that he keeps his special valuables in.

He opens a second drawer, where he has his toy collection: windup Godzillas, gnomes, fairies, and various Disney characters. He adds a tiny *Millennium Falcon* to the collection, something from Yolanda's son.

Then he lies down on the bed and passes out.

31

The next morning Howard is awakened by a knock on his door. Howard doesn't move. He lies there hoping whoever it is will just go away. They don't, and the knocking continues.

"Sir, could you open the door please," comes a determined voice.

Howard, still dressed as Einstein, gets up and goes to the door.

"Who is it?" he asks.

"Los Angeles Police Department. Can we have a word with you, sir?"

"I'm a little busy at the moment."

"Sir, I think you need to open the door right now."

So he does.

The two policemen standing at his door recoil from the stench.

"Jesus," the younger officer cries.

"Is there a problem, officer?" Howard innocently inquires.

"We have a warrant to search these premises," the older one says.

"Well I'm sorry, but I have a show today, and I really need to get going," Howard says apologetically. Then his mustache comes undone and dangles precariously from his upper lip. Howard pulls it off and puts it in his pocket.

"Just give us a minute. This won't take long. Could you stand aside, sir?" the calmer, more mature officer asks.

Howard stands aside.

"What's this all about, officer?" Howard yawns.

The older one shows him a search warrant and stands in front of the doorway while the younger officer squeezes past with a handkerchief over his face. He points to the bloodstains on the carpet. The older officer nods, confirming that he's already seen it, and then the younger cop continues to search the apartment.

"We're investigating your wife's disappearance, sir."

"Disappearance? What happened?" Howard sounds properly shocked by the news.

"She's missing," the cop tells him.

"I didn't know. That's terrible."

"You didn't know?" the cop asks suspiciously.

"We're separated. She's been gone a few months already. I haven't heard a peep from her. I had no idea, truthfully."

"We've gotten complaints about some bad odors coming from here, sir," the cop says while trying not to gag.

"Really?"

"Yes. Really."

"Hmm," Howard says. "I wonder what that could be. I've been out of town for a few days. Maybe I forgot about the garbage."

"Bill," the younger cop calls from the bedroom. "You better come in here!"

"Sir, let's see what he found in there, shall we?"

The older officer gently takes Howard by the arm, and they go into the bedroom together.

The younger officer is at the dresser by the window next to a stiff dead cat.

"It's a cat. Been dead a long time."

"What happened to the cat, sir," the older cop asks?

"Nothing. I don't know."

"Its neck is broken, Bill. Did you kill the cat, sir?"

Howard has a completely perplexed look on his face.

"Oh man," says the older cop. "Check that closet. I'm getting it really strong here."

"I'm not feeling very good all of a sudden, guys." Howard is indeed looking pale. "I'm sorry, but I really must ask you to leave."

Howard falls to his knees, but the cop doesn't let go.

"Check the closet!" the older cop repeats but with much more urgency this time.

"I need my flashlight," Howard pleads.

"What?"

"Officer, may I borrow your flashlight. It's kind of an emergency. Oh, God, did you feel that? He's coming!"

The cop tightens his grip.

The younger cop opens the closet door, and Howard's dead wife falls into the room.

"Holy shit!" The young cop stumbles away from the gruesomely decayed body.

Howard pulls away from the cop. It's an amazing maneuver—as if someone grabbed him by his other arm and was dragging him into the living room.

Howard screams.

The cops follow him and can't believe what they're seeing. Still on his knees, Howard is being slammed into the living room wall over and over again, as if someone is trying to pull him through to the other side. He begins to levitate, sliding up the wall. He starts hitting himself in the face, and the blood is spattering everywhere. Then—*boom!*—into the wall, then up and—*boom!*—into the wall again.

The cops rush toward him and with a monumental effort they get him down on the floor and handcuffed. Howard screams the whole time.

32

oward had killed his wife, too. They were never divorced; he just threw out all her stuff. Over a five-year period, Howard had dressed like Einstein and killed thirty-six people, mostly women and children. Howard was found unfit to stand trial and is now serving a life sentence in an institution for the criminally insane. He gets a tremendous amount of fan mail and has many female admirers who have proposed marriage. He has given countless interviews, and he wrote a book. The rights have been bought, and *Cellar Man* (the movie) will be released this coming Halloween. Most of the time Howard is charming and funny. Some of the time he needs to be isolated.

Howard Dudek made it big. He showed them all.

BILL'S APPOINTMENT

Bill stands at his kitchen counter staring at his new Krups coffee maker. He checks for a third time to be sure the thing is plugged in. He smacks it, it gurgles once, and then nothing. Lots of switches and buttons and blinking lights, but apparently they forgot to program the thing to make coffee.

Exasperated, he pounds his fist on the Corian countertop and his toaster (which doesn't work either) rattles in response. He considers the appliance—it's an extremely cool toaster. It looks like a vintage radio with lots of interesting-looking gizmos. You can set the toasting levels a thousand different ways, but it doesn't make any difference—the toast always comes out burned. The thing isn't satisfied until it sets off the fire alarm.

While staring at the toaster, Bill feels a great weariness and literally begins to fall asleep on his feet. He shakes his head to snap himself out of it, and his gray hair flops down in front of his eyes. He checks his bathrobe pockets for a tissue and blows his nose. The snot comes out red. That happens once in a while. Maybe because it's been so dry in LA. It hasn't rained since—he can't remember when. Or maybe it's the late-night drinking.

He thinks again about going for a checkup. He still has the insurance, but he just can't seem to drag himself in there. Maybe the blood in the tissue will inspire him. When you get to be over fifty, you need to watch stuff. You have to suck it up and let them do things to you—check the prostate and get that camera up your ass before something really bad starts growing in there.

Damn, I need a cup of coffee.

He has an interview across town in about an hour, and he was drinking last night until three in the morning. Bill got laid off his job last month. His longest stretch of being unemployed since the good old bad days. Bill used to be an actor. He had done a few films, some TV commercials, and spent a fortune on acting classes. But his career wasn't going anywhere, and he got tired of constantly being broke and the soul-crushing rejections. There was also an ill mother who had to be dealt with, who he couldn't ignore anymore, so one day he just quit. Turned his back on the whole thing. Dropped his agents, his friends, all his theater connections—completely deserted what he once believed to be his reason for being.

He went to an employment agency and got a temporary job at a swimwear company. He worked his way up into the customer service department and started making good money there. He was with the same company for twelve years, until he got laid off. Budget cuts and the trade wars were hitting the garment industry hard. So now he has a big house with lots of fancy stuff that doesn't work. He has health insurance, a big mortgage, a new car, and no job.

The coffee maker beeps and blinks and then shuts itself off. Bill has to laugh, and when he does, some blood sprays out from his nose and spatters onto the kitchen counter.

"Jesus…"

Then he feels unsteady as if the ground has shifted beneath his feet, and he has to brace himself against the kitchen counter to keep his balance. His ears start ringing, and Bill thinks he's about to pass out. He hangs on to the counter until the ringing stops and the kitchen floor is done moving around. Bill takes a deep breath, grabs a paper towel, and starts cleaning up his mess.

Everything is falling apart. It hit home last night when he got in from the Dodgers game. He only goes once or twice during the season these days. It's gotten way to expensive, and then it takes forever to get out of the parking lot after the game. He lives ten miles from the stadium, but it took him almost an hour to get back home. When he walked in the door, the ADT alarm system started to beep, as it's supposed to, but when he went in to disarm the system—nothing happened. It wouldn't stop beeping. He pushed the code on the key pad over and over, but the system wouldn't respond. He ran into the bedroom where the other keypad is, but that one didn't work, either. Then the alarm went off, and it was screaming bloody murder. One in the morning and all hell was breaking loose. Bill's two neurotic cats completely freaked out and started bouncing off the walls. Bill got a stepladder and tried to disconnect the alarm box from the ceiling in the hallway, but he couldn't get the thing to budge. The alarm company finally called after about ten minutes of this ungodly noise, and somehow they managed to disarm the system from their office. Then Bill was informed that he had to pay ninety-five dollars to have a technician come out to the house to diagnosis the problem. We're all worried about somebody breaking in and stealing our stuff, but it's the alarm company that you really have to watch out for.

After that, Bill made himself a drink, a scotch on the rocks, and then sat down in the TV room to relax. But the TV didn't work, either. First he couldn't get any sound out of the Bose sound system, and then his five-thousand-dollar four-month-old big-screen TV just blinked out and died. While staring dully at his dead TV, his black cat, Ernie, made his presence known with a deep, psychotic howl. He was hanging by his claws from curtain he just shredded. Bill carefully removed the cat and then fixed himself another drink. Then he went into the living room to read for a while. He turned on the lamp, and a puff of smoke came up from the wall socket. The light bulb crackled and popped, and then everything in the house went black. Bill collapsed in his big overstuffed goose-down sofa to drink his scotch in the dark and then felt a sharp pain behind his left eyeball, and a blood-red tear rolled down his cheek.

Bill knew something was coming for him. He'd felt it for a while—cancer, death, a horrible accident—something was stalking him. He finished his drink, fixed the thrown breaker switch, and then got ready for bed.

So Bill is not particularly surprised to find himself cleaning blood off the countertop this morning. He chucks the bloody towel into the garbage and then makes his way toward the bathroom. The interview this morning is important. It's a good position with a well-established sportswear manufacturer, and they're looking for somebody with Bill's kind of customer service experience. He might have to take a pay cut, but he is more than willing to do that.

Then there's a knock at the door. He should just ignore it—but he doesn't.

Bill opens the door and looks into the hopeful but distressed face of a big man in a tattered raincoat and pants that are three sizes too small for him. His eyes are bloodshot and intense.

More and more these people are making their way into the neighborhood. When he first moved to Glendale, if somebody knocked, it was probably a kid selling cookies. But this is no Girl Scout standing before him. The times they are a changin', and Bill is kicking himself for being so reckless.

"Can I help you?" Bill indignantly asks.

"Is that your stuff in the driveway?" asks the stranger.

"What stuff?"

"You got all those things piled up in the driveway next to the garage."

"Its old stuff. I'm throwing it out, so what?"

"You shouldn't do that. People see that and they want to take a look. Do you want people snooping around like that?"

Bill studies him for a moment. He's not sure what's happening here. It'd be almost funny if it wasn't so annoying. "Listen, I don't have time for this right now."

"Hon-Jon."

"What?"

"Hon-Jon, that's my name, but you can call me Juan."

He offers his hand. Bill doesn't shake it.

"Anyway," he continues, "I'm just trying to tell you, if you leave stuff lying around like that, you're asking for trouble. There are people looking for signs, you know? And you got a big invitation out there for bad things to happen. I'm here to warn you. I'm trying to do you a favor, Bill."

Hearing him say his name stops Bill from ruminating about how to get rid of this guy.

"How the hell do you know my name?"

Juan smiles but doesn't answer the question.

"Are you looking through my mail or something?"

"No!" Juan answers as if insulted by the question.

"I have to go now. So…goodbye."

Bill starts to close the door, but Juan puts his hand up against it and locks his elbow. He's strong and easily stops Bill from putting an end to their encounter.

"Where are you goin'?" Juan asks with a troubled look.

Bill feels himself starting to sweat. This is not good. This might be a real nightmare scenario developing here.

"Look, if you want that stuff in the driveway, just go ahead and take it," Bill suggests.

"I don't want that stuff."

They stare at each other for a moment.

"I have an appointment, okay? Can you please step away from the door now?"

"Why don't you just put the stuff in the garage?"

"Why? Because the garage door is broken, that's why."

"What happened to it?" Juan asks.

"It's the spring. The spring snapped in there."

"The what?"

"The spring. You know those big coils that hold the door open and closed. Why am I even explaining this to you? The spring broke and the door is jammed, so I can't open it any-more, okay?"

"You should get that looked at because you got computer stuff and a TV and that toaster oven just sitting out there for all the world to see. That's going to attract the wrong kind of people. Uh, you got a little something…there's some blood on your lip."

Bill self-consciously wipes his face with the already blood-ied tissue.

Juan smiles.

"I really have to go now." Bill tries to close the door again, but Juan won't let him.

"You're that the guy in that movie, huh?" Juan asks with a knowing grin.

"Look…I'm not kidding. I have a very important appointment–"

"Yeah, that drug dealer. You were good. What was that mov-ie called again?"

"That was a long time ago…*Dirty Habit*. It was called *Dirty Habit*."

"Yeah, *Dirty Habit*. That was a good movie. You were great in that."

"Thank you."

"Very believable. I liked that you started out bad and then found your higher calling when the little girl got into trouble. And you changed your whole outlook for her and the whole neighborhood. And then you kicked the holy crap out of those bad guys."

"Well, somebody had to do it."

"Do you get a lot of nose bleeds, Bill?"

"Come on, man—"

He tries pushing the door closed again, but Juan holds firm.

"There's something important I have to tell you," Juan says.

"If you don't let me close this door right now, I'm calling the police. Do you want me to do that?"

"Don't be an asshole, Bill. It will make this more complicated than it needs to be."

"That's it—we're done now."

Bill tries again to close the door, really putting his weight into it this time, but Juan thwarts him again, this time blocking the door with his shoulder.

"We really need to talk," Juan says with blazing bloodshot eyes.

"No, we don't. Goodbye!"

They struggle against each other for a moment, and then Juan bulls his way inside. Bill stumbles back; shocked and gasping. Juan slams the door shut behind him and throws the dead bolt.

"Nice place. Love the wallpaper."

"Get out!" Bill's voice sort of sticks in his throat, and it comes off more scared than commanding.

"We have destiny, you and me."

"I'm calling the police."

"I'm here so that we can save each other."

"Oh really?" Bill picks up the landline, but the phone is dead. "It's dead isn't it?"

Bill abruptly turns and starts toward his bedroom. He jerks around so quickly that he loses his balance. Juan, close on his heels, grabs his arm to keep him from falling. Bill roughly pulls his arm away from him.

"What the hell are you doing? Don't follow me!" Bill scolds.

"Oh, okay, you're right. That was rude. I'll check the windows, then."

"Yeah, you do that."

Bill goes into his bedroom and grabs his cell phone from the bedside dresser. But the cell phone is dead, too.

"You got to be kidding me!"

He gets on the bed and rummages around behind the headboard until he finds his aluminum baseball bat. He always has it back there for just such an eventuality. Bill takes a few practice swings but then has to sit down on the bed to steady himself. He is alarmingly light-headed and about to faint again.

"Okay, what am I doing?" he gasps. "I'm going to hit this guy?" He thinks about it for a second before answering himself. "He just invaded my house. Hell yes I'm going to hit him!" Bill takes another deep breath and stumbles out of the bedroom.

Juan is indeed checking the locks on the windows and pulling the curtains closed.

"Hey!" Bill tries to sound intimidating, but he's not quite up to it.

Juan turns toward him.

"You see this?" Bill waves the bat and tries to look intimidating.

"That's it? Don't you have a gun?"

"If I had a gun, I'd be pointing it at you right now, don't ya think?"

"We could use a gun." Juan takes a peek through the curtains. "They're out there…I don't see them yet, but we better get ready."

"What are you talking about? Who's out there?"

The look on Juan's face is disarming—not threatening at all. In spite of the bloodshot eyes, it's a kind, compassionate face, and Bill is momentarily mesmerized by the warmth of this man.

Then they hear someone whistle from outside as if signaling for a cab or trying to get a distracted person's attention.

Juan turns to Bill and signals for him to be quite. Then there's a rush of soft footsteps from right outside the door. Juan, with impressive agility, leaps behind the sofa and then frantically waves for Bill to join him there. Bill hesitates, but after another whistle from outside, he rushes over to join him.

"What the hell is going—?"

Juan grabs his robe and pulls him to the floor with him, so that they're both hidden by the sofa.

"Shhh!" Juan orders.

There is some muted conversation and scraping noises at the door—they both freeze.

After a moment—Juan carefully gets to his knees so he can take a peek at what's going on. Bill gradually finds the courage to take a look as well. Side by side, and as still as statues, they peer together at the front door. But whoever was out there has moved away, and it's completely silent again.

"What was...?" Bill starts, but he runs out of breath and then something clicks in his throat. "What the hell was that?" he finally manages.

Juan chooses his words carefully. He speaks slowly and deliberately. "They are dangerous. And they are crazy, and the situation needs to be taken seriously. Do you understand?"

"No."

"Did you see that movie *Fight Club*?"

"With Brad Pitt? Yeah I saw it."

"Well, these guys, in their club...they hunt people. They go after the homeless, run-a-ways, desperate people who have lost all hope. They come like ninjas. They have an hour to get you once it starts. That's the game."

"And then what happens?"

"They take you away."

"They take you away?"

"They kill you."

"Okay, wait a minute—"

"So we have to work together, Bill. We're partners now."

"No, no, no—let's get something straight. We are not partners, okay? And if whatever this is—if it's true, they're after you, right? Not me. I've got nothing to do with this."

"That's not entirely so, Bill. We're in the same boat. You're on the list, too, just like me. We're both fighting for our lives...together."

"You know what? I am seriously running out of patience now. You are in some deep shit, my friend. So let's just cut the bullshit. I don't know what your game is, but if you don't leave my house this instant—"

Juan puts a hand on Bill's shoulder. Bill shudders and then winces from another pain behind his eye, and then collapses back down behind the sofa. Juan joins him there.

Try to relax," Juan says with a most earnest expression. "Or you might miss something important."

"Oh, really?"

"Yes. The truth of it is...you probably won't make your appointment today, Bill. You've reached a time where you need to expand your perceptions. You have to open your mind if we are going to survive this thing. We have to work together. We have to help each other. You do for me; I do for you. Then after an hour we're done and hopefully...everything will work out. Just like your movie did."

"No, Juan. That doesn't work for me. I want you gone. Now!"

"If I leave now, this will have a very bad outcome. For both of us."

Bill stares at him, and then he starts to laugh. Not that he thinks anything is particularly funny, it's just, well, what else can he do?

"You're too much, Juan. You really kill me."

He laughs a little harder and slaps a hand against his leg as if he's just heard a terrific joke. When the forced hilarity is over, Bill gets serious again.

"Okay...you know what? I'm done. That's it. I'm going in to take a shower and get ready for my appointment. If you want to rob me. If you wanna kill me—go ahead because I tell you something, Juan, I don't give a shit anymore."

Bill starts pulling himself up when there's a low demonic howl from right outside the door. Bill drops back down again.

"What the fuck was that?"

"They're signaling to each other."

They listen for a moment. But it's quiet again.

"You know what I think you should do, Juan?"

"What?"

"You should go over to the neighbor's. That guy...he loves this kind of thing. He's big and strong—loves trouble like this. He even rides a Harley. You need a fighter, Juan. Not a customer service guy like me. He's got guns, too. He's your guy, Juan. Just go over and knock on his door. He won't mind. He's a drug addict and a little psychotic—but if you stay off his grass and bring something alcoholic, you should be fine."

Juan laughs and slaps Bill on the back. Bill feels an instant wave of nausea and a sharp pain on the side of his face.

"What a sense of humor you have!" He mimics Bill—laughing and slapping a hand on his thigh. "You kill me, you really do."

And then Juan gets serious, just like Bill had before.

"I can't go next door, Bill. Because this was meant for us to do. This is our moment. This decides everything."

Bill's two cats come out to see what's going on. They see Juan, growl, back up, and then run back into the bedroom.

"They don't like us," Juan says. "They smell something."

"They don't like anybody. Don't take it personally. But I gotta tell you. There is a smell."

"Really?"

"Nothing terrible, a little...sulfurous, maybe. There's a sprinkler outside in the backyard. Go ahead, hose off a little, be my guest."

Juan overlooks the suggestion and gets up from behind the sofa and begins to examine the room.

With some difficulty, Bill gets up as well. Thankfully, he still has the bat to steady himself with—his knees are killing him. He limps out and watches as Juan looks behind curtains, under rugs, and opens furniture drawers to see what's inside.

"That's kind of rude, don't you think?" Bill asks.

"What is?"

"Well, snooping around in somebody's house like that."

"Oh, is it?" Juan stops snooping and they stare at each other.

"Can we lock ourselves in here?" Juan asks. "Can we close off the rest of the house?"

"How about I hit you over the head with this bat instead?"

"Why do you have to hurt my feelings like that? We have a situation here, and if we are going to be partners—"

"I didn't ask to be your partner, buddy! You just barged into my house, remember?"

"Okay, okay, okay!" Juan looks angry. His eyes are blazing, and he's breathing like a mad bull. But it's way over the top and consequently a bit comical, like Harpo Marx trying to look intimidating.

Bill raises the bat and takes a batters' stance, anyway. If Juan should stop mugging, and really comes at him, Bill is absolutely prepared to start swinging.

Juan falls to his knees instead. He hits the floor hard, with a suddenness and violence that makes Bill wince and take a step back.

"Go ahead then." Juan bows his head and extends his arms like Jesus on the cross. "Give me a whack if it makes you feel any better." And then he starts to cry. But not real tears—they're performance tears. Like a bad actor trying to be dramatic. It's very odd.

Bill is confused and starting to feel nauseated.

Juan looks up at him, smiles, and wipes nonexistent tears from his eyes.

"Okay, here's the thing," he begins. "I thought somehow I could have a friend who would like me and would be willing to help me out, and we could learn about each other. Maybe I don't deserve that, I don't know. No, forget that. That's not entirely true. Here's the prepared story. I should have started with this, forgive me. I was a Yale graduate. I have a PhD in the history of ancient civilizations or something like that. No, I was a military strategist or a high-ranking officer. Or was I a hostage negotiator? Oh, wait, that's right. I was a politician. No…was I secret agent?"

"What the hell are you talking about?"

Bill is starting to sweat again, and he's getting floaters in his eyes. Juan is becoming blurry, and it seems as if he's fading in and out of existence. Bill shakes his head to clear the floaters and loses his balance. He stumbles awkwardly to the side, and if he didn't have the bat to steady himself, he would have surely taken a fall.

"Are you all right?" Juan asks.

"Floaters. It'll go away in a minute."

"Let me start over. It gets so muddy sometimes. Oh wait, it's coming to me now. It was a girl, broke my heart to pieces. You know how that is, right? We should talk about that because it happened to you once, didn't it? Just like it happened to me. That's why I'm here, I think. Because of what we have in common. How are you feeling?"

Bill says nothing so Juan continues.

"We had it all, eh Bill? The world on a string wrapped around our finger. But after the girl broke up with you and moved away, something started dying inside. And it got worse as the years flew by. You lost your way. You turned your back on everything—didn't care about anything anymore. Why struggle?

Why be an artist? Why act? Who cares? So you got greedy and selfish and just did things for yourself and didn't pay attention anymore to the people who needed you. You lost your way. You lost yourself."

Juan takes a nasty handkerchief from his pocket and blows his nose.

"And this girl who left?" he continues. "She was pregnant, but she never told you. She was afraid of what you'd say and what you might ask her to do. So she moved away and had the baby. It was a girl, and she grew up without ever knowing you. But she knew about you. She got into a lot of trouble, your kid. Bad trouble. You had a—what do you call it—an inkling that there was another part of you. Something was missing, and it made you feel alone and sad, didn't it Bill?"

Again Bill says nothing, he just looks stunned.

"Well, don't worry, Bill. I was hurt like that, too. We survived and did what we had to do, but eventually you lost your spirit. Your soul was in trouble, and you felt like giving up. You wanted to kill yourself. There was nobody who really cared about you, and you didn't care about anybody, either. You went a little crazy, didn't you? But it's okay. I was selfish and I did bad things, too, just like you. Well, that about covers it. How do you feel?"

Bill stares with his mouth open.

"You can hit me with your bat now if you want."

Bill takes a step toward him.

"Who are you?"

"You're getting a second chance, Bill. And now we are here for each other. The important thing is that we have to work together. You and me. Not the guy next door. We have to help each other. Thank you, Bill, in advance. I really appreciate the help."

There is a sudden eruption of crows outside, and then shadows move in all directions across the drapes and window shades. Juan quickly gets to his feet. "Okay, are you ready?"

"What?"

"How do you feel?"

"Sick."

"It will pass. Close the hallway door!" Juan orders like the general that he might or might not have been.

"Wait a minute! You can't give me orders in my own house!" Bill protests.

"Lock it!"

When given a direction, especially a forceful one, it's hard for Bill not to do as instructed. A remnant from his old acting days—he wasn't the greatest actor in the world, but he followed directions well.

Bill stumbles toward the door but abruptly stops before he gets there. "That door doesn't lock, Juan!"

"We need weapons." Juan races into the kitchen."

Bill lurches after him, but Juan is gone. And Bill is not in his kitchen anymore.

* * *

He's sitting on the couch in his mother's old one-bedroom apartment in Florida. He can hear the sound of an oxygen machine pumping air so that his mother can breathe. The place is littered with medical supplies and pill bottles. Everything looks worn out. The carpet is dirty, the paint is old—everything is falling apart.

Bill looks around completely flummoxed about how he's wound up here.

His mother died three years ago. She was in poor health for a long time. Near the end he made many trips from LA to Fort Lauderdale to visit and maintain her apartment and manage her care at home. His mother was terrified of winding up in a nursing home, so Bill did everything he could to keep her in this apartment—right up to the very end. That required a full-time aide, and that cost a fortune. His mother's savings and all her supplemental insurance ran out years before she died, so her care, her apartment, and all her expenses became Bill's burden to bare. If he hadn't given up acting and taken a full-time job, there would be no way he could have handled it. But even with a good-paying job—it wasn't enough to cover everything. There were other things he had to do for extra cash. Side deals with contractors to secure contracts with the company. And there were drug things, too. Things that he still has nightmares about.

Even though he never really liked his mother very much, he felt a responsibility to take care of her. He resented her for it, though.

A thin hospice nurse who looks to be in her sixties comes out of the bedroom and stretches her arms in the air, trying to take some pressure off her aching back. She wears a sweater over her medical attire. She doesn't seem to notice, or doesn't care, that Bill is sitting on the couch gawking at her in his bathrobe and underwear. She takes out her cell phone and makes a call.

"Hi, Tasha…case 479…we're almost done here. No, any moment now…I'm preparing the paperwork…yes, that close… we won't need another shift here tonight. The daughter is here…I will…thank you."

She disconnects the call, sighs heavily, and then goes back into the bedroom.

"What the hell is this?"

Juan's disembodied voice answers him.

"As children we have unreasonable expectations of what our parents should be. We want them to be perfect. But they're not. They are human and flawed and they do the best they can. As we mature, we hopefully come to realize this. You never did, though. And you never said goodbye. You never said I love you."

"I had my reasons."

"Go in and say goodbye, Bill. It will do you a world of good."

"I'd really rather not."

"Yes, but this is important. Even if you'd rather not."

"I don't understand what's happening here?"

"Go in Bill. Tell her what she needs to hear."

"My mother was a pain in the ass."

"Yes, and so are you, but it doesn't matter now."

Some blood from his nose distracts him.

"Jesus Christ."

He cleans himself up with the bloody tissue that's still in his bathrobe pocket. He hesitates, but then gets up and goes into the bedroom.

His older sister, Doris, sits in a chair looking haggard and at the end of her rope. Mom already looks dead—lying there in her hospital bed with oxygen tubes in her nose. The hospice worker sits in another chair calmly filling out paperwork.

Bill is not sure what to do. He hates the look on his sister's face—the worry and concern. The devotion she's always had toward this woman has always baffled him. It makes him angry. He never felt his mother deserved such loyalty. She was not a kind woman and she was particularly mean to his sister.

"You're okay, Mom," his sister says, while patting Mom's hand. "Everything will be okay. Bill will take care of everything. It's okay to go now if you want to. You don't have to worry, Mom. Everything is handled. I love you. We both love you very much."

Bill lets her words linger for a bit and resists the urge to run out of the room. He feels a nudge at his back, and then somehow the distance between him, the bed, and his mother is instantly eliminated. He's standing bedside, holding Mom's other hand. It's cold and clammy and that brings on another wave of nausea.

Another nudge from behind, and Bill turns to defend himself.

"Cut it out, Juan! Jesus Christ you're annoying."

A shove on the shoulder this time spins him back around, and he's looking down at his dying mother again.

"Oh, man…"

In spite of himself, he leans down to talk to his mother.

"You did the best you could, and I've probably been too hard on you. I'm sorry I wasn't here. I had business. And I'm sorry I didn't turn out how you wanted me to and that I never said things that you probably needed to hear."

Bill looks to see how his sister and the nurse are reacting to what he's telling her. They aren't reacting at all, so he continues.

"Truthfully, you just pissed me off. But, I have to say, you could be really funny sometimes, too. There were two people in this world who could make me laugh out loud, and you were one of them. I'm pretty sure that back when I had a sense of humor, I must have gotten that from you. So thanks for the laughs, anyway.

"I guess I never really told you much about myself. I was afraid of what you'd think. That you'd get angry. You were always so angry. What happened to you? Maybe because you knew this was coming. That this would be your life. Bedbound and helpless like this for longer than anybody should ever have to be, and I'm sorry about that. I should have done something, but I couldn't. Anyway, in case you can hear me—and in case you didn't know—we kept you in the apartment right up until the end. And we took care of everything after you died, although apparently you aren't quite dead yet, wherever this is. But you don't have to worry anymore, Mom. That might be difficult for you because I know how you love to worry. Made yourself sick and drove everybody else crazy with the worrying. It was psychotic, really—fucking ridiculous. But we should let that all go now. Doesn't matter anymore. Anyway, I've come to say goodbye, I guess. And to tell you…that I love you. Because I couldn't before, and I'm sorry about that, too."

Mom opens her eyes for a moment and manages a smile. His sister gasps. Mom takes a final short, halting breath, a long rasping exhale, and then she's gone.

"I think that's it," says the nurse, and then she gets up to check Mom's vitals.

Bill let's go of his mother's hand and backs away from the bed.

"Yes, she's gone now. I'm so sorry," says the nurse to his sister and then rubs her shoulders to offer some comfort.

Doris starts sobbing.

Bill can't stand to see her cry. He can't stand any of this.

"How is this doing me any good? I'm sorry, but I'm just not getting it."

And then he has to get out of the room.

In the living room there are strange scuffling noises coming out of the walls.

"Could use a little help here, Bill. Three of them got in through the back," Juan's disembodied voice tells him.

"What do I do? I don't know what to do."

"Think of your house and walk through the wall."

"Think of my house and walk through the wall?"

"Yes, hurry!"

So that's what Bill does.

***

Bill finds himself in his bedroom, looking at himself lying on his bed, flat on his back, with blood all over his face and down the front of his T-shirt and bathrobe.

"Oh, shit," says Bill. "That can't be good."

He slowly backs away and makes his way into the kitchen. Three men dressed in black have Juan on the floor and are about to cut him to pieces with their nasty-looking daggers.

"No!" Bill screams at the top of his voice. He leaps at the largest one, but the ninja is quick, sidesteps, and Bill catches nothing but air, landing hard on the kitchen floor next to Juan, who smiles as if he's extremely pleased about seeing him again.

"Thanks, Bill. I'll take it from here."

The tall one lunges with his knife, but Juan is quick and grabs hold of his arm before he can do any harm to Bill. The tall man shutters and collapses, hitting his head hard on the Corian counter before crumbling to the floor in convulsions. Although their faces are covered by black masks, Bill can tell by their movements that the two remaining assassins have become unsure of themselves. Juan takes advantage. He grabs hold of the shorter one's ankle, and he also falls to the floor convulsing like a fish out of water. The last one backs up and makes a run for it into the living room. He struggles with the deadbolt for a moment, nervously looks back to see if Juan is coming after him, and then manages to fling the door open and run like hell.

"I better get these guys out of here before they snap out of it," Juan says.

Bill is mute and can only stare wide-eyed as Juan gets up and drags the men from the kitchen. In the living room, he effortlessly hoists the still convulsing tall man onto his shoulder. Juan steps outside and tosses him like a sack of potatoes onto the concrete walkway that leads up to the porch. Bill has made his way into the living room and watches as Juan grabs hold of the other guy. This time it's the old heave-ho. Juan picks him up by the collar and the belt of his pants. The guy is squirming and shaking, but Juan is not distracted by that. He starts swinging the guy, like a pendulum one, two, three times—and then he lets go. The guy goes flying out the door and lands with a sickening thud on the concrete outside.

Juan closes the front door and throws the deadbolt. He smiles at Bill, who is watching him in utter amazement.

"Don't think we have to worry about those three anymore," Juan says.

"You really didn't need my help at all, did you?"

"It was the effort. That's what mattered. You gave me the power."

"I just saw myself in the bedroom. I don't look so good."

"You're starting to see."

"What am I seeing, Juan?"

"Another stop to make on this trip. Are you ready?"

"Wait a minute—"

Juan points a finger at him, and Bill is out of the room again.

* * *

He's standing on the ledge of a roof. It's the hotel right next door to the world-famous Comedy Store on Sunset Boulevard. Next to him is his ex–best friend Steven. Steven wears all black. Black sports jacket, a black T-shirt, and black chinos—same thing he wears when he goes onstage to perform his comedy. His long black hair is greasy and disheveled. He wears a pair of Ray-Ban rose-tinted sunglasses even though it's nighttime. He stares down at the driveway, which is five stories below.

A sudden gust of wind causes a frantic balance correction—Bill being much more frantic about it than Steven is.

"What are you doing here?" Steven asks.

"I'm not watching this. I'm sorry. I don't need to see this."

Bill steps off the edge to get back on the roof and then nervously looks around for a way out of there.

"Hey, are you holding? You got anything for me?" Steven dully asks.

"No, I don't. I don't have anything for you, Steven! I can't take this shit anymore, do you understand?"

"Well, fuck you then."

Steven swan dives off the roof.

Bill's knees buckle, and he screams into his hands.

* * *

Mid-scream he's transported to an alley. He slowly straightens up and looks around. It's winter. There's snow on the ground, and a green dumpster is overflowing with snow-dusted black garbage bags. Bill is still in his robe and underwear, but he doesn't feel cold at all.

Next to the dumpster is a pile of blankets covered by a blue plastic tarp. When the tarp starts to move, Bill suspects that whatever comes out of there is what he's come to see.

A head in a red ski cap pokes out from under the blankets. Bill thinks it's a woman.

"Oh, it's you again," this person says in a husky voice.

He hears a noise—a rustling. He looks out toward the end of the alley and sees three more black-clad ninjas standing shoulder to shoulder, watching. On the street behind them, more ninjas (or whatever they are) swoop in from the sky and swipe up pedestrians who wander aimlessly. These people don't scream or yell when they get abducted. They don't seem to recognize what's happening to them.

The men in the alley take a synchronized step forward but stop when Bill looks at them—as if playing a child's game of Red Light, Green Light. Then he attempts to engage with the person under the blankets.

"Are you my daughter?"

"Your daughter? No, no, no, God forbid. Your daughter is gone. Long gone. She wants nothing to do with this."

"So who are you, then?"

She takes off her ski cap and vigorously scratches her balding head.

"I've got something here, something official so you'll know who you're dealing with."

She half-heartedly looks around in the trash, finds something that might be eatable, smells it, makes a face, and then tosses it away.

"Oh, hell. I don't know where it is. I used to have something nice in a frame with a seal. You don't have any cigarettes on you, do you?"

"No."

"Anything to eat?"

Bill doesn't answer her.

"Anyway, your daughter died in a place like this—in case you're interested. Alone and drug addicted, thirty-three years old, completely fucked up, and alone."

"What happened to her mother?"

"Dead. Breast cancer. Died young. Very bitter."

"And it's all my fault? Is that what this is about?"

"Partially."

"I never knew the girl. I didn't even know that she existed."

"Just out of curiosity. Would you have helped if you had?"

"I really don't know how to answer that. It's a ridiculous question."

"What about your best friend who committed suicide? You knew he was having problems, right?"

That freezes him.

"Bill?" she asks as if calling on a high school student to answer a geometry question.

"Sometimes the best thing to do is leave it alone, you know?" Bill tells her.

"That call when he got that bad speed, though. Lord—he pleaded with you for help. How could you just ignore something like that?"

"I just thought he was better off without me. I helped him out plenty, believe me. For years I put up with all his problems and his addictions and all his other crap. He was a taker. He was just using me. He wasn't the same person anymore."

"He was your best friend. The man who knew you better than anybody else in the world. The man who made you laugh like nobody ever could. The man who loved you like a brother. Man oh man-o-schewitz—some friend you are."

She puts her ratty ski hat back on and wipes her nose on the sleeve of her tattered jacket.

"Well, Bill, what we got here"—she gestures grandly to the alley trash—"this is about where you go from here. What you go on to."

"Am I dead?"

There's a whooshing noise, and the ninjas are right next to him now. Bill shutters and feels cold for the first time since arriving here.

"You're in limbo." she says. "Have been for quite a while."

"What's with these guys?"

"They're escorts to a place you probably don't want to go."

A black cat suddenly rushes out from under her blankets and darts away through the alley.

She laughs. "Oh shit. I was wondering what happened to that cat."

"What do you mean by escorts?"

"Huh?"

"What do you mean by escorts?" he says slower and louder this time. As if he were talking to someone who might be mentally deficient in some way.

"They're here for when you give up," she responds in the same condescending fashion. "If you're too arrogant to change, then you go with them."

Then she drops the attitude and starts searching for something else in the rubbish.

"Have you given up yet, Bill?" She continues. "Do you feel anything? Can you let go of your bullshit yet?"

She finds an old mirror and looks at herself in it.

"Oh my God!" She is truly startled by her own reflection. "What a difference a day makes—holy mother of God! You don't have any mascara or lip gloss, do ya?"

Again, Bill doesn't answer her.

She puts down the mirror and starts searching for something else.

"It's all about what you can do for others. Grace and forgiveness. Be kind to your fellow human beings. All of this,"—she searches with one hand, and with the other gestures again to the filth and the garbage—"this was only the training ground. Then there's a whole other thing to go on to—if you qualify. And things are looking a little iffy for you at this point, Bill."

She finds a cat toy—a squeaky mouse. She squeezes the toy for Bill to hear the funny noise that it makes.

Bill has no reaction to this.

She shrugs and tosses it under the blankets with her.

"Not too many chances left for you, Bill. And they don't let just anybody in. Somebody, for reasons I can't begin to understand, still thinks there's hope for you. Maybe it's that movie you did. But if you can't make certain adjustments, then you go with them."

She waves a hello to the ninjas, but their attention is riveted on Bill—like attack dogs waiting for the kill command.

"And you don't want to know what that's like."

"I took care of my mother."

"And you resented her for it. You still do."

"I'm human."

"Actually, no. Not yet. Come here for a second. I want you to see something."

"What?"

"Come over here. I won't bite."

She picks up her mirror and turns the glass toward Bill.

"Take a look at yourself in here. I want you to see this. It's very interesting."

Bill reluctantly approaches her. When he gets close enough, she puts the mirror up to his face.

What he sees chokes the breath right out of him. His reflection in the glass only resembles what he once was. It's more of a possum's face than his own. His eyes are small and black, and he has a muzzle with pointed teeth, and there's dirty bug-infested fur all over his face. Bill stumbles back, properly horrified.

"You're changing."

"What was that?"

"That's you, Bill."

"This can't be happening."

"It's happening all right. If you want to be human, Bill, you're going to have to feel something first. You can't push it away anymore."

An alarm clock goes off from under her blankets.

"Well, that's it. Your hour is up. Open your heart, Bill. It's the only chance you got."

"But wait a minute! Who is Juan? I don't understand."

Upon hearing his name, the ninjas get uncomfortable and take a step back.

"He's the one to take you if you figure it out."

"And who are you?"

"Me? I'm nobody. I'm the one who punches your ticket, that's all."

Bill feels a tear run down his face.

"How did I die? I don't remember."

"You got shot in the face. The neighbor next door did it."

"The Harley guy?"

"Yup. One of your best customers, too. I guess he figured out a way to cut out the middle man—literally."

"How did he get in? Why didn't the house alarm go off?"

"Remember? It wasn't working. That was the night it happened. You wrecked a lot of lives and then a wrecked life broke in to wreck you. That's the way it works, I guess."

"I only did business with those guys because I had to...she wanted me to kill her, did you know that? I couldn't do it. I did the best I could for her."

"A little compassion would have been nice. Did you think she didn't know how you resented her? How you blamed her for everything you did wrong in your life? Spare me, Bill. I've got more important things to do than to hang around here and listen to this crap. You've been hurting people for a long time, Bill."

"Yes, that's true, I guess."

"You missed the whole point of living, Bill."

And then she starts working her way back under the blankets like a worm wriggling backward.

"If I don't see you again—good luck," she says. "You're going to need it where you're going. Gonna need those teeth, too."

"I'm..." There's a click in his throat again from where the bullet is lodged. "I'm sorry for everything. If there's a way to make it right for people...I don't think what I became is who I really am. I got lost in it all. If there's anything I could do, I'd do it now to try and make things right."

This time there's enough pain and genuine remorse that it feels like he means it.

She stops. Her ski cap is all of her that remains visible. She lingers a moment as if to consider the ramifications of his apology. Then the cap follows the rest of her, and she disappears under the blankets.

"God help me for being such a fool," Bill moans.

The alarm stops ringing, there is a *poof* sound, and like a magic trick the bulges under the blanket go flat. There's nothing under there anymore—she's transported elsewhere.

Another tear rolls down Bill's face. It's a red tear. And then there's a flood of them. He falls to his knees like Juan did in the living room, but this is no performance. Bill grieves for the things he's lost, for those he's hurt; feeling in this moment what he's spent a lifetime trying to ignore. While Bill mourns, the ninjas float backward and begin to dissolve into mist.

＊ ＊ ＊

Bill is back in his kitchen, staring at the coffee maker, feeling weak and broken, but with no conscious memory of where he just was or what his face looks like. The coffee maker gurgles and then shuts itself off. Then the ground shifts under his feet again, and he has to grab on to the counter to steady himself. He sees dried blood on the countertop and is confused about how it got there.

He looks around the kitchen. It seems dingier than before. Some wallpaper has begun to peel from below the dish cabinets, and everything looks dusty and old.

Bill shakes his head, trying to dislodge a deep feeling of melancholy. The hair he has left is white now, and it flops down over his eyes. Blood comes from his snout, but he doesn't seem to notice. Then he goes toward the bathroom to get ready for his appointment.

A knock comes at the door.

He should just ignore it—but he can't. He is compelled to answer it, as if his life depends on it.

Bill opens the door to find a younger version of himself staring back. The way he looked in his thirties. The way he'd like to look again. This man at the door has a warm smile, and there is kindness in his eyes. Juan stands a few steps behind him, and he's grinning like a loon.

"Are you ready, Bill?" asks his younger self.

"I don't understand," Bill says as his face starts morphing back to its human form.

"I'm from a different time. It's not the same where we're going. We're operating in a whole different system now, and sometimes you can run into yourself."

"Should I get dressed?"

"No need," young Bill tells himself.

"What about my cats?"

"Oh, they've been gone for quite a while now."

And the three walk out together onto the concrete pathway and then vanish from this world.

HANUKKAH GHOST STORY

With Additional Material by Douglas Dickerman

PROLOGUE

My name is Moe Zell, and I had an experience awhile back that I'd like to tell you about. It has to do with my friend Mike and a stage play we did that almost broke up our friendship. It's also about my aversion to all things religious, which I think precipitated a lot about the story I'm about to tell. I've been through some changes because of what's happened. In the past, I preferred to stay mostly uninvolved and as far away from problematic people as humanly possible. In fact, if I never had to deal with another complicated personal relationship for the rest of my life, I would have been fine with that. I had thought about getting a dog. But then there's all the walking and the danger of possibly having to socialize at a dog park somewhere. A fish or a turtle would have been more my speed. But now I'm trying to get out a little more and hopefully do a little good in the world. My intention is not to preach about how you should live your life—that's not my style. But if you are like I was—if you've stopped believing in magic and the good that we are sometimes capable of—then this is for you.

CHAPTER ONE

HOW DO YOU SPELL CHANUKAH?: *THE STAGE SHOW*

As the audience is entering the theater, Mike and Moe sit at a card table staring at each other. They are dressed in suits—like what you'd wear to a Bar Mitzvah. Upstage from where they're sitting, extending down from the ceiling, is a screen where images are projected. At the moment there is a picture of a menorah—all candles lit. There is a dreidel on the table. Mike has a big pile of gelt in front of him. Moe's pile is tiny. In the middle of the table is where the antes are placed. On the floor in front of the table is a litter of gold foil gelt wrappers.

(Moe eats a gelt chocolate from his own dwindling pile and drops the foil onto the floor.)

MIKE. If you keep eating them you won't have any left, and I'm not giving you another loan.

MOE. (*Feels around the glands in his throat.*) Hope I'm not coming down with something. Do my glands look swollen to you?

MIKE. (*Sighs.*)

MOE. I think they're swollen. Here, feel them. (*Stands up and leans across the table so that Mike can feel his glands.*)

MIKE. No.

MOE. (*Sits back down.*) Do you want some orange juice?

MIKE. Sure, why not. What else have I got to do?

MOE. (*Stands up.*) Ice?

MIKE. Cube.

MOE. How many?

MIKE. *A* cube

MOE. (*Starts to go but comes back.*) Do you want me to put some water in it? Cut it a little.

MIKE. Cut orange juice? It's orange juice. Who cut's orange juice?

MOE. Well, so it's not so Hassidic…

* * *

That's how we opened *How Do You Spell Chanukah?*, a show for members of the tribe to gather and celebrate the holiday and one another. But Mike and I (probably me more than him) were really not very good Jews. We were just pretending to be. I have played Jews in many productions without suffering any consequences for it. But *How Do You Spell Chanukah?* was a different kind of animal. Not to be too dramatic, but it was a kind of unholy deception and, apparently, there was a price to be paid for that.

I first met Mike, fittingly enough, while playing Scrooge in a production of *A Christmas Carol*. Mike was cast to play my nephew, Fred. When he walked into the first read-through of the play, he definitely had that serious New York actor vibe—a little above it all—but he also looked like John Garfield. I've always been a big fan of John Garfield's, so I nodded a hello. He nodded back reluctantly, as if he'd much rather be left alone.

As I was deciding that this guy is just another stuck-up actor who I'd rather have nothing to do with, he looked at me again and made a face. He transformed his handsome leading-man features into the most ridiculous clown face I'd ever seen. I started to laugh. I mirrored back my own clown face, but he turned away from me, went back to serious actor mode, put his attention back on his script, and left me hanging there with a stupid look on my face.

Thus our relationship was born. Now that I think about it, the whole foundation for *How Do You Spell Chanukah?* was born that day as well.

CHAPTER TWO

JUST SO YOU KNOW WHO YOU'RE DEALING WITH:

ACTORS' PROGRAM BIOS FOR
HOW DO YOU SPELL CHANUKAH?,
THE STAGE SHOW

Moe Zell (Actor/Writer)

I am thrilled, I tell you, thrilled to be performing here for you tonight in my second-favorite play of all time, *How Do You Spell Chanukah?*. My first-favorite play has been banned in New Jersey and certain parts of Lithuania. I'm not even allowed to talk about it, that's how good it is. Anyway, where was I? Oh yeah…my old friend Lawrence Steinberg, the artistic director at South Shore Repertory Theatre in San Diego, asked me if I'd be interested in putting together a holiday show for their Jewish patrons. Our last venture together was a one-man show called *Einstein Comes Back*. We cowrote, he directed, I acted, and it was sort of like a dream come true for both of us. Now we call each other Al all the time. I'm frankly getting a little tired of it, but he likes it, and he's the artistic director so I'm not complaining. Anyway, when Al asked me to do this, I was thrilled, I tell you, thrilled! I thought to myself, if I could only get Mike Spector to do this with me—oh man, that would be great! I got him, and here we are, so look out! I've done Shakespeare with Mike, and we did (are you ready for this?) *A Christmas Carol*. I was Scrooge and he was Fred, the kind, forgiving nephew. In real life Mike is not so kind and forgiving, so hopefully, doing this show with me will make him a better Jew and a better person in general.

Because of my age and my alarming profile, I am a veteran performer of over fifty-five stage shows in the LA area, including a regular stint with the Kingsmen Shakespeare Festival, where I actually met Mr. Steinberg—oh, sorry, Al—for the first time. There was a time when I was all over the TV. I was a series regular and guest starred on everything from *Hardcastle and McCormack* to *The Famous Teddy Z*—well, not everything, but I'm trying to make this look good. I also made a lot of money in commercials. But all that money is gone now, and I sure do miss all those checks coming every week in my mailbox, but I'm not complaining. I have a place to live, and I'm busy writing and developing projects for film, TV, and the theater. So don't worry about me. I get plenty to eat and try to exercise at least three times a week; lately I've started taking naps in the afternoon sometimes, but that's just between us. Happy Chanukkah (I still don't know how to spell it), and thanks for coming out to see us.

Mike Spector (Actor/Writer)

As I sat at my desk, staring through a window of my tiny Hollywood apartment, transfixed by the decaying pink apartment building next to mine, I dreamed of another life, a life of hope and purpose. Then I got a call, a call that would thrill my parents to no end. Mr. Moe Zell's slightly nasal and only just tolerable voice echoed on the other end of the line.

"Hey, Mike. Moe Zell here. You wanna write a Chanukah show with me?"

Now I have worked with Moe a few times, mostly at the Susana Repertory Company. We appeared together in *A Christmas Carol*, where I, a nice Jewish boy, played Fred the nephew, the epitome of Christmas magic, to Moe's enthusiastic but sadly misguided and annoyingly nasal Ebenezer Scrooge. Shortly thereafter we did *Hamlet* and the Scottish play (*Macbeth*, for those of you with real jobs), and he was nasal in that, too. What I didn't realize upon accepting this *gezunte* undertaking was that Moe wasn't really Jewish. I mean he is Jewish, but he had a basic Jewish information deficit disorder. This fact became glaringly obvious all too soon. Like, in the third rehearsal. He kept looking at me funny when I used Jewish words like *prayer*, *oppression*, and *kvetch*. After falling over, I got up and we got to work. It felt like training Rocky—just the Jewish version, you know the one where Rocky can't stand getting hit or the sight of blood, and doesn't like to sweat much, either. Training this Jew who had lost his way was hard work, but, by God, I think I done good, and here he is today: not only does he look like a Jew, but he actually sounds like one, too. There's nothing I can do about the nasal thing. He needs to see a specialist about that.

Aaand back to me! Now, my past in the theater includes playing a dog. Yes, yes, I actually was on all fours barking like a dog. Two things, though: first, I got paid for it; and second, I did and do an amazing barking dog. I wanna get that out in the open so I can tell you that I have appeared off Broadway, as well as at Carnegie Hall in *The Jeweler's Shop*, written by Pope John Paul II. I kid you not. In LA I graced the stage in so many small theater productions that I've considered killing myself a few times. I have also appeared on TV and in film. Perhaps you are a slow blinker and caught my stellar work on *Law & Order*, *Numb3rs*, or *Law & Order: Criminal Intent*. If you'd like to troll the internet for more info on me, go ahead, I won't tell. Go already!

*** * ***

We were also in a production of *Merchant of Venice*. I played Shylock the Jew, and Mike played Antonio, the merchant I try to get my pound of flesh from. Shylock is a man scarred by discrimination, anger, and resentment. I used my grandfather as my model for Shylock. He was the religious grandfather on my mother's side, but his beliefs never filtered down to me. I had no connection to my Jewishness or to God. Religion just seemed like something somebody made up to keep people in line, give them a little connection to the great and powerful Oz, and provide some comfort for living in a hard and unforgiving world; something satisfyingly supernatural to make sense of the randomness of the human struggle and the terrifying fact that we will all die a gruesome, painful death. It's also why alcohol was invented, by the way.

CHAPTER THREE

JEWISH INFORMATION DEFICIT DISORDER

Regarding my grandfather, I never got to know him that well. I don't think my parents wanted me to. His father was a rabbi, so, needless to say, he was raised in a strict Jewish home. I remember my grandfather to be a no-nonsense straight shooter; sarcastic, critical, and not pleasant to be around. Perfect for my Shylock role model. My sister and I didn't have a lot of contact with him. I think we were being protected from the resentments and the rage that this man carried around with him.

I found out when I got older that my mother had another sibling, a younger sister who was killed while out shopping with my grandmother. The little girl ran out into the street and was hit by a car. My grandfather never forgave his wife for that, and he held it against her until his death. I remember my grandmother to be a kind woman, and when she came to visit she would always bring candy for me and my sister. She died when I was still quite young.

My grandfather died of a stroke shortly after my parents put him in a nursing home. I went to visit him in the hospital the day he died. When I went into his room, I found him looking tiny and frail with a little smile on his face. Dead as a doornail—as Charles Dickens liked to say. Whether that smile was a result of the stroke or because whatever he saw or felt at the time of his death finally brought him some peace—I've always wondered about that. After his death, I remember hearing my mother and father talking about how angry he was that he had a stroke—*How could God do this to me after a lifetime of being a devoted Jew?* The story goes that he renounced God and his religion while in the hospital. What a waste—all that praying and davening for nothing.

My most vivid memory of him, besides seeing him dead in the hospital, was the day he came over to our apartment to help me with the haftarah that I had to learn for my Bar Mitzvah. I was a lousy Hebrew school student—I'll get into that in a second. My grandfather and I sat at our kitchen table, and he listened patiently as I pathetically stumbled through the Hebrew. Then he abruptly got up, threw his hands in the air, and started shouting at me, "Why are you doing this? Do you know what this even means? You don't care about any of this, so why waste everybody's time?" Truer words were never spoken. Then he stormed away, leaving me feeling even more stupid than I usually did.

I knew that my grandfather didn't like me or my parents very much. Oddly, I respected him for that, but I didn't know how to deal with him. We didn't get a whole lot of honesty back in those days. We were, I guess you'd have to say, Jewish phonies. My mother would hide the shrimp and anything else in the refrigerator that wasn't kosher when my grandfather came over, which thankfully wasn't often or else I would have starved to death.

So you get the idea. We were the new generation of sort-of-Jewish Jews, and he hated us for it. We went through the motions, but the whole Jewish thing, including the Bar Mitzvah, was just a farce that even a dumb kid like me could recognize. Still, I was thirteen. I had to become a man, and the Bar Mitzvah was part of the deal. If I had really wanted to be a man, I should have turned my back on the whole thing. But that would have been a devastating embarrassment for my parents, and their lives were hard enough already. Even if I had taken a stand against

Jewish hypocrisy, friends and neighbors would have construed that the Zell kid was just too dumb to learn his haftarah. Besides, my mother had already bought a dress, and the invitations had gone out in the mail.

So I had a Bar Mitzvah, but I never did get the Hebrew down. I had to write it out phonetically. The party afterward was pretty good, though, and I did get a lot of envelopes with checks in them. There was a band, a photographer, and a lot of adults getting drunk, including my mother. My grandfather was there and drank schnapps and pretty much kept to himself. I don't know what happened to all the money we got. Probably went to pay for the Bar Mitzvah party that my parents couldn't really afford. My father did take out a life insurance policy for me, though. Probably because he was thinking about killing me for how badly I screwed up my haftarah.

⁎ ⁎ ⁎

All the Jewish kids in my neighborhood in Paterson, New Jersey, went to the same Hebrew school. Classes were held on the second floor of the shul. We had to go three times a week after regular school, and it was a major pain in the ass.

The rabbi, Rabbi Tannenbaum, was a nice man. He and his wife taught the classes. His wife always had a runny nose and a body odor that was hard to be around without getting sarcastic. Of course we were aware that *Tannenbaum* means "Christmas tree," which probably contributed to the inability of me and my friends to take the rabbi seriously. We liked to play cruel pranks on the rabbi and his wife. We tortured them, really. The rabbi was a patient man, but we would test his limits until he would get so upset that he would throw us out of class and make us go sit with his wife in another room. If you could piss her off enough, she would threaten to call your parents and send you home. I was sent home a few times, but she never called my parents. Not that I knew of anyway.

I wanted to be outside playing after school, not stuck inside listening to the rabbi drone on and on about things I couldn't care less about and read Hebrew that I couldn't understand. And the stories he told were just preposterous. Not only were the Bible stories farfetched, but he used to come up with some other stuff too, some real humdingers. Here's one that's stuck with me through the years, a classic, and a perfect example of the kind of stuff the rabbi was trying to get us heathens to swallow:

> *A Jewish soldier in the navy was on the deck of his ship during a battle at sea. It was Yom Kippur and this soldier had been praying and fasting all day. A cannonball was fired from another ship, and it hit the guy right in the gut, actually putting a hole right through him. But he survived because of all the praying and fasting he had done.*

The rabbi's point was that if you're a good enough Jew and follow the laws of the Torah, God will protect you no matter what—even from cannonballs. I mean, really?

Anyway, I was a terrible Hebrew student and a spoiled brat to boot. To kill time, I would throw things out the window just so the rabbi would make me go outside to get them. He would choose a student at the beginning of every class to pass out the prayer books. If it was me, I would find a way to drop them all. If you drop a prayer book, you're supposed to kiss it after. That was a good way to kill even more time and get some big laughs. Why he continued to call on me to pass out the books, I'll never know. Maybe he was worried about my soul and was trying to give me a chance at redemption, but there was no hope for me. I had absolutely no respect for the rabbi, his wife, or anything to do with the Hebrew school or the religion.

One of my favorite things to do was to try and get the rabbi to do his letting-off-steam routine. If you could get him mad enough, he would do this thing where he would lift his yarmulke up and down as if he were releasing steam from his head. He would start to sweat, and his eyes would bulge behind his nerdy glasses, and then he would actually start to hiss like a radiator. My nasty friends and I (when torturing a holy man it's best to do it as a mob) would try and get him to this point as often as possible. I feel terrible now for how we treated this very decent man. But Hebrew school was a great imposition on the other moronic things that I'd rather been doing, and somebody had to pay for that. For me, Hebrew school was a sham, just a means for getting to the obligatory Bar Mitzvah. But when it was done, my plan was never to set foot in a temple again for the rest of my life. Little did I know.

CHAPTER FOUR
MOE AND MIKE'S NEVER-PERFORMED SKETCH IDEA 151

MIKE. By the by, will you be fasting for Yom Kippur this year?

MOE. Will you?

MIKE. I asked you first.

MOE. Well, I'll probably just be cutting back. I've got to watch that blood sugar lately. If I don't eat, I get kind of light-headed and nauseous.

MIKE. But you're not going to watch any baseball games on TV or anything like that, are you?

MOE. What kind of Jew do you think I am?

MIKE. Well, I think Friday is the first playoff game for the Dodgers, isn't it?

MOE. Friday is Yum Kippur?

MIKE. Yes, Moe, it is.

MOE. It's not fair, Mike. First the Dodgers make that pitiful Time Warner Cable deal so I can't watch any games on TV. Then, finally, it's the playoffs, the drought is over, and Fox is broadcasting the games for all to see—and now this. Whoever is in charge of scheduling, whoever that is, they should be ashamed, and they should definitely stay the hell out of my way for a while.

MIKE. But you're not going to watch the game are you?

MOE. Mike, I'm really too upset to even talk about it now.

MIKE. You are being judged. That's what this holiday is about. You know that, don't you?

MOE. The person who scheduled the first game of the playoffs on Yom Kippur, that's the guy who should be judged. If you look in that big book in the sky...that's this holiday isn't it?

MIKE. Yes it is, Moe.

MOE. Well, there's going to be a big red X next to that guy's name, let me tell you.

MIKE. Yom Kippur is a time for reflection. A time to consider your actions in the year that's past and resolve yourself to do better in the coming year.

MOE. I for one will try harder than I have ever tried before. I'm just a little upset right now, Mike, and forgive me if I sound a little harsh, especially with our most solemn holiday soon approaching.

MIKE. Okay, just try to remember the meaning of the holiday. At least in between innings.

MOE. I will.

MIKE. And if you have to eat—just make sure it's kosher.

MOE. Hebrew National, Mike. It's from a higher authority.

MIKE. That a boy.

MOE. We do what we can.

CHAPTER FIVE

PHONE CALLS

I was sitting at home, anesthetizing my brain by playing a game of *Candy Crush* on my computer, when I got the phone call from my old pal Lawrence Steinberg over at South Shore Repertory Theatre.

"Al! How have you been?" he asked.

"I'm good," I said as if I really wasn't.

I always feel like there's something wrong with me, and simple phone questions often become ridiculously complicated. A normal person would just say, *I'm great. How are you?* But I didn't ask him how he was. I was much too self-involved for that, and that made me feel guilty and strange about myself and about my shallow personal relationships. I really should let all phone calls go to voice mail. They're much too emotionally challenging for me.

"It's not the same around here without you, Al," he lied.

I'm sure it's exactly the same without me. Why is this man calling me out of the blue like this and making me feel so bad about myself? He probably wants something from me. He's plotting something. He's a plotter, this Steinberg. It's how he got to be artistic director.

"So, listen," he said. "I've got an idea. I'm thinking about doing something different this year for the holidays. What do you think about writing a Chanukah show and performing it at the theater?"

"A Chanukah show?"

While I was breaking out in a cold sweat, he continued.

"I was thinking it's about time that we do something for all our Jewish patrons for a change, and I'd love to have you back here performing again. You can have a whole weekend, three shows. It'll be fun. Make some money, see some old friends. How long's it been anyway? Two years already? It's been way too long since I've seen you, Al. You won't believe how big the kids are now."

"Wait…" I was compelled to interrupt his small talk at this point. "You mean…we write a show and perform in it together?"

"No, I don't really have the time. I'm thinking more like you write the show. A one-man thing, like we did before. Something easy to produce. Something funny, you know?"

I was flattered and gratified by his offer but felt completely unqualified for the job.

"Think about it," he said. "Five hundred for the weekend plus a royalty for the show. But don't think too long. It's only three months away."

"How long of a show are we talking about here," I asked, and I'm sure he could hear the panic in my voice.

"You know. Ninety minutes. A full show."

"Ninety minutes?" I squawked.

"It'll be fun. Like old times. I'll direct, you act—it'll be like putting the band together again. Oh, shoot—there's another call." (Al always has another call.) "Let me know. I'm excited. It'll be great to see you again. Call me!"

And then he was gone, leaving me with a twitching eyelid. A one-man show about Chanukah? In three months? That'd be hard enough for a good Jew, let alone the likes of me. I mean, I could think of a thousand things I'd rather do than write a Chanukah show, but unfortunately nobody was offering to pay me for any of those.

Okay, so what kind of show could a Hebrew school thug like me possibly come up with to make Jews feel good about themselves during the holiday? What do I know about Chanukah? Me, alone onstage, relating to real live Jewish people? A guy who had to write out his haftarah phonetically?

If I was going to do it, I sure as hell wasn't going to do it alone. I needed to pair up with a Jew who could add a little authenticity. I thought about the Jews I knew and who I might be able to wrangle into something like this. Mike Spector was the obvious choice.

I hadn't seen him for a while, but we did have a great time working together. He's a Jew. He's talented. He looks like John Garfield. He's crazy funny. He's perfect! I gave him a call.

He picked up on the first ring, and he already sounded annoyed.

"Yeah?" he answered.

"Hey, Mike, how have you been?"

"Who is this," he asked, even though I knew he knew it was me.

"It's Moe…remember? We met in that lesbian bar?"

"Oh yeah. Jewish fella. Short. Bad hair. Don't you have a rash that won't go away or something like that?

"I got that taken care of. Now I have hemorrhoids."

"Don't strain on the toilet. How many times do I have to tell you?"

"Listen, do you want to write a Chanukah show with me?"

"Do I have to?"

"I just got a call. It'll be at South Shore Rep. It'll be fun."

"Is that where you did the Einstein thing?"

"Yeah, it's a really good theater—they pay."

"Call me about it later. I can't talk now. I'm on the toilet, and something is about to happen."

"But do you want to do it?"

He grunted before answering.

"Sure, what else have I got to do?" And then he hung up.

"Well, thank you Moses, Buddha, Jesus, and all you apostles, too," I said out loud to whichever God might be listening.

And then there was an earthquake. Not a huge one—a 4.0 maybe. A picture of my father (who had died a few years ago) fell off the hutch in the dining room, and the glass shattered when it hit the floor. I waited a moment to make sure this wasn't the "big one," and then I went to clean up the mess. My father's face was staring up at me through the broken glass in the picture frame, and just for a second I thought his lips moved as if he were trying to say something to me. I got a chill that made me shudder, and then I quickly tried to rationalize.

The broken glass just made it look like his lips moved, that's all.

I didn't dwell on it. I had shit to do.

I had never written anything with Mike before and wasn't sure how this kind of partnership would go. I usually write alone. On the Einstein show that I did with Al, I would write, he would review and critique, and then I would revise. If that happened with Mike, I'd be fine with that. Anyway, ideas started coming to me pretty quickly. I was thinking of a vaudeville-type show. A comedy duo talking about Chanukah from their own perspectives. Get some songs in there, some jokes, some witty banter—what more could a Jew want?

The thing about Mike, though. He's always busy doing twenty different things at the same time that are much more important than the thing he's doing with you. So in order to really get him on board, I knew I had to knock it out of the park.

After the earthquake, and checking the news to see if anything had blown up or if a tidal wave was coming, I did some research about Chanukah, and here's what I wrote and sent to Mike the next day in an email:

MIKE. You know the story of the dreidel, don't you?

MOE. The story? The story of Hanukkah Harry delivering the

dreidel from the mountaintop after his meeting with
God? That dreidel story?

MIKE. No. Listen, this is pretty cool. The dreidel was actually
invented by the Greeks. The Jews were under Seleucid
Greek rule at the time, and a guy named Antiochus—

[Photo of Antiochus on the screen.]

MIKE. —rose to power and decided it was time once again to
wipe out the Jews.

MOE. So what's new? Take a number.

MIKE. And this was a time when a lot of Jews were trying to
assimilate into the Greek culture.

MOE. Bad idea, that's when we always get in trouble.

MIKE. So a Jew named Mattityahu—

[Photo of Mattiyahu on the screen.]

MIKE. —decided enough was enough.

[A photo of a bag of Lays potato chips on the screen.]

MOE. Yeah, but nobody can eat just one.

MIKE. What?

MOE. Nothing. Go ahead. (*Yells to the projection booth*) Forget it!

[The lit menorah photo comes back on the screen.]

MIKE. Are you done?

MOE. For now.

MIKE. Anyway, he started plotting and building an army to
revolt against the Seleucids.

MOE. And they were going to fight them with dreidels?

MIKE. No. See, if they were discovered by the Greek soldiers
while they were plotting, they would pretend to be

playing dreidel, which apparently at that time was a popular game and the thing to do.

MOE. I thought we invented it. It just seems so Jewish to me.

MIKE. It's okay. We invented everything else.
(*They walk downstage to talk to the audience.*)

MIKE. Hi, my name is Mike.

MOE. And I'm Moe.

MIKE. Welcome all to this grand celebration.

MOE. A new tradition.

MIKE. And a long time over-Jew.

MOE. Oy vey.

MIKE. Happy Hanukkah everybody!

MOE. Yeah!

MIKE. Or is it *CCC*hanukah?

MOE. What?

MIKE. *CCC*hanukah! (*spoken with much spraying saliva*)

MOE. Say it, don't spray it.

MIKE. I mean…how do you spell it? It's confusing. You see it spelled sometimes with a *C*; sometimes with an *H*. Sometimes with two *K*s; sometimes with one *K*.

MOE. If it's three *K*s, then you went to the wrong party and get out of there fast!

Much to my surprise, Mike was excited about what I had written, and I was thinking that we might actually pull this thing off.

✳ ✳ ✳

That night I had a dream: I'm walking down a hallway and then enter a room through a red door. There is no floor in this room. Well, there is, but it can't be walked on because the floor goes straight down at a 90-degree angle from the doorframe. If I had taken another step into this room, I would have fallen straight down. There is a bed that I guess has been bolted to the floor, but it's starting to slide down. Then I see my father. He's hanging on to the bottom of the bed. He's grasping a bed leg with one hand, and he's trying to hammer a nail into another leg with the other hand, I assume so that both he and the bed don't slide off into God knows what.

He drops the nail, which disappears into the blackness beneath him. He frantically tries to reestablish his grip on the bed, his feet dangling precariously at the edge of oblivion. He looks up at me in the doorway with a strained expression on his face.

"Hey, Moe. Give me a hand, will ya?"

"I don't think I can, Dad."

"Yeah, but…I can't hang on much longer."

"I don't even know what's going on here," I say.

"I think I'm here to warn you," he tells me.

"Warn me about what?"

"It's going to piss him off."

"What? Piss who off?"

Then he lets go of the bed and falls, reaching out for me before disappearing into blackness.

Thus begins my bad-dream period.

CHAPTER SIX
PUTTING THE PIECES TOGETHER

My friend John had done a one-man show. Onstage with him was a projection screen, and throughout the performance, images were projected that related to what John was talking about onstage. It worked well, so I figured it would probably work well in this show, too. Mike and I also decided that it would be a cool idea to have a video of an expert who could answer some questions that might come up during the show. I suggested that we dress Mike up in a big beard and a funny hat and have him impersonate a rabbi. Eventually, we decided this to be a bad idea and probably sacrilegious as well. We needed somebody with real authority. Somebody the audience could respect. We needed a real rabbi who would have a sense of humor, would be willing to have us videotape him (all we had was an outdated Sony video camera), and wouldn't mind us profiting off his image. We didn't know anybody like that, so I called Al at the theater.

"Hey, Al! How's it going, boss?"

I sometimes call people that I like, or people who I work for, boss. It makes them feel good, and I figure it might increase my odds for not getting fired.

"Hey, Al!" he responded as though he were glad to hear from me.

"Do you know any rabbis?"

"A rabbi?"

"Yeah. We're thinking of putting a rabbi on tape."

"We?"

"Yeah. I'm bringing in a partner. Do you know Mike Spector?"

"No…"

He seemed a little put off about my bringing somebody new into the mix.

"He's great and a much better Jew than me. It's going to be like a vaudeville show but without the jugglers and the naked dancers. Like a Chanukah comedy team."

"I can still only pay the five hundred," he told me.

"That should be fine," I said, not being sure if it actually was. "You still have a place for us to stay down there, though, correct?"

"Not the one you had last time by the beach. We had to give that up. But a board member lets us use his condo. He'll be away for the holidays, so it should work out. Hey, you know what?"

"Probably not. I know very little."

"I do know a rabbi. He's a subscriber."

"Really?"

"Yeah, I'll call him, see if he's interested. When are you coming down? I should meet Mike, and you guys can talk to Billy about what you'll need for the show. Nothing too fancy, though, right?"

Billy is the theater's technical director. I've worked with him before—he's great.

"No. I'm thinking real simple," I promised. "Just a card table, and we'll bring down all the props and whatever we're going to wear. Very self-contained. We'll just need a screen and a projector."

"We have that."

"Piece of cake, then."

"A comedy act, huh?"

"Yeah, what do you think?"

"Interesting. Who knows, maybe this will turn into a regular holiday gig for you guys."

"That'd be weird."

"What do you think about *How Do You Spell Chanukah?*" he asked.

"What do you mean?"

"As a name for the show. Because nobody ever knows how you're supposed to spell it."

"I just wrote a joke about that, actually. Brilliant idea!"

"Well, they don't call me Al for nothin'. I'll get back to you after I call the rabbi. The more I think about it—putting a rabbi on tape? I like it."

"Yeah, somebody the audience can respect. Two clowns and a rabbi. Something for everybody."

"I'm excited," Al said. "How about you? Are you into it? Are you excited?"

"I'm not sure yet. I feel a little something, but it might be gas."

"There's another call. I have to take this. I'll call ya."

∗ ∗ ∗

Turned out that Al's rabbi was agreeable. So Mike and I took the two-hour trip down to San Diego. I did the driving. Road trips with Mike can be hysterical, annoying, and sometimes personally revealing.

"Did I tell you that I'm taking a new class?" Mike told me as he looked through my glove compartment.

"Another one?"

"Yeah, on-camera technique. It's really good."

"Expensive?" I asked although I was already sure that it was. The bilking of actors in Los Angeles is a profitable and despicable business.

"A little expensive, but it's worth it, and I love the teacher. She's honest, and she knows a lot of on-camera tricks that I never even thought of. You should try it. It demystifies film acting. She's tough but encouraging."

"Glad to hear it. Enjoy."

"Are you interested in doing it?" he asked while poking me repeatedly in the shoulder.

"No."

"I get a discount if I bring somebody in."

"Sorry, not for me. I'm not big on classes."

"This is really good, though. You'll get a lot out of it."

"I don't like classes."

"Yes, but that's stupid."

"I know."

"Actors have to take classes. You have to stretch. How else are you going to do that? You have to have a place to grow, a safe place to try and fail and learn something new."

"I have a full-length mirror in my bathroom. It's cheap, and it's right next to the toilet in case I nauseate myself."

"You should take this class. Break you out of some bad habits."

"I like my bad habits."

He didn't respond to that, but I could feel him staring at me—studying me, judging me, and purposely making me feel uncomfortable.

"Stop staring," I said.

He leaned in closer until I could feel his breath on the side of my face.

"That's a very limiting artist view you got going there, bud," he whispered right in my ear. Then he started poking me in the shoulder again.

"You're not supposed to embrace bad habits, you're supposed to get rid of them."

He abruptly threw his hands up, just like my grandfather did when I was butchering my haftarah at the kitchen table, and said in a perfect Yiddish accent, "I give up on you. I'm finished, kaput."

He slapped his hand against his open mouth and made a loud popping sound.

"And that's the last I'll say about it!"

"Thank God."

But he couldn't help himself.

"Why don't you like classes?" he asked, as if it hurts him that I don't. "You're, like, pathological about it."

"It's a long story."

"Go ahead…we've still got an hour and a half to kill in this fucking traffic, otherwise, believe me, I couldn't give a shit."

"I have a bad history with classes, that's all."

"Why, did you get a boner in history class?"

"What?"

"You know, those unexpected childhood boners? The bell rings, you get up from your desk, and there's your thing tent for all the world to see."

"Thing tent?"

"Yes, if I could pitch a fastball as well as I could pitch a thing tent, I'd be a wealthy man today."

"I'm sorry, I didn't realize you had such an affliction. It must have been humiliating for you."

"Not really. It actually made me popular. But maybe you're not as well-endowed as I am."

"If you must know, I never did well in school. I had a hard time concentrating, no pun intended."

"I don't get it."

"Hard?"

"Oh."

"Anyway, I was a slow reader, so I got put in the slow classes. It was like a scarlet letter. Each grade was split into three different categories. The really smart kids. The average kids. And the dumbass kids like me. It was humiliating, especially because all my friends were in the smart classes. My mother panicked about having an idiot child so she took me to a special reading center for idiot children. When my friends found out, it made going to school even worse than it was before. I used to pretend to be sick all of the time so I wouldn't have to go.

The year before they started splitting everybody up. I had this one teacher—Ms. Golden—in fourth grade, and she would classify kids as different types of flowers. She had the orchids, the daisies, and the weeds. She'd write your name on the blackboard under whatever flower you were so everyone could see. I was a weed. I was always a weed. I hated school, and I hated Hebrew school even more. And just so you know, I did take some acting classes in New York and here. And for the record—they were stupid, and I hated those, too."

"I think you should see somebody. All that childhood trauma just doesn't go away, you know."

"Therapy you mean?"

"Yeah, I've been doing it for years. Stuff about my father."

"Does it help?"

"Oh, yeah. I'm almost completely functional now."

"How are those thing tents doing? Does therapy help with that?"

"I'm down to only twice a day. But seriously, folks, you might want to stop being such an asshole about not taking classes and get some help with your issues. It's probably holding you back from realizing your full potential. Trust me on this. I'm certifiable—I know what I'm talking about."

"I didn't know you had father issues."

"He's demanding and impossible to please."

Then Mike found some old trail mix in my glove compartment.

"Ooh, are you eating this?" He made a screaming baby noise and then devoured my trail mix.

* * *

First we met with Billy. I love this guy. A tall, skinny tech nerd with long, stringy blond hair that he tucks under a beat-up John Deer cap, and I've never seen him not wearing a dirty white T-shirt. Billy is the most even-keeled person I've ever known. No airs. No ego issues. He loves what he does, and he does it well. Not unexpectedly, Billy was absolutely fine with everything we told him about the pictures and videos that we were thinking about using in the show. "No problemo," he said.

Then Al came over from his office to meet Mike. I was a little surprised when I first saw him. He'd put on a lot of weight, and his hair was almost completely gray. I guess being artistic director can get pretty stressful. Al has expressive eyes and a big, warm smile that he always greets me with.

Unfortunately, there was a thing, an uneasiness between Mike and Al. It started with Mike trying to be funny and Al not laughing. Mike doesn't like that; he takes it personally if people don't think he's funny.

"So you're a writer on this as well, Mike?" Al asked in what seemed more like a challenge than an actual question.

"Uh, yeah…we're a partnership, so we have a system."

"We had one, too. He writes and I criticize. Is it something like that?"

"No, not really like that at all. It's more collaborative."

"Ah, good. That's good. And listen, like I told Moe, if you guys want to come down and have me look at what you're doing—"

Mike responded with a raised eyebrow.

Al raised an eyebrow back at him. "You decide. I just think you should get a little feedback before you throw it up in front of an audience."

"Might be a good idea," I offered. "Certainly don't want to be throwing up on anybody."

"We'll talk about it," Mike said with a patronizing grin that said something more like *we don't need any help from the likes of you.*

"Just offering." Al turned away from him and back to me with a *What's with this guy?* look on his face.

Sometimes I do believe that I've gone into the wrong line of work. I'd rather not have to deal with this kind of thing. Personality clashes happen much too frequently in this business, and it stresses me out. I'm not good with confrontation. If I hadn't been categorized as a weed by my fourth grade elementary school teacher, I could have been an oceanographer by now. People are just annoying. I'd much rather work with octopuses.

"We'll be paid the weekend of the show, correct?" Mike asked while taking a step closer to Al.

"What do you mean?" Al replied turning back to face him.

"I mean we'd like half the money up front and half after the last show. I just don't want to be waiting for something in the mail six months later. Been there. Done that."

My jaw must have been hanging open. He had never said anything about the money before. I can't believe Mike sometimes, I really can't.

Al was getting steamed.

"What the hell is going on here?"

He looked back at me, and it felt like an accusation—like I went around talking trash behind his back or something. Then he turned back to Mike again, stepping toward him and getting right up in his face.

"We've never been late paying talent here. And, frankly, I find that rude and insulting. I mean, where the hell are you even getting that shit from?"

When Al gets aggressive, people tend to back off. He's a big guy, and he can be quite intimidating. I've seen his friendly smiling eyes get fierce before, but this was on another level. Mike didn't budge, though. Because Mike is a maniac.

I'm not getting it from anywhere," Mike coolly told him. "It's just business. I just want to be clear about how payment is going to work, that's all."

There is an excruciating silence.

"I'll run it by the business manager, how's that?"

Al waited for a response, but Mike didn't give one.

"Did Moe tell you about the royalty?"

"Yeah, he mentioned something about it." Mike deadpanned.

"Well, I got you a couple hundred for that, too."

"Yeah? What's a couple hundred mean?"

Al was getting a little red in the face at that point.

"A couple is two," he said in a deliberately measured tone.

"So seven hundred for three shows?"

"That's correct."

Mike shook his head to show he couldn't believe what a shitty deal we were getting, and then Al continued with increasing ire and volume.

"And the apartment, all the publicity, we sell the tickets, and print the programs…that's pretty good, I'd say, wouldn't you?"

Mike didn't respond. He just stood there looking unsatisfied.

They stared at each other like gunslingers waiting for the other guy to twitch.

I felt I had to say something at this point to ease some of this ridiculous tension before I had an aneurism or something.

"Well, sounds great to me!" I chirped like the stupid next-door neighbor in a bad sitcom.

I was ignored. They continued to stare at each other, and I didn't know what was going to happen next. Then Al suddenly decided he'd had about enough of Mike. He abruptly turned away from him and back to me.

"So, you like my title idea?" Al asked, his friendly smile attempting a comeback.

"I do. I think it's great," I said.

"What title idea?" Mike asked, refusing to be ignored.

Al's smile instantly vanished.

"*How Do You Spell Chanukah?*" *I told him.* "A title for the show. I forgot to tell you about that. Al's idea. I like it."

Al reluctantly looked to see how Mike reacted to this. Mike frowned and nodded but didn't say anything, brilliantly non-committal. What we had here was an epic battle of thespians behaving like assholes.

And then Al was done with us.

"I have to get back to the office," he said while walking away. "If you want my help, the offer still stands. Call me, Moe. Let's talk about this."

And then he was out the door.

I looked at Mike feeling completely mortified by what had just gone down.

He shrugged as if it were no big deal.

An old Jewish joke suddenly came to me—which I guess was a good thing at that point. Do you know what happens when you put three Jews in a room together? You get five different opinions. I'm not sure why I was reminded of that, but I welcomed the distraction nonetheless.

* * *

After that particular stickiness was over, we drove toward the temple in the next town over. We had a lot of time to kill before our scheduled meeting with the rabbi, so we toured the area, and I pointed out some hot spots that I remembered from the last time I was there. We didn't talk about the meeting with Al. We talked about what we're going to do with the rabbi and reviewed the questions that we had for him. Then Mike surprised me.

"Actually, *How Do You Spell Chanukah?*. That is a pretty good name for the show."

"Oh, good. I'm glad you like it. I think it's perfect."

"I just hope he doesn't try to mooch in on this thing and start trying to control what we're doing."

"He's fine. I've worked with him. He's a good guy."

"Yeah, we'll see. I get a weird vibe from him."

Then I drove over something, we felt a bump, and I had a blowout—*boom*. The car swerved sharply, and I nearly rear-ended the driver in front of us. Horns were blaring and tires were screeching, but I managed to maneuver over to the side of the road. It was a scary moment, and my heart was pounding. I looked over at Mike who seemed abnormally calm about the whole thing, considering I almost got us both killed.

"Well, that's another fine mess you've gotten me into," he said in a perfect Oliver Hardy.

Anxious to assess the damage to the car, I carelessly opened my door into oncoming traffic, and the screeching and beeping started all over again. I quickly closed the door and tried to compose myself.

I looked over at Mike, and he still had that unnervingly calm demeanor.

"I can't take you anywhere, can I? Mm, mm, mm," he said in an even better Oliver Hardy than before.

I think he was trying to smooth over his annoying behavior from the meeting. But at that moment, I wasn't at all receptive to whatever he was attempting to do.

* * *

Turned out I had a temporary spare in the trunk but no jack.

We were standing off to the side of the road, waiting for AAA to show up, when Mike got back to the Al business. He turned his head to the side over his shoulder until there was a loud pop in his neck. He had deserted his calm demeanor, and now he was antsy and short-tempered.

"And I definitely don't want him directing us or having any kind of say about what we're doing with the show," he said.

"He's not saying that he's got approval about anything," I told him. "He just wants to help."

"Don't be so sure about that."

"It'll be fine, relax."

"I'm just telling you; I'm not putting up with any bullshit from this guy. And we should have a contract with everything written out. Was there any negotiation? No, he just gives you a price, and you say sure, okay, sounds good, let's shake on it. You're too easy. I know he's your friend, but this is business, and we should be getting a lot more than seven hundred for this. You can't let people take advantage of you, Moe. No matter who they are."

"He's not taking advantage of anything. It's a little theater, Mike. Two hundred seats. It's not Carnegie Hall we're playing here. Maybe you should call your therapist about it."

"What's that supposed to mean?"

"Nothing," I said with passive-aggressive perfection.

He gave me a nasty look, and I gave him one back.

"I can't believe you don't have a jack," he said, getting off the subject.

"I thought I did."

We didn't say anything else until his stomach growled.

"Are you hungry?"

"I could eat," he said.

* * *

After AAA got done we still had an hour before our meeting, so we got something to eat at a Panda Express. Mike had momentarily put the AI business behind him and had returned to goofball mode. He made faces at little kids and did spot-on dog noises that equally delighted and annoyed everyone around us. Mike eats twice as much as I do, and when I took a little breather from my own dish, he wanted to know if I was finished because he was still hungry. I gave him the rest of my chicken with string beans and watched as he wolfed it down. If I ate like Mike does, I'd weigh four hundred pounds. I don't know how he does it. I opened my fortune cookie. It said: "The fortune you seek is in another cookie. Come back tomorrow." Everybody's a comedian.

After Mike made some more disturbing animal noises, we drove to the temple. The temporary tire wasn't the same size as the other ones, so the car was driving unevenly. The spare made thumping noises on the road that sounded like heartbeats, and it was putting me on edge. It can't be good driving around too long like that, for me or the car. So now I had to buy a new freaking tire because no way could I drive all the way back to LA like that.

If it weren't for bad luck, I'd have no luck at all.

CHAPTER SEVEN

MOE AND MIKE'S NEVER-PERFORMED SKETCH IDEA 147

MOE. Hey, Mike!

MIKE. Didn't we just do one of these?

MOE. Yeah, but it's Chanukah and all, and besides something interesting happened last night that I want to share with everybody.

MIKE. You didn't use that wood menorah again did you?

MOE. No, nothing caught on fire or anything like that.

MIKE. You didn't dress up like Hanukkah Harry and dance on the roof again, did you?

MOE. No, I'm not drinking during the week anymore.

MIKE. So what happened?

MOE. Okay, I come home last night about ten thirty, and it's pouring out—

MIKE. Oh, yeah, that was intense last night. You were out in that?

MOE. Yeah, I was in Encino, and I'm telling you, Mike, there's something about that place. When it rains, the whole city just floods. It was like driving through a river, I'm not kidding you.

MIKE. Nasty.

MOE. Yeah…so I finally get home and guess what happens?

MIKE. Alligators started coming up from the sewers?

MOE. No, there's no lights. My whole block is out.

MIKE. Power failure?

MOE. Yup.

MIKE. You get a lot of those over there in Glendale, don't you?

MOE. We do. I'm not sure why, but I think the raccoons have something to do with it.

MIKE. You have to watch those raccoons. They're power hungry.

MOE. What?

MIKE. Never mind…

MOE. So it's pitch-black in the house, but I manage to find my menorah and the candles. I say the prayer, but instead of just lighting two candles, I light them all.

MIKE. Well, you know there are several schools of thought about that. Some rabbis think that's actually the way to do it. You light all the candles on the first night and then remove one candle on each of the following nights.

MOE. Seemed like a good year to try that out.

MIKE. Did the power come back?

MOE. It came back a few hours later.

MIKE. Too bad. It would have been interesting to see if the candles would have burned for eight days and eight nights.

MOE. Probably not, I get the cheap ones at Ralphs. Anyway, the point being—the Chanukah candles literally brought light to the darkness for me this year. It just made the whole thing a little more significant somehow.

MIKE. Cool.

MOE. Sort of my own private Chanukah miracle.

MIKE. Mazel Tov.

MOE. Raccoons—power hungry—I think I get it now.

MIKE. Two miracles in one sketch. What a day.

CHAPTER EIGHT

THE RABBI IS A HUNK

When we walked into the reception area, I got a chill down my spine. Like how the Antichrist must feel when he gets near a church. The place was huge. It was a whole community center with classrooms, meeting rooms, and auditoriums. There was art everywhere you looked. Paintings done by kids adorned the walls, and in glass cases they had some expensive-looking antiques and jewelry. Higher up on the walls (twenty-five-foot ceilings in this place) were framed paintings depicting biblical scenes that looked like they should be in a museum. It was a whole different esthetic than what Rabbi Tannenbaum had going on.

We hooked up with an administrator in the main office, and then she led us to the temple. It took forever to get there—that's how big this place was. The administrator told us that the rabbi would be with us shortly, and then she left us alone with our outdated recording equipment and $30 tripod. I had bought an external microphone that hooks up to the camera, so hopefully the sound would be a little better than if we were just to use the camera mic. That's all we had equipment-wise.

The temple was, without a doubt, the most impressive temple I'd ever seen. Not that I've seen that many of them, but still it was impressive. It had long curving pews made of polished maple, and they must be able to seat a thousand people. Huge stained glass windows adorned the walls, and there was a big stage where services are conducted. This was high-class Jewry.

Not like the kind I grew up with. Center stage was an ornate cabinet where the Torah was housed—the ark, is what Mike told me it's called, and the stage is called the bimah. Mike couldn't believe I didn't know that. Once a weed, always a weed.

So we started setting up our equipment, and in case somebody might be spying on us, we pretended to know what we were doing.

We had a list of questions for the rabbi and hoped that he would have some fun with what we were going to ask him to do. Our idea was that we'd ask him questions, the rabbi would give his answers, we would respond—hilariously of course—and the rabbi would react to our responses. Later we'd edit our questions and hilarious responses out of the video and then ask those same questions and give those same responses when we were live onstage. Hopefully, if our timing was good, it would feel as if we were having a real conversation with the rabbi. As if we were Skyping him and he was actually there, live onstage with us, and we were all having a lovely time together.

When the rabbi finally came into the temple, he threw me for a loop. I was expecting a Rabbi Tannenbaum–type rabbi, but what we got instead was a big, handsome, athletic-looking rabbi with a perfectly trimmed black beard. He was young and dressed well enough to be on the cover of *GQ* magazine. He told us that he was an ex-football player, a hospital chaplain (the chaplain thing confused me; I'd never heard of a Jewish chaplain before), and then after getting his law degree, he became a rabbi. Don't hear that every day.

The rabbi was cooperative and listened patiently as we described the show and what we were hoping to do with the video. He smiled and seemed to be a good sport, but he also let us know that he had a busy day ahead, just in case we weren't aware of how valuable his time was. We treated him respectfully (which was a new experience for me—considering my history with rabbis), thanked him profusely for helping us, and promised that he and the temple would receive many thanks in the theater program and free tickets for him and anyone else he'd like to bring. He seemed unimpressed by our generosity.

As we were about to start taping, we ran into some technical problems. I couldn't get the camera to record, and the external mic wouldn't register that it was connected to the camera. I couldn't figure out what was wrong, and every time I touched the camera, I got a little electric shock. Even with my limited technical abilities, I figured that couldn't be good. The rabbi and Mike were both getting frustrated, and I could feel the energy draining from the situation. The rabbi was starting to look at his watch (a very fancy watch, I might add), and Mike was giving me nasty looks. I was about to ask the rabbi if he knew a prayer for old decrepit video equipment when Mike came over to try his hand at it. He turned the camera off and then on again (without getting shocked), and then everything seemed to be fine. I had tried the same thing and it hadn't worked for me, but Mike got it going right away. Weird.

So we eventually got things set up as best we could. The rabbi stood behind one of the beautiful wood podiums on the bimah, and we fed him our questions. I had sent an email the day before to give him a heads-up about the kind of things we'd be talking about, and he seemed to understand what we were going for style-wise. But he was a particularly stiff ex-football playing/chaplain/lawyer/rabbi.

We had a few jokes for him to tell, which I had also included in the email, but I think he had over-rehearsed, as if he had performed them for his staff and bombed and now had comedy shell shock. Although our rabbi was tall, dark, and handsome, he was also extremely unfunny. We tried to help him, making some timing suggestions that he might try, but nothing helped. You either got it, or you don't—you can't teach funny. But he did know his Chanukah stuff. And in case you're wondering—there really is no proper way to spell *Chanukah*. "So long as you get the *KKKhaaah* sound in there, then you're doing okay," quoted verbatim from the rabbi's on-tape explanation.

We spent about an hour and a half with the rabbi. But the more we tried to get him to be funny, the worse he got. Ultimately, though, his complete lack of comedy timing began to grow on us. It was oddly charming. He was trying so hard and being so unsuccessful at it that you just kind of loved him for it. Yes, we had ourselves a complete original: an ex-football playing/chaplain/lawyer/rabbi with absolutely no sense of humor. An unfunny Jew. A rare and remarkable thing to behold.

* * *

After I bought a new tire to match the other three that hadn't blown up yet, we made our way through ridiculous traffic and finally got back to LA—all tires still intact.

The next day I got an urge to do more videotaping. I decided it would be a fun idea to ask strangers on the street what they thought about Chanukah and videotape their responses. After a few threats of violence and an attempted robbery, I decided that it'd be easier, and a lot safer, just to talk to people I already knew—Jewish people with big personalities and strong opinions—I know lots of those. Mostly I'd ask them how they spelled *Chanukah*, what their religious upbringing was like, how they celebrated the holiday today, and what, if anything, it means to them now. I wasn't sure if we'd wind up using any of this stuff, but I figured it'd be a good thing to have in the back pocket.

A good friend, who taught at the campus where I did Shakespeare in the summer, agreed to help me out and do an interview on camera. He wasn't a Jew but a very interesting guy and one of my favorite people. He'd been a professor of religion, a professor of philosophy, a published author, a rock and roll fiend, a wine and beer lover, and a wild party animal. A sensitive, complex, and profoundly deep human being.

We got together on campus and found a nice shady spot under a big sycamore tree. I set up the equipment (which seemed to be cooperating), and then he talked nonstop for an hour about religion, the human condition, our responsibilities to our fellow man, the importance of God in our lives, and what he thought the future held for the human race. He talked about his struggles with faith and his insecurities about how he'd spent his time. He was worried that he might have been too selfish and that he hadn't contributed enough to help improve the human condition. As he talked, he was sweating profusely and seemed more agitated and uncomfortable than I had ever seen him before.

Shortly after we made the tape, my friend was diagnosed with pancreatic cancer. He battled bravely but not long after our meeting on campus, he died. I still have the tape in a desk drawer in my office. I was going to give it to his wife after he passed but thought the timing wasn't right, so I've held on to it. But in reality, I just couldn't let it go.

We didn't wind up using anything from what I recorded with him that day. It was too heavy for a comedy show. But I've watched the tape over and over again, and it has consistently moved me to tears. He had a premonition about what was to come, and our meeting that day was a chance for him to lay it all out there. A record of his philosophy, his regrets, his concerns, his hopes, and his failures—it was a farewell.

His courage and calm while facing his illness was inspirational. He was more concerned for the people around him than he was for himself. He told me one time after he got very sick, "A lot of people say, why me? I say, why not me?" On his office door he had printed out in big, bold letters, **LOVE RECK-**

LESSLY. I think that is profound. I don't know if I'll ever be capable of that kind of generosity, but it's certainly something to aspire to.

Was it his faith in God that gave him this strength? Was that what allowed him to put things into such a beautiful perspective and fearlessly face what he knew would be a tragic end? Of course he would say that it wasn't tragic and it wasn't the end. I admire that, I envy it, and I wish I had that kind of faith and that kind of perspective. It's what my grandfather might have been trying to get at but lost track of when his time came.

CHAPTER NINE
REHEARSING WITH MIKE

I pounded out a first draft in about two weeks. I bought some gelt, a dreidel, and some Chanukah candles from a Jewish-supply store online to use as props during rehearsals. I set up a card table and a couple of folding chairs in my living room and then waited for Mike to come over and read through the script with me. I was excited and nervous about starting this part of the process.

Mike was late. He's always late. I'm always on time or a little bit early. People being late bugs the crap out of me. Mike knows this, but I think he enjoys getting under my skin about it. He called me about fifteen minutes after he was scheduled to arrive.

"I had to wait for a repair guy," he told me. "My brand-new water heater isn't getting hot, and then I had too much coffee, and now I'm stuck in the bathroom because coffee does that to me sometimes." Then he groaned to underscore the situation.

"Well, when do you think you'll get here?" I asked with just enough aggravation in my voice to hopefully make him feel guilty for wasting my time.

He didn't.

I'm on my way," he told me. "Keep your panties on."

* * *

When Mike parked in my driveway about thirty minutes later, he was in complete comedy mode and doing his old-man routine—loudly. He was grunting and groaning while struggling to get out of his car, painfully straightening his old-man's body and shaking a fist at God.

"What'd I ever do to you to deserve this kind of pain? What, you're having a bad day or something?" he yelled in a perfect Yiddish accent. "You got a headache? Well take an aspirin and leave me the hell alone already!"

I was watching him through the dining room window. He was putting on a show for me and any of the neighbors who might be interested. His old-man physicality was brilliant, and in spite of my foul mood, I couldn't help but laugh.

He was slowly making his way toward the house when he started to lose his balance. It was a master class in physical comedy. He struggled mightily to stay upright, turning and swirling and desperately trying to stay on his feet. He nearly went down several times, but somehow, just when I thought he was going to hit the deck, he managed to correct himself and find his balance again. Finally, he steadied himself, took a gasping breath, and then continued toward the house again. But on the first step he stumbled, and the ballet began anew. This time, however, he was going down in a slow motion collapse that was reminiscent of Harold Lloyd or Buster Keaton at their best.

So Mike was in my driveway, rolling on the pavement like a turtle who got flipped on his back.

"Whhhyyyy? What'd I ever do to you that you make me suffer like this?"

He was rolling and yelling and kicking his feet in the air, and I knew he wouldn't stop until I went out there to join him. So rather than have the neighbors call the police, that's what I did.

"It's all right. He's crazy but he's not dangerous," I yelled on my way out the door.

I helped him up and started leading him toward the house.

"Did you forget your medicine again?" I asked, also in a Yiddish accent.

"What do you care? Do you ever call? Do you ever take me shopping? Eccht! You don't know what love is. You don't care about how I suffer."

Then he fell to the ground again, shaking his feet in the air and screaming in that high-pitched baby noise that he does.

I tried to get him back on his feet, but somehow we both wound up on the ground rolling and cursing at God. Eventually I got back up, and after a series of slapstick attempts, I finally managed to get him off the ground. Once on his feet, he grabbed my face and gave me a wet kiss on the cheek.

"You're a good boy. You're a bad Jew and an idiot, but I love you anyway." He said this in another old-man voice. This time it's a Russian Jewish accent.

It's been a lifetime since I'd heard my grandfather's voice, but that was it. And the grin on Mike's face was the identical grin my grandfather wore when I found him dead as a doornail in his hospital room. Freaked me out.

When we finally made it inside, the Mike show continued, and I was gladly along for the ride. We were cracking each other up with rapid-fire impromptu character bits. We fed off each other, and it was so smooth and easy; it really felt as if we were meant to be doing this. There was a chemistry we had that was special—that just doesn't happen often.

Eventually, we started reading and rehearsing the play. We sat at the card table and played to the fireplace as if it were an audience. Some of the things we said to the fireplace—I wish I had on tape. We went back and forth from the script to just riffing and taking off on tangents, and most of that stuff was funnier than anything I had written down on paper. It was filthy, irreverent, and hilarious. Working on *How Do You Spell Chanu-*

kah? with Mike, even with all the problems we had, was by far the most fun I've ever had rehearsing a play. If we could crack up an audience half as much as we were cracking each other up, we'd be in great shape.

During that rehearsal, Mike and I worked out the music for the first song lyric I had written for the show. Besides being a funny actor and a sometimes annoying human being, Mike is a talented musician. For this song, Mike played guitar and sang the melody, while I sang harmony.

THE JEWISH ENEMIES SONG
Assyrians and Babylonians
They were our enemies
Hittite, Moabite, Persians
Midianite, Philistines, Syrian Greeks

They tried to kill us
We won
Let's eat (Don't forget the Seleucids…that's right!)

The Romans and the Nazis
Tried to bring us down unto our knees
Egypt, Jordan, Lebanon (not all of them)
Iran, Iraq, Palestinian (ehh)

They tried to kill us
We won
Let's eat (Don't forget the Seleucids…that's right!)

The Saudis and the Syrians
The list is long and doesn't end
We wish these troubles would go away

Then there're the skinheads and the KKK

They tried to kill us
We won
Let's eat...everybody

They tried to kill us
We won
Let's eat...one more time

They tried to kill us
We won
Let's eat. (Don't forget the Seleucids...that's right!)

I loved singing this song. I'm not a trained musician, but I have a good ear for picking up harmonies. I would rather sing harmony than do just about anything else, except for drinking single malt scotch whisky, but I can't do that much anymore. So I was thrilled that Mike picked up the melody part and played guitar, and I could just concentrate on being harmonic.

In spite of that ideal first rehearsal, Mike was constantly being distracted by his phone. As I mentioned before, Mike has a lot of irons in the fire. He was serious about building his acting career—his real acting career, not the fooling around that we were doing (he would never hesitate to tell me). He knew that it bothered me, but I think he enjoyed watching me stew about it. Not unlike how I enjoyed watching Rabbi Tannenbaum let off steam, so maybe there was some poetic justice going on.

At the rehearsals, I didn't comment about how his phone was driving me crazy. How his baby noises made me want to throttle him. How I thought his always being late was rude and disrespectful. I didn't want to make waves. I knew the show would work if we were having a lot of fun doing it. If we weren't—we'd be in trouble. So I tried my best not to let Mike provoke me, which I think irked him almost as much as his baby noises annoyed me. It was my passive-aggressive way of getting some payback. I knew that he was looking for the confrontation—he enjoys that—but I didn't give him the satisfaction.

It was a dangerous game we were playing. On the upside, the friction going on between us could be a helpful tool for finding our characters and what our relationship would be like onstage. I think we both intuitively understood this. Like Bud and Lou. Like Stan and Ollie—there was always conflict. But on the negative side, this kind of thing could easily get out of hand and do more harm than good. It happens all the time. It breaks up rock bands and comedy teams, and destroys marriages. It gets competitive and eventually causes enough resentment to overwhelm any of the positives that might be going on. So you have to be careful. And just for the record, if you're thinking Mike had the upper hand in this little competition we had going on, let me enlighten you.

There was a thing I understood about Mike, and if I chose to, I could use it as a terrible weapon against him. Mike is a gifted comic actor. He is out-of-control hilarious, but he wants to be Robert De Niro when he is really Will Farrell. He was always auditioning for the Actors Studio, but he never got in. He needed to prove to himself, and to the world, that he was a serious dramatic actor—which, unfortunately, he really wasn't. He read constantly about acting and was always taking acting classes. He compared himself to his heroes and then felt small in comparison. So he paid good money to therapists and tried in vain to deal with the devils that tormented him. That left him exposed and vulnerable to the likes of me. Mike was a sitting duck. I knew he thought himself superior to me intellectually, morally, physically, and artistically. But the truth was that he was being lied to by his acting teachers and his therapists. They were just telling him what he wanted to hear. I knew the truth, and I could have crushed him like a bug.

See what I'm talking about? This stuff can get ugly. And I know that I'm easily prone to vengeful thinking. Probably got it from my grandfather. I would hazard to guess that I can be much more vindictive than Mike ever could. It's the passive-aggressive guys you need to watch out for. All that ugly stuff that gets unsaid and percolates under the surface can come out in explosively destructive ways. Mike thought he knew me, but he really didn't. I knew him, though, because he'd told me everything. He was an open book, and he was exposed. Mike had no idea what I was capable of.

Yes, I have to be careful with this stuff.

CHAPTER TEN

MOE AND MIKE'S NEVER-PERFORMED SKETCH IDEA 172

MOE. I'm looking for a painter. Did I tell you that?

MIKE. No. To paint what?

MOE. The outside of my house.

MIKE. BIG JOB.

MOE. I'm getting bids from five different painters. So far one guy didn't show, one guy was drunk, and another guy threw his back out getting out of his truck.

MIKE. I'd definitely go with the drunk.

MOE. Painters can be odd, you know? All those paint fumes. It gets to you after a while.

MIKE. You used to do that kind of work, didn't you?

MOE. I did.

MIKE. They used a lot of oil paint back in those days, didn't they?

MOE. Yes, and let me tell you, it got to you after a while.

MIKE. Apparently so.

MOE. It was bad. I remember doing cabinets and closets with oil paint. After an hour or two of that, my head would really start spinning.

MIKE. Probably still had lead in the paint back then, too.

MOE. Many of the mental problems I have today I can attribute back to my painting days.

MIKE. Like forgetting lines and stuff like that?

MOE. Yes. And missing time, imaginary animals—you know, general confusion-type stuff. What were we talking about again?

MIKE. The depleting ozone layer and declining polar bear habitat.

MOE. Oh, that's right. It's a crime what's happening to those poor polar bears.

MIKE. You're kidding, right?

MOE. What?

MIKE. Nothing…

CHAPTER ELEVEN
SOUTH SHORE REPERTORY THEATRE

When we got to San Diego with all our props and costumes, we were feeling anxious. We had put in plenty of rehearsal time in my living room, but no one had seen any part of the show yet, and we had no idea if any of it would actually work. The first thing we did was check the box office to see how the show was selling. The first two nights were sold out, and the third night looked pretty good, too. The original agreement was that we'd be performing on Friday, Saturday, and Sunday, but that got changed for reasons we weren't privy to. Now it was Saturday, Sunday, and Monday. Monday is usually a dead night in the theater, so I was pleased to see that it was selling as well as it was.

We went into the theater and found that the stage was all set up for a Christmas show that was running there through the holidays. There were wreaths and Christmas decorations everywhere—hopefully, we could get some comedy mileage out of that.

We had a technical rehearsal scheduled with Billy. I had made up a special script for him with all the cues highlighted—around fifty of them. The overhead projector was in place, and the projection screen was already set up for us. We put our card table and folding chairs up on the stage, and I covered the table with a Chanukah tablecloth I had found online. It had dreidels and menorahs printed all over it, which helped us stand out a little from all the Christmas stuff.

When Billy showed up we went through the script, and he felt like he would have no problem running the show. I was worried about having only the one rehearsal with him. The cues were complicated, and a lot of our jokes depended on certain pictures coming up at exactly the right time. But Billy was cool as a cucumber.

We had a cue-to-cue rehearsal. That's when you just do a few lines leading into a sound or light cue, or, in this case, a cue for a picture or a video to come up on the screen. Billy's timing was spot-on. He did everything perfectly—the guy's a wizard. The only problem was that the pictures didn't transfer well from our computer to the projector and then onto the screen. Some of the shots looked blurry. The rabbi video was okay, but the photos left a lot to be desired. Actually, they looked like shit. We tried adjusting the focus on the projector, but that just made it worse. My bad. I didn't realize that stealing pictures off the internet would result in such poor-quality photo projections. Live and learn, as I'm sure many internet thieves before me have been heard to say.

Mike and I were getting along pretty well. There was some tension from time to time but nothing too evil or vindictive. A few things were still simmering underneath, mostly on my end, but as expected these conflicts helped us find our characters in the show. Nothing was getting out of hand enough for me to consider pulling out my secret weapon to destroy him with.

Mike had gone through many disappointments during our rehearsal process. So there'd been periods of him being depressed. He'd been rejected by agents, had countless failed auditions, tried again to get into the Actors Studio, and again he was rejected. So I think Mike was grateful for having the Chanukah show to help restore his disintegrating self-esteem. In case you don't already know, the acting business is brutal on the ego. And actor egos are the most delicate egos of all.

The condo where we were staying was a nicely furnished two bedroom. We were asked to be respectful of the property and to their neighbors while we were there. I guess they've had some rowdy actors in the past who caused some problems. The condo was, as Al had mentioned, just blocks away from the theater, so it was convenient. We got ourselves some food and hung out there until showtime.

Mike was able to take a nap; I was not. I didn't sleep the whole time we were there. I'd been having some bad dreams, dreams that made me feel guilty and ashamed because I'd screwed something up or had been found out to be a liar. My grandfather made his first dream visit the night before Mike and I came to San Diego. I was my younger self standing in the doorway of his hospital room. He was lying in bed with that smirk on his face. His lips trembled and he tried to speak, but he couldn't.

I was sitting in the living room of the condo, reading a *National Enquirer* that we had picked up at the supermarket. I was looking at a story about a man who claimed that he saw an alien spaceship while working at Area 51, when Mike started shouting from his bedroom.

"Phony! There will be a price to be paid. There is always a price."

It was the Russian Jewish accent again. I was frozen there on the couch, completely freaked out by what I was hearing. Was it possible that my grandfather was using Mike to tell me what he couldn't say in my dream the night before?

Then the TV turned on by itself and started flipping channels. Mike was moaning and grumbling from his bedroom, something that I couldn't understand. I think it was Russian, though.

I seriously couldn't wait for this whole thing to be over.

CHAPTER TWELVE
THE FIRST SHOW

We arrived at the theater, got situated in the dressing room, and put on our suits. Mike gave me a tie to wear. An obnoxiously loud tie that no normal human being would be caught dead in—so it was perfect for the goofy version of myself that I played in the show. We were both nervous. We ran our lines in the dressing room and then went onstage to check our props. We made sure the guitar was tuned and then sat at the card table with the Chanukah tablecloth. We looked at each other and shrugged—whatever will be, will be. I gave the house manager a nod, and she opened the doors so the audience could start coming into the theater. A chatty and excited mob of Jews if ever I saw one.

We joked and talk with them as they filed in to find their seats. Mike took a small wreath off the wall, put it on his head, and then sat back down at the table. He looked like Jesus in a suit wearing a halo.

"Too much?" he asked.

"For this crowd? Probably yes," I said.

That was our first laugh, and Mike did figure a way to use the set to our advantage.

Mike put the wreath back, and I ate gelt, throwing the foil wrappers on the floor by my feet, which would aggravate Mike and illicit his disapproving anal-retentive glares. Were we going to pull this off? I could tell from the audience that this was an important event for them. This was something personal. A show to celebrate who they are, what they believe in, and what they're proud of.

What was it for me? Not only did I feel like a phony, but I felt like a hustler and a thief. I had to be funny and charming for the next hour and a half, and I suddenly wasn't in the mood for doing that anymore. I tried to keep engaging with the audience, but I was starting to flounder. I had to get my head straight. Mike picked up the slack and continued to schmooze as the theater started filling up. He's much better at it than I am anyway.

CHAPTER THIRTEEN

HOW DO YOU SPELL CHANUKAH?: *THE STAGE SHOW*

MIKE. Okay, I think we're going to need a little help from the audience at this point.

MOE. Really? I thought we were doing pretty good on our own.

MIKE. We know that the lamp oil burned for eight nights, but is that all there is?

MOE. What, now you're Peggy Lee or something? That's not enough for you?

MIKE. No. Because I don't think that's the whole story, and that's my question for the audience. What is the true meaning of *CCC*hanukah, and what are we really celebrating here?

MOE. It is his nature to question. To doubt. To argue. To nosh.

MIKE. Those who respond with meaningful answers will have our undying gratitude and will be immediately rewarded with two fresh chocolate gelts. Not the old melted ones we've been saving from last year.

MOE. And those with less-meaningful answers will be removed immediately from the theater by beefy Jews with slingshots.

MIKE. So, ladies and gentlemen—the floor is yours. With all sincerity we ask—what is the true meaning of *CCC*hanukah? Please enlighten us with your wisdom.

MOE. I have a question.

MIKE. Anybody? Anybody?

MOE. Mike, I have a question.

MIKE. Why are you asking a question when we're trying to get an answer?

MOE. Because I think my question might be relevant to the answer.

MIKE. But we don't even know the answer yet, so how could you know if your question is relevant to something that you don't even know the answer to?

MOE. Let me think about that for a few days, and I'll get back to you. In the meantime…now I forgot my question.

MIKE. There is a God. So, ladies and gentlemen, without further ado…

MOE. Wait! Did you ever hear about the Great Dreidel War?

MIKE. No.

MOE. That's why they needed the oil.

MIKE. To spin the dreidels?

MOE. Right, and it was a miracle because the dreidels spun for eight days and nights when everybody thought the game would just go on for a couple of hours.

MIKE. Are you finished?

MOE. I hope so because I'm giving myself a headache.

MIKE. Imagine how we feel.

[The rabbi appears on the screen.]

RABBI. You know, you guys asked a very good question, and I'd be happy to help you with it.

MOE. Whoa, what the…

RABBI. Hello friends. My name is Rabbi Fanberg from congregation Beth El.

MIKE. A real live rabbi, ladies and gentlemen. And not a moment too soon.

MOE. Rabbi, I might be wrong about this, but I heard through the manischewitz grapevine that at one time you were quite the football player.

RABBI. Yes, that is true. And not only that, I was a hospital chaplain, a poet, and a lawyer.

MOE. (*Aside to the audience.*) His mother must be exhausted from being so proud.

MIKE. So tell us, Rabbi, because the anticipation is killing me. What is the real meaning of Chanukah?

RABBI. Well, there is a lot of symbolism in the holiday. But what the menorah really represents is the wisdom of the Torah. The holiday itself is not so much a celebration of the war between the Greeks and the Jews; it's more of a celebration of the reclaiming of our right to religious freedom—to keep our own wisdom without being forced to keep the wisdom of the Greeks.

MOE. That's good. The man knows what he's talkin' about.

RABBI. By the way, do you know the difference between Jewish food and Chinese food?

MIKE. Yes, but go ahead anyway.

RABBI. With Jewish food, *in two days* you're hungry again! (*The rabbi waves goodbye as he dissolves from the screen.*)

[Photo of the lit menorah comes back on the screen.]

MOE. Sorry, folks, no chocolate tonight. But come back tomorrow and hopefully he won't show up again.

MIKE. So *CCC*hanukah is not really commemorating the battle that we were talking about before, with the Greeks.

MOE. The Seleucids?

MIKE. Right. It's more about the Jewish struggle against assimilation and the reclamation of our Jewish identity.

MOE. Every time we turn around, someone tries to put us down.

MIKE. And, ironically…

MOE. Uh oh, here he goes…getting all ironical again.

MIKE. *CCC*hanukah has become the Jews' most assimilated holiday.

MOE. Hmm. That is ironical and paradoxical, coincidently at the same time together—if that makes grammatical sense.

MIKE. And because Jews don't celebrate war.

MOE. Although we're pretty freaking good at it.

MIKE. We celebrate the lamp oil instead.

MOE. And latkes. Don't forget the latkes. Eight days of them. That's enough grease to keep those lamps lit for twelve days. Maybe even a month.

MIKE. Did you do eight nights of presents?

MOE. Yeah, what did you do?

MIKE. We didn't fool around with all that. My family was pretty straightforward about it. We lit the candles, did the prayers—one night of presents, that was it.

MOE. Just one night?

MIKE. That's right.

MOE. We did eight nights. But, truthfully, it got a little old after a while. One night right foot sock, one night left foot sock, thank God there were eight nights or I'd have to wait a whole year to get a complete set.

* * *

Much to our shock and delight the show was a success. After getting off to a slow start playing a seemingly endless game of dreidel and arguing incessantly about the rules, we started to hit a rhythm, and the audience was actually having a really good time. We got big laughs; in fact we were killing it. There was lots of audience participation, and even the rabbi was a hit. It went better than either one of us ever expected. We were funny, musical, educational, and it was the best damn Chanukah party I've ever been to. Actually, it's the only Chanukah party I've ever been to—but still.

Then we went out for drinks to celebrate.

* * *

We found a nice upscale bar that was still serving food. I ordered scotch and Mike had a margarita. Our consumption levels with alcohol is much different than it is with food. I can drink like a fish. Mike is a lightweight—half a margarita and he's flying.

We were both feeling euphoric about how things had gone, and we were having a wonderful time, laughing and riffing and reveling in our favorite moments from the show. We flirted with the waitresses and were doing character voices all over the place. It was like that first rehearsal at my house, and I couldn't recall seeing Mike so excited about anything before.

"This could be big," he said. "We can make a real business out of it. Seriously, we could book this thing in every JCC and every temple all across America."

I tried not to put a damper on things, so I just smiled and drank. But the truth was that turning this show into a big business was about the last thing in the world I wanted to see happen.

"It's a goddamn gold mine!" he shouted to the waitresses and the drunk at the bar.

Then I got a call from Al, right there in the restaurant. He wanted to know if Mike and I could meet him for breakfast to talk about things. Mike shook his head—no way was he going to subject himself to a breakfast with Al. I felt obligated and agreed to meet him, but I was also nervous about what he would say. After disconnecting the call, I tried to get Mike to go with me.

"We should really talk to him," I said.

"You talk to him. He's your friend, not mine."

"He's a smart guy, Mike. And a good director."

"I gotta pee."

He got up to use the toilet, and that's all that was said about it.

CHAPTER FOURTEEN
SECOND NIGHT CURSE

I met Al the next day at a trendy little breakfast place with a great view of the ocean. To avoid making things emotionally complicated, I told him that Mike was feeling a little off and wanted to sleep in to make sure he was well rested for the second show.

"First of all, congratulations," Al said. "I really am impressed by how you guys were able to put this together. Like you pulled the ideas right out of the air."

Okay, so far so good.

"I mean, that takes a discipline I don't think I have. I couldn't have done it. And it felt so spontaneous, too. Like you were just making it up on the spot."

"Oh, good. That's what we were going for," I said. "But I tell you, truthfully, we had no idea if any of it was going to work."

"So how did you think it went?" he asked.

Usually, when somebody asks you that, it means they don't think it went so well.

"Well, I was happy about it. You heard them. We were getting huge laughs, and people seemed to be having a really good time," I said.

"I have a couple of things," he said, and then pulled out a notepad from his back pocket.

Okay, here we go. Something tells me that when he was talking about how we pulled ideas out of the air, he was really talking about how we pulled them out of our asses.

"I think you can tighten it up some. And you need more music. And more audience participation. And the pictures—"

"I know, some of those didn't work so well," I admitted.

"And the whole opening…"

He made a sour face, shook his head, and then took a drink of water—I think to get the taste of our opening out of his mouth.

"You really should rethink how you open the show. It's tedious."

I was starting to think I should have slept in as well.

"The other big thing, though," he said. "I think you need to decide who the straight man is. You might have noticed I don't like Mike very much, as a person."

"Yeah, but he's okay. I don't know why you guys—"

"It doesn't matter, though. Because he's really good. He's really funny. And you guys are a good team, so I'm not saying any of this because I don't like him. Anyway, something like this needs a straight man. I think you should be the clown and Mike should be more straight."

"I thought he was pretty straight."

"Yeah, but when he gets excited he gets really crazy. It's funny, but he becomes another character altogether, and then you have two clowns up there, and it doesn't work so well."

"Oh, okay…"

I was feeling deflated at that point. I thought we were a hit; I had hoped that Al would be thrilled by what he had seen—apparently not.

"I mean, not for tonight or tomorrow, but for when you do it again. And you should definitely get a director."

He went on like this. A whole notepad full. Al did all the talking, and I was just drinking coffee as though it were the last pot in town. I wasn't hearing very much of what he was saying anymore. My head was spinning, and my stomach was threatening to erupt.

When I got back to the apartment, I gave Mike a thumbnail rundown of what Al had to say. I gave him the condensed, softer version of it. I didn't want to upset him.

* * *

Sunday night we had another enthusiastic crowd.

The doors opened, the audience started coming in, and we joked and welcomed everyone. All was going well. We got into the dreidel-playing portion (the overly long and tedious opening that Al was talking about) and were arguing about the dreidel rules when something extraordinary happened. Never have I seen it before in all my years onstage. We both went completely blank at the same time. Neither one of us had any idea where we were in the show. I couldn't rescue Mike, and Mike couldn't rescue me. Then the projector went crazy. Our pictures started flashing on the screen. The rabbi video started and stopped, interrupted by more images that appeared in random order, thereby ruining all the jokes that they were connected to. I looked up at the control booth and saw Billy shrug at me. Like us, he had no idea what was going on.

Then it got worse. Things started coming up on the screen that weren't even in the show. I had no idea how they got there. Grainy, ghostly images from my Bar Mitzvah. My grandfather and his father (the rabbi who I only met once). My old house in Paterson, New Jersey. The outside of the Hebrew school where I had tortured Rabbi Tannenbaum. My parents' wedding photo. My grandfather and my grandmother when they were still young and happy, proudly holding the daughter who was later killed in the car accident. I couldn't figure out what the hell was going on. Was it only me seeing this? Or was the whole audience seeing it, too? Then the table started to shake and all the gelt started jumping up and down like popcorn in a hot pan. I looked over at Mike, and he was staring at me with a stroke-like grin on his face. Then he erupted and angrily wiped everything off the table.

"This is your fault," he yelled in a Russian Jewish accent.

"What?" I thought I was about to have a stroke myself.

"You're a phony, a coward, a fool, and a liar! You're living a lie! It will destroy you. Do you want to wind up like me? You need to find your truth! You need to find what you love. I'm here to warn you. Don't be like me, don't be like me, don't be like…"

Mike's voice faded to a whisper, but he continued to repeat himself like a stuck record, as if he were in a trance. "Don't be like me, don't be like me…"

We were staring at each other. The rage in his eyes morphed into something more like panic and confusion, but he wouldn't stop, or he couldn't stop, repeating, "Don't be like me, don't be like me…."

I was trying not to lose my mind and run screaming from the theater. I didn't know what to do, so I tried talking to God, something I'm sure I've never done before, unless the Bar Mitzvah qualifies as a discussion with God. I don't think it does though, especially the way I did it.

"God," I started in a voice I hoped only the Lord and I could hear. "I know I haven't been worthy of any help from you, but I think I'm getting the message here. I'll do better. I promise. Just stop this now. Please. We're right in the middle of a show here. No offense, but it's a little over the top, don't you think? Anyway, we'll talk later if you want, and I'm sorry. I'm sorry about everything."

Mike stopped mumbling and seemed to come out of his trance. I don't think he had any idea of what he had just said. He looked desperate, his eyes pleading for help, but I could offer him nothing.

Then a stage light directly above us blew out.

The audience gasped.

That's when it hit me. It's *A Christmas Carol*. I marveled at the symmetry of it. What a perfect example it is. I was not so much in a panic anymore. I was more in awe of the moment.

"It's *A Christmas Carol*, Mike. I'm Scrooge, and you just came to warn me."

"What?" Mike looked like he was about to cry.

"You were my grandfather's ghost! You were Jacob Marley come to warn me!"

There was a long pause after that. The type of pause that should never happen onstage—especially in a comedy show. In desperation, Mike threw me a random cue line. We skipped over at least four pages. We were not spontaneous or clever in our attempt to regain control of the show—we were deer in the headlights. We had lost our connection to each other and to the audience. We weren't funny. We were playing by the numbers, just to get through the play. The audience had come to see a light-hearted holiday celebration but got a confusing tragedy instead—a complete train wreck.

* * *

After sneaking out the back door, we did some drinking, but it was not the celebratory kind. There was no fooling around with the waitresses, either.

"Was Al there?" Mike asked.

"No, I don't think so."

"Did he pick up the bill for the breakfast at least?"

"We split it."

"Figures."

We drank a little before getting into the rest of it.

"I think I blacked out," Mike said. "I don't remember the whole start of the show. That's happened to me before, when

I've been really good. But this wasn't good. This was…I don't know what this was."

"I'm telling you…" I'd told him about five times already, but he just couldn't seem to absorb it. I leaned in across the table. I whispered it this time, slowly and purposefully. "It was my grandfather. It was a warning. He took over your body. He talked through you to warn me. That's what it was."

"That's insane," he said.

"Well, that's what happened."

"So what did he come to warn you about?"

"That it's a lie. I can't do this show anymore."

"What are you talking about? It was one show. Shit happens. It's the lack of a logical through line. That's why we got lost. We can fix that. You need sleep. You don't get enough sleep."

"That's got nothing to do with it!" I was getting really frustrated by what he was not recognizing about this. "I'm trying to tell you, the reality is—"

"You're giving up again. Like you give up on everything else in your life. It's not a lie. It's a show, that's all. Your problem is that you can't handle success. You can't handle classes. You can't handle a challenge. You want everything easy. Well, guess what? Sometimes it's just not easy, but that doesn't mean you give up. You want some reality? This is the best thing we've got right now. I don't like it any more than you do, but that's where it's at. And that's the reality."

I thought for a moment about bringing out my secret weapon to crush him with, but that idea passed as quickly as it came. I felt bad for him. I felt bad for what I'd done to him and what this had turned into.

"I'm sorry, Mike. We'll do something else. Anything. Just not this."

"I need some air."

He took some money out of his wallet and threw it on the table.

"I'll walk back," he said.

He shook his head disdainfully to let me know how pathetic I was, and then he left the restaurant.

⁂

Monday it rained all day and into performance time. The attendance was light—the word of mouth could not have been good. If I were at a play and saw one actor get possessed by a ghost and the other one plead with God to make it stop, I might have talked that up a bit. No accounting for taste, I guess.

The few who did brave the rain were enthusiastic and looking to have a good time. The show was much better than Sunday (which isn't saying much) but not as raucous as the Saturday show. No ghosts showed up, so I guess my grandfather figured that I had got the message.

After the show, we said goodbye to Billy, who was definitely the most consistent performer over the three days. He had an envelope for us with our check inside. No note from Al. Just the check for the agreed upon amount. We never did get a contract or any money up front. I was afraid that maybe something would be deducted because of what happened, but it was all there.

We thanked the volunteers and the theater staff who were still around and not too embarrassed to be seen with us. Al had only come to the first show. I'm sure he got reports about what happened and was either too embarrassed or too pissed off to see me in person. We quickly packed up our stuff—props, costumes, and card table—and then slunk out into the night. We drove back to LA in the pouring rain, listened to music on the radio, and didn't say a word to each other during the whole trip home.

CHAPTER FIFTEEN

MOE AND MIKE'S NEVER-PERFORMED SKETCH IDEA 150

MOE. Do you believe in ghosts?

MIKE. I'm kind of on the fence about it, to tell you the truth.

MOE. Well, I was at this party last night, and everybody was talking about it.

MIKE. Is that right?

MOE. Yeah, and they were saying that our departed loved ones are always with us.

MIKE. Well, I think there is something to the fact that we are energy, and energy doesn't really die. Starlight continues on long after a star has died, so maybe it's the same with people.

MOE. You know what bugs me about it, though?

MIKE. What's that?

MOE. The always being with you part. I'm not so sure I like that so much. I think the dearly departed should call first or make an appointment. I mean, what if I'm in the bathroom?

MIKE. If those spirits weren't already dead—that would surely kill them.

MOE. I'm just saying—

MIKE. Spirits beware.

MOE. Just give me a little heads-up is all.

CHAPTER SIXTEEN
THAT'S A WRAP

I dropped Mike off at his house and haven't heard from him since. I thought he'd call and want to do a little post mortem on the show, but nothing. Not a peep. I guess it is really over—just a creepy little story to tell the grandkids about one day—but I don't have any of those, so I guess it's just a creepy little story.

At first, I found myself in a kind of artistic limbo. I couldn't act, I couldn't write, and I was sleeping only about two hours a night. I had considered for a time that maybe I was losing my mind, that none of this really happened, and that I was even crazier than I thought I was. But the evidence was there. It was undeniable. So even though I'd like to push the whole thing away, to run and hide in some dark corner somewhere, my hand had been forced. I had to do something so my grandfather's efforts would not have been in vain.

I was truly flattered that he had made the trip to see me, coming all the way back from the dead as he had. I guess he had more feelings for me than I realized; he couldn't stand to watch me live such a pointless, faithless, meaningless life. The Chanukah show was the last straw for him—the final insult.

Don't be like me. Don't be like me. It took me a while to work out how I could have been like him. It was hard to see the similarity. Unlike me, he was never afraid to take a stand. Never afraid to be brutally honest. He would never hold back, and he always said what he felt and meant what he said. But maybe if you get too callous with that kind of thing, it's just another way of shutting people out, as he had with my family. And even though we had different approaches to how we dealt with life, he must have recognized that the final destination would be the same, and he couldn't bear to see me go there. That's what I think it was anyway.

I still don't know where I'm at with God. I want to believe in something. The people I've admired most in this world are the believers. Not necessarily the believers in God, but the ones with faith enough, who care enough about their fellow human beings to try and make a positive difference in the world. But my belief in God, even after what's happened, remains tenuous at best. If there's a ghost, does that mean there's a God? Are they necessarily a part of the same story?

So I'm not jumping to conclusions, but I am on a quest. I'm searching for God, or for whatever else will inspire me to be a better person, and for what I won't be tortured by if I decide to do a show about it one day.

I'm willing to give Judaism another try and see if something clicks for me, more than it did the first time around. To my grandfather, and to any other departed friends or family who might be interested—I'm working on it. It's kind of like what Scrooge said when he was pleading with the ghost to grant him more time to live a better life—*I'm not the man I was!* Scrooge went on to do good deeds, and I will strive to do the same. I will try to find the things I love, and love them as recklessly as possible.

I started going to services at a temple not far from my house. There're nice people there, and I got involved in doing community service things: food drives, collecting clothes and toys for the needy, helping the homeless—those kinds of things.

I finally did make a copy of my friend's tape, by the way, but I'm still hesitant about sending it to his wife. I can't seem to let it go. I know it's something she should have. I guess I'll do it eventually. Maybe include a note about what's on there, and then she can decide if she wants to watch it or not.

* * *

It's been six months since we did the show. I called Al once to apologize for what had happened. I left a message, but he never got back to me. I still haven't heard from Mike. A mutual friend from the Shakespeare Company told me that Mike was branching out into other things now. He was in a band playing drums and studying to be a life coach—whatever that is. I hope that our relationship isn't completely over. I miss him. I've started writing little sketch ideas for us, the "Moe and Mike's Never-Performed Sketch Idea" stuff, and I hope that we can laugh and get goofy again someday, and that he won't hold this whole Chanukah experience against me for the rest of his life. But I guess I'd understand it if he did.

As I'm getting ready to go out for Shabbat services—the phone rings.

"Schlomo?" a Jewish-sounding voice asks.

"Mike-ness?"

"I love you," he says.

"What?"

"Let's get together and run through this thing. I'm not saying that we have to do the show anymore, but we should talk about it and try to understand what happened."

"Okay."

"Hey, I'm a life coach now," he tells me.

"I heard something about that."

"I'm really good at it, but I need forty hours of counseling before I can get a certificate. Do you mind?"

"Do I mind what?"

"Can I practice on you? Don't worry. You don't have to sign up for classes or anything. I just have to register the hours with a real live human person, and you somewhat qualify for that. It might even help you, who knows?"

"Uh…okay, I guess."

"And I meant what I said. I love you. I miss your face."

"Thank you, Mike. I miss you, too."

"Hey, are you sitting down?"

"Yes, how'd you know?"

"I got cast in a play in Portland."

"You did?"

"It's a period thing—very dramatic. I leave in two weeks, and I think they want me for their second show, too. So I'm going to be gone for a while and thought we should get together before I leave. Sort things out, you know?

"Mike! That's fantastic! Congratulations."

"How about lunch at the coffee shop tomorrow?"

"Okay, but don't be late."

"I'll try, but give me a break. I have issues."

I wasn't able to tell him that I love him back. But I can't wait to see him. And I can't wait to see how much he eats. Mike has finally made it. He didn't give up. He's a serious dramatic actor now. I've apparently lost my secret weapon to use against him, but I can't be happier about that.

CHAPTER SEVENTEEN

MOE AND MIKE'S NEVER-PERFORMED SKETCH IDEA 168

MOE. Well, that was weird.

MIKE. What?

MOE. Just in general.

ACKNOWLEDGEMENTS

Special thanks to my kind sister Sandy, for her encouragement and her determination to plod through early versions of this book. And thanks to Ruth Strother, my editor, for her patience, wisdom, and willingness to answer all my ridiculous questions.

ABOUT THE AUTHOR

 Marc S. Silver is a journeyman actor who has performed on stage, screen, and television sets for over forty years. But the things that happened when he was growing up in Paterson, New Jersey—the really weird stuff—that's what inspired him to stop running around to auditions and spend more time hunkered down at his desk. He's had five plays produced, two screenplays optioned, and was a finalist in the World Series of Screenwriting. Phony Einstein is Marc's second book, and he's currently hard at work on the sequel to his first novel, Still Harping on my Daughter. As of this moment, and now more than ever, having been sequestered at home, and his favorite Mexican restaurant shut down—Marc has even less going on than he did before.